THE GIRL I WAS BEFORE

Lily McDermott Series Book 1

Do you believe in second chances?

by

Izzy Bayliss

This novel is entirely a work of fiction. The names, characters and incidents portrayed in it are the work of the author's imagination. Any resemblance to actual persons, living or deceased, events or localities is purely coincidental.

http://www.izzybayliss.com

About the Author

Izzy Bayliss lives in Ireland with her husband, children and their dog. A romantic at heart, she loves nothing more than cosying up in front of the fire with a good book. Her motto is that reality is over-rated and she is happiest staring into space and day-dreaming.

You can find out more about Izzy Bayliss on **http://www.izzybayliss.com**

She can also be found hanging about on Facebook as @izzybaylissauthor **or** Twitter @izzybayliss

For my children - my best creations

Chapter 1

The Worst Moment of My Life

It all started after I had just come in the door from work. I'd had a horrible day – a day from hell actually. I was tired and hungry and longed to come in the door and into Marc's arms where he would instantly make me feel better. I climbed the steps to our duplex, rooted my key out of my bag and with a sigh of relief to finally be home, I let myself in. I dumped my handbag on the console table inside the door and saw that the TV was on, but there was no sign of him. So I walked down the hallway to our bedroom, and it was then that I saw it. Well it was the socks that I saw first. He was wearing his red-soled Paul Smith pair, the ones with the coloured stripes going up towards the ankle. For a man, Marc always did have rather good taste in socks. He specifically co-ordinated his socks to the outfit he would be wearing that day and would happily spend money on designer socks made from silk knits or even cashmere, whereas I would be getting five pairs for a fiver in Tesco. It probably only lasted seconds but it felt as though my eyes were travelling up towards the head of the bed for an eternity. I wish I could say that my first reaction was something witty and clever like, "Aren't you going to introduce me to your friend?" But no. Instead my first thought, I'm ashamed to say was the rather weak, "What a great bottom". And it *was* a great bottom. It was smooth and toned with not even a dimple of cellulite, which when you consider all the jiggling she was doing, was pretty remarkable. It wasn't a bottom like mine – no mine was at least twice the size of this arse. Her olive skin was naturally tanned and her long brown, caramel highlighted hair cascaded mane-like down her arched back. This woman obviously worked out.

I noticed the photos of us from our wedding day were lying face down on the locker. In shock, I dropped my Marks & Spencer's bag containing the meal deal spaghetti bolognese and garlic bread for the dinner that I had planned on cooking him for our three-month anniversary that evening. I had decided to go with an Italian theme to remind us of our honeymoon on the Amalfi coast.

The noise of the bag crashing to the floor disturbed them and they both swung around towards me. Marc's eyes met mine. I could see panic. He pushed the woman and her long lanky limbs off him and jumped up off the bed with his dangly bits swinging in all their glory before me. He was completely naked except for his bloody socks, which for some reason he never seemed to take off when he was having sex. As an after-thought he cupped his hands over his manhood - as if I had never seen it before!

"Lily!" he said in shock.

It took me a moment, but I recognised the woman who was

smiling smugly at me from my Egyptian cotton sheets. She was starting to wrap herself in the throw we got from my Auntie Flor as a wedding present. It was Nadia, Nadia Williams.

"Lily – I can explain. This is not what it looks like – I swear!" Marc was pleading desperately.

"Lily – I've been dying to meet you," Nadia drawled before holding out a long slender hand to shake mine.

Marc shot her a look and sullenly she folded her arms back across her chest again. Marc started to walk over towards where I was standing, reaching out to me with one hand while trying, but failing miserably to cover-up his meat and two veg with the other.

The room seemed to be spinning around me and I thought my legs were going to give way. I knew I was probably doing a good impression of a goldfish right then. Beads of perspiration had broken out all across my forehead and on the back of my neck. I started to back out of the room. Suddenly I was feeling ill. Very ill. And nauseous. The blood had drained from my head and I thought I might pass out. My heart sounded as though it was beating in my ears. I could hear Marc trying to talk to me, but it sounded like he was speaking to me through a very long and far away tunnel. I turned and ran out of the room. Somehow I managed to grab my handbag from the console table where I had placed it just minutes earlier, before racing down the steps of the duplex where we lived. The cool fresh air was a welcome relief as I breathed it in deeply to my lungs.

"Come back, Lily - if you'd just let me explain -" I heard

Marc calling from behind me.

I turned around to see him standing in the doorway stark naked.

"It's not what it looks like, Lily - please!"

But what else could it look like? They were hardly playing Doctors and Nurses in there.

The neighbours' blinds started twitching as they started peeking out from underneath. They had obviously heard the commotion. I put my head down and started to run. Even though normally I couldn't run more than a hundred yards without thinking I was going to have a heart-attack, somehow the adrenalin kicked in and I kept on running the whole way back down towards the bus stop that I had only just come from half an hour earlier with my M&S bag laden with goodies, full of excitement and anticipation for the evening I had planned for Marc.

My mind was whirring from everything as it tried to process what had just happened. In our house. *Our home.* I tried to tell myself that this wasn't happening, that it was just a dream - an awful, terrible dream. I prayed that I had imagined it and I even tried pinching myself. But it hurt, so no, I was definitely awake. What was I going to do? It felt as though Marc had taken my heart in his two hands and twisted it dry. How could he do this to me? I was his wife! We were newly-weds for God's sake, didn't that mean anything to him? I thought we were rock solid. He had said he could explain, but I couldn't see any explanation that he could offer me to make this okay. I felt the weight of big fat tears building in my eyes, and it wasn't long before they were spilling over and running down my face as the shock of what I had just witnessed started to sink in.

The sky was full of inky blue clouds that threatened to burst at any moment. I prayed it wouldn't rain, because all I had on me was a cotton vest top with a light cardigan over it and a pair of linen trousers. In the shock of everything that had happened, I hadn't thought about grabbing a jacket. As I waited for a bus that would take me back towards the city centre, I wasn't even sure where I was going to go; I didn't want to go to my Dad's - he would only worry. I could have gone to my sister Clara's but I really couldn't face her in those circumstances. So I decided that Frankie was my best bet.

Soon the heavens opened and it began to pour rain. I stood there getting soaked as my hair began to cling to my face in rat's tails and the water dripped down from my fringe and into my eyes but I didn't feel any of it.

There was only a skeleton service operating to Ballyrobin at that time of the evening, and I must have stood waiting in the rain for nearly an hour, by which stage the water had seeped up through the thin soles of my flimsy ballet pumps, which threatened to fall apart at any minute.

Marc and I had bought this "two-bed-in-the-middle-of-nowhere-but-commutable-to-Dublin" duplex at the height of the market because it was all we could afford. I had wanted us to buy our own place for ages, but Marc had held out, saying the housing market was going to crash. But we had kept on watching as prices rose and one by one our friends all bit the bullet and became mortgage holders. Of course when I did finally convince him to take the plunge, the housing market did collapse, six months later. So in fact he had been right all along.

Finally I caught sight of the red and white bus snaking its way along the road in the distance. When it pulled up, its wheels sent a shower of muddy water over me. I didn't care at that stage because I couldn't have been any wetter. I climbed aboard, wiping the dirty water from my face, and through tears and snot and grit, paid the fare and made my way down the back of the bus to where a gang of teenagers had taken over the entire back seat. They were all dressed the same, wearing hoodies pulled up over their heads and jersey tracksuit bottoms that gathered just above their ankles, to reveal white sports sock and trainers. I sat in a seat about midway down the bus.

"What's wrong wit yer' one?" I heard one of the gang grunting, ignoring the fact that I could obviously hear him.

"Ah she's probably just a psycho or somethin'," one of the others replied to him.

I stared straight ahead, pretending I couldn't hear them.

"Yeah I'd say you're right, Aido - look at de state of her. She's like a bleedin' banshee!" They all started laughing at that.

As I sat there, listening to them, the tears kept on coming until soon my whole body was shaking with sobs. I kept thinking about the scene I had just seen in my own home. It was so hard to take it in. What had happened to me that evening was bad enough without having to endure the humiliation of these teenagers too.

When we finally reached the city centre, I got off at the quays and was glad to leave the teenagers behind me as I made my way towards Frankie's apartment. Frankie is my best friend in the whole wide world. Chalk and cheese we are, but I think that's why it works. We met on our first day in junior infants when Mrs Trevor put us sitting beside each other on the Blue table. My first memory of Frankie is of a tall, skinny child with Pippi Longstocking style pigtails, screaming *"Don't Leave Me Maaammy"* and running back out the classroom door after her mother. She was always dramatic even at five years of age. She was christened Francesca, which is what I knew her as all through school but at the age of fifteen she declared she wanted to be known only as Frankie from then on. Stubbornly she wouldn't answer to anyone who dared to call her Francesca anymore, even teachers.

Frankie worked for herself as a very successful freelance fashion stylist. She had a knack for pulling outfits together, things that look nothing on the hanger work when Frankie puts them on. But alas, despite having been her friend for almost the last thirty years, it has had absolutely no effect on my own dress sense.

"Lily? What's wrong?" Frankie exclaimed when she opened the door to me. "Are you okay? You look desperate!"

She was never one to beat about the bush. I shook my head

11

and the tears started again.

"What's after happening – here come in." She shooed me inside and I plonked down on her red velvet seventies bowl shaped sofa, the one that just happened to be thrown into a skip on a shoot she was working on. She thrust a box of tissues into my hands.

"Okay now speak -"

"I-I-I. . ."

"It's okay, take your time, deep breaths now. In and out, in and out."

"I - I . . . Marc -" was all I could manage to get out through the sobs.

"Marc, what? Did you have a fight, is that it?"

I shook my head and blew my nose into the tissue again.

"I caught him -" I couldn't say the words.

"You caught him what, Lily?"

"I caught him . . . in bed with someone else -" My voice had lowered to a whisper as if saying it out loud would completely break my heart in two. Suddenly I felt my mouth begin to water and my body broke out in a cold sweat. I ran into Frankie's bathroom and threw my head over her toilet bowl to be sick.

When I was finished I sat on the cool floor tiles with my back against the bathtub. Frankie was perched on the tub beside me.

"Here," she handed me what I thought was a glass of water and I gulped it back quickly but the liquid burned my mouth and throat.

"Jesus Christ, Frankie – you could have warned me!" I spat the neat vodka straight back out again.

"Sorry – it's for the shock," she said apologetically. "You okay?"

I nodded and started to sip on the vodka even though it tasted awful.

"I can't believe it, Lily!"

"Me neither," I sobbed as she pulled me into a big hug and stroked my hair.

"I had wanted to surprise him for our three-month anniversary – I was going to cook him an Italian themed dinner to remind us of our honeymoon. I had bought loads of stuff in M&S and I even stayed up late to make a tiramisù last night. I worked through my lunch-break so I could finish an hour earlier and go home to surprise him. But it turns out the anniversary surprise was on me. It was horrible, Frankie - seeing them like that in *our* bed . . ."

"Do you know who is she?"

I nodded my head weakly. "It was Nadia."

"Nadia - as in Nadia Williams?"

"Yes," I whispered.

Her hands flew up to her mouth and I think the normally unflappable Frankie was just as shocked as I was. "I can't believe it, Lily."

Nadia Williams was an actress; she was Ireland's golden girl of the moment. Having appeared in a few relatively low-budget films, her most recent role as a domestic abuse victim had garnered her a best-supporting actress nomination in the Oscars, and had catapulted her to international success. She was currently one of the most sought-after actresses in the world, and the Irish media had really taken her to their hearts. Marc, also an actor, had had a minor role in the latest movie that Nadia was starring in, which was being filmed in a remote part of the Wicklow Mountains. Nadia was playing the character of a reclusive writer, and Marc was playing the part of a village man who delivered firewood to her. But although I had known they were filming a few scenes together, Marc didn't even have a speaking part, so never in my wildest dreams would I have thought that they would be moving in the same circles, let alone sleeping together.

"Well, if I saw that wanker now, what I wouldn't do to him – I'd string him up by the goolies, I tell you!"

"We've only been married for three months. Three months!" I wailed. "Oh, Frankie, what am I going to do?"

Chapter 2

That night Frankie tucked me up into the bed in her spare room. But even though I was exhausted, I still couldn't sleep. I tossed and turned, watching the hours change on the LED alarm clock. I was thinking it all over and playing the sequence of events over and over in my head. The pain of seeing my husband in bed with another woman was almost physical. I felt like someone had kicked me in the chest and knocked all the air from me.

I must have eventually fallen asleep at some stage because when I woke up, I didn't know where I was. I looked around the unfamiliar room where fuchsia walls, clashed with orange accessories, and then with a horrible sinking feeling I remembered where I was and what had happened. The events of the night before came rushing back to me with full horror – I had found my husband in bed with another woman. This was the stuff of films - I couldn't believe it had happened in real life – *to me*.

With trepidation I reached for my phone on top of the locker. I wanted to see if Marc had tried to get in contact with me to explain himself but I was shocked to find that there were no missed calls or even messages from him. My heart sank even lower. At the very least he should be trying to track me down and begging me to come back shouldn't he? I put the phone back up on the locker and sank back down onto the pillows. The tears started up again. *How could he do this to me?*

Frankie knocked softly on the door soon after. "You awake yet, Lily?"

"Come on in."

She entered the room with a cup of tea and some toast on a tray. "I thought you might be hungry," she offered, setting the tray down beside me on the bed.

I shook my head, for once in my life the very idea of food made me feel like being sick again. This really was serious, I *never* refused food.

"Any word from him? Although I don't think anything he could say could get him out of this one."

I shook my head again.

"What a prat – I always said that anybody who introduces themselves when you meet them for the first time as *'Marc - spelled with a C'* is a tosser anyway."

"How could he do this to me, Frankie?"

"I don't have an answer for that, honey I'm afraid," she said softly.

"I just have so many questions spinning around in my head. Like how long has it been going on for? I still keep thinking that maybe it was all just a bad dream. I can't believe it. We're newly-weds, we're meant to be in the throes of post marital bliss - surprising each other with little post-it notes when you open the fridge, making each other breakfast in bed with toast cut into heart shapes. We're meant to be watching our wedding video on repeat and freezing it on the bit where we say our vows. We should be running out of wall space in the living room because we've hung so many wedding photos up, all that sort of thing - he's not meant to *sleep* with someone else!" I spluttered. "I mean I haven't even sent out our bloody thank you cards yet!" The panic started to rise inside me again as I thought about what all of our family and friends would think. "What am I going to do?"

"Don't worry about all of that yet. You can stay here for as long as you need to, but that bastard better not come within an inch of my door because he will be going home minus the bits that God gave him."

I sent my boss a text message to say that I had food poisoning and that I wouldn't be coming in that day. Frankie was able to call in a favour from a friend to cover the shoot she was supposed to be working on, so the two of us spent the day laying back on her double bed drinking endless cups of tea. We were both wearing what Frankie termed "lounge wear" but essentially they were just like really baggy tracksuits. She flicked on Jeremy Kyle and we both stared brainlessly at the screen. It was car-crash TV, like a bad accident – you knew you shouldn't look but you just couldn't help it. I realised that after the drama of the night before, I could star in my own episode of Jeremy Kyle with the headline *I found my husband in bed with another woman.* Suddenly the guests didn't seem quite so pathetic, I could relate to these people. I wished *I* could have Jeremy put his kindly arm around my shoulder while the audience tutted with sympathy, before he would give Marc a good stripping down.

After two more episodes, titled *Is my boyfriend my brother?* and *Three men could be the father of my baby,* I made up my mind – I couldn't take anymore. I needed to get some answers. I swung my legs over the side of the bed and jumped up.

"Where are you going?" Frankie asked.

"I need answers, Frankie. He hasn't even bothered his arse ringing me. I'm going back over there to ask him what the hell he is playing at!"

"Are you sure you want to do that?" she said cautiously.

"No, not really but it's something I have to do. I need to know how long it's been going on and *why*? All the questions are driving me demented." My voice waivered and threatened to break into tears again.

"Okay, if that's what you want, then I'll come with you."

Frankie threw me a pile of clothes from her wardrobe. She didn't even check to see what she was giving me, which I thought was odd for a stylist, so I got dressed into a pair of beige harem pants, suede ankle boots and a mint-green vest top. Then she handed me a khaki parka jacket to throw over it. It was still Spring after all. When I asked her if she was sure the whole ensemble matched, she assured me I looked fine, but I wasn't so sure. It was the kind of outfit that she could pull off, but on me it just looked plain stupid. I felt like MC Hammer in the trousers, plus they didn't fit me properly. They were digging into my waist and the boots were pinching my toes, but I dared not complain.

Once we were dressed, we hopped into Frankie's electric blue Mini Cooper, left the city behind us, and headed for Ballyrobin.

"Jesus, Lily – how do you do this commute every day?" Frankie moaned lowering down the Lady GaGa CD.

"We're not even half way there yet!" I said.

Soon we had left the suburbs behind and were in the greener territory of the countryside. As we drove along I fell silent, as I thought about everything that I wanted to say to Marc.

An hour after we had left Frankie's apartment, we finally turned into my estate. We drove down the back to where the developers had decided to hide all the cheap box-design, flat-roofed duplexes. A quick scan around the car park told me that Marc wasn't there. My heart sank – I had spent the whole journey psyching myself up to confront him.

We got out of the car and climbed the steps towards the house. I hesitated at the front door, afraid to cross the threshold into my own home. After the events of the night previous I thought I would be scarred forever, and that fear would always stay with me.

I looked around the living room briefly, but there were no obvious signs of last night's events, so with trepidation I walked down the hallway towards the scene of the crime. As I stood in the doorway to our bedroom, to my horror the evidence of what I had seen the night before was plain to see. The photo frames were still lying face down on the locker, and the frozen spaghetti bolognese and garlic bread that I had picked up on the way home for dinner were now sitting defrosted in a pool of water. The paper bag had split, from where the water had seeped through onto the carpet. He hadn't even bothered to pick it up. I noticed that there were two champagne flutes left on the locker that I hadn't remembered seeing the evening before. The duvet lay tossed in a messy pile on the floor. Now what on earth had possessed me to think they would have a shag and then stop to tidy up the place afterwards was beyond me, but it felt like more salt in the wound. I automatically went to lift the duvet back up onto the bed.

It was then that I noticed that all the wardrobe doors were wide open. With trepidation I walked across the room and saw that all of Marc's clothes were gone.

Tears gave way to anger. "He's gone, Frankie! He's left me!"

"How do you know that?" she asked rushing over behind me to take a look.

"He's taken all his stuff. Look!" I showed her Marc's side of the wardrobe.

I turned around and bent down to check under the bed.

"They're gone!" I wailed.

"What are?" Frankie asked swinging around to see what I was after finding now.

"The suitcases - the new Samsonite ones that we got as a

wedding present! How dare he do this," I cried angrily. "Shouldn't he be here in tears waiting for me? Shouldn't he be all remorseful saying what a terrible mistake he made and begging me to come back?"

Frankie put her arm around my shoulder and guided me down onto the bed. "Lily, I'm so sorry, for once I don't know what to say – I can't believe the audacity of that bastard, I really can't!"

"You don't think –"

"What?" Frankie asked.

My voice started to tremble. "That he's gone . . . with her . . ."

Frankie wouldn't meet my eyes.

"You do, don't you? You think he's gone to stay with her?"

"Lily, I don't know, but well . . ." She paused to choose her words carefully. "You found him in bed with someone else, and now he's packed his bags - you don't need to be Sherlock Bloody Holmes to figure out he is probably staying with her."

"You're right, oh God what am I going to do? I'm only thirty-two years of age - only just three months married and already my husband has left me? God I'm such a fuck-up!" I held my head in my hands.

"No you are not – it's Marc, he's the fuck-up!" Frankie said grabbing hold of my shoulders and forcing me to look her in the eye. "You've done nothing wrong here. Do you hear me?"

"Pass me my phone," I said.

"Why?"

"I'm going to ring him."

"Are you sure that's a good idea?"

But I grabbed the phone out of her hands before she could try and talk me out of it.

With trembling fingers I speed-dialled his number, but it just rang through to his voicemail. His familiar rhyming greeting played: "*Hi, this is Marc - spelled with a C. Leave a voicemail . . . I'll call you . . .*"

I thought about leaving a message, but no message I would leave could begin to express how desolate I was feeling right then. I was about to hang up when Frankie grabbed the phone out of my hand just as his mailbox beeped to record a message.

"Hey, 'Marc - spelled with a C' – this is Frankie with an F a big fuck-you wanker!" And then she hung up.

"Frankie!" I cried out in shock.

"Sorry I'm just so mad with him, Lily!"

"I suppose I should say thanks," I mumbled.

"Don't mention it."

She then started to strip down the bed, pulling off the sheets, taking off the duvet cover and pillowcases like a woman on a mission. When she was finished, she gathered up the pile of dirty laundry and proceeded to walk out to the kitchen. I followed behind and watched in horror as she started stuffing my luxury 100% Egyptian cotton bed-linen (another wedding present by the way, because we could never have afforded such fine bed-linen), into the bin.

"What do you think you are you doing?" I cried in horror. "Those sheets have an 800 thread count!"

"Lily, do you honestly think you will ever want to sleep on these sheets again?" she replied as she grappled with a sweeping brush to shove them down further into the bin.

She had a point. They would be forever tainted by what had gone on between them.

"Well no, I suppose you're right . . ."

"There!" she pronounced rubbing her hands together when she finally had managed to stuff the remainder of the pile in. "All done!"

I gave her a grateful smile. I really couldn't have faced stripping off those sheets, where they had done the deed. "Thanks, Frankie you're the best."

"I know!" she sang. "Do you want me to order you a takeaway – you must be starved at this stage?"

It was only then that I remembered I hadn't eaten anything since lunchtime in work the day before. I had purposely starved myself of my daily four p.m. Mars bar because I had wanted to save my appetite for the special dinner I had planned. Almost instantly my tummy started to rumble, but the thought of food made me nauseous.

"I'm okay, really, Frankie, I think I'm just going to have a bath and get an early night."

"You can't stay here on your own!" she protested. "Come

on back to my place, we can share a bottle or three of wine."

"No really, Frankie I want to be here." I didn't dare say it to her, but I wanted to be there just in case Marc decided to come home.

"I don't know, Lily . . . I don't like the idea of you being alone right now. I can stay here if you'd prefer?"

"Please, Frankie, my head is in a spin - I think I just need some time alone."

"Well if you're sure . . ." she said hesitantly. "Ring me if you change your mind and I'll be straight back."

"Honestly, I'm fine."

She gave me kiss on the cheek, and promised she would ring later.

As soon as Frankie had gone I reached for my phone again and dialled Marc's number. I waited for an eternity for him to pick up. But yet again, it just went to his voicemail.

"Hi, this is Marc - spelled with a C. Leave a voicemail . . . I'll call you . . ."

I hung up again in despair. I sat looking around the living room - the house, although not big by any stretch, felt so empty and lonely without him. What had I done wrong? What on earth had I done that was so awful that it had caused my husband to walk out on me after only three months of marriage? I thought we were happy. We had a good sex life, or so I thought, but maybe I just wasn't good enough – maybe I should have tried spicing things up - like maybe . . . I don't know, by getting some kinky new underwear instead of my usual M&S sets, or dressing up in a nurse's outfit. Didn't you always hear how men love that kind of thing? Or even tantric sex, although I wasn't too sure what exactly that was, all I knew was that Sting and his wife raved about it. Then there was the little voice inside my head that was saying maybe it was because I just wasn't attractive enough – I had put on a few pounds on honeymoon what with the free cocktails and the all you can eat buffet every night. Marc was always jiggling my tummy. And Nadia Williams had such an amazing figure – I could never compete with that. Was that the reason? I felt sick just thinking about it. And where was he? Yes I was angry, but we were married, we had things to talk about. I had so much I needed to say to him, so many questions. How had it happened, and how long had it been going on for? But I didn't even know where Nadia lived. I felt a knot in the pit of my stomach as I thought of them together. I was wracking my head trying to find a reason for Marc's behaviour. None of it made any sense. I kept trying to come up with some reason for it all. It wasn't like Marc – was he going through a crisis of some sort? But at thirty-four surely he was a bit young for a midlife crisis? Maybe he was depressed? But he certainly hadn't seemed depressed - I would have noticed something like that. I tried to think of a reason – what had happened to make him run into the arms of another woman after only three months of marriage? The only thing I could think of was maybe it was because I had recently started to mention that we should think about starting a

25

family? But I hadn't meant *right now*, I had just meant someday in the future. I thought that was what married couples *did* - but maybe I had completely scared him off? It wasn't as if I was in a hurry! Hell I wasn't even sure if I was ready yet myself.

But no matter how I tried to make sense of everything I still couldn't stop wondering how on earth had I let it happen? How did I always manage to ruin everything that was good in my life? Well at least I was consistent in constantly messing things up. I could feel the weight of fat tears bulging behind my eyes before spilling down my face. I sat there sobbing until I could taste a horrible mixture of snot and salt in my mouth. They kept on coming, I just couldn't stop them. How do you go from one day being a fresh out of the box newly-wed, to walking in on your husband shagging an A-list actress in your bed the next? Only I could manage to achieve something like that. Good girl, Lily McDermott - you have gone and fucked up your life yet again!

Chapter 3

I woke sprawled uncomfortably on the couch. My neck was stiff and sore and a round damp patch stained the cushion where I must have been drooling. As I opened my eyes, it all came flooding back to me like it did every day when I woke. The pain washed down through my body. I instantly checked my phone, which I still was clutching in my right hand, but there were no missed calls or messages from Marc. I lay back on the cushions and closed my eyes to try and stop the tears from streaming down my face.

It had been three days since I had found Marc in bed with Nadia. I had been living a zombie-like existence. I couldn't face sleeping in our bedroom, so I had been sleeping on the sofa because our spare room didn't actually have a bed in it – I had never got around to getting one. My body hadn't seen any other clothes besides Frankie's outfit and the too small boots. My routine was watching Ireland A.M., followed by Jeremy Kyle to make me feel better about my own situation. Then it was time for Oprah, and then Ellen. Judge Judy was on at three, which helped to pass another chunk of time, and somehow the mornings turned into night and this was how I got through the day.

I had told my boss that it was a really severe case of food

poisoning, and once I started the descriptions of my bowel motions, he seemed happy enough just to accept my word for it.

I had been working in the call centre of Rapid Response pregnancy tests for the last eight years. Initially it was only meant to be a summer job, but it had ended up turning into one long fulltime one. I was promoted to supervisor two years ago, so it was my job to deal with customer complaints. These usually took the form of distressed customers, and I have faced all sorts of questions over the years from "What do two lines mean?" to the more common "Why isn't there a second line on my test?" It's very hard to bite your tongue in those situations. Then there are those people who need instructions on how to do a test, "Eh – *hold it under your pee and wait three minutes* – read the back of the box, moron!" The worst part of the job is that all the used tests that are faulty are sent back in to the lab for analysis, but we have to process them first. No matter how many pairs of latex gloves and facemasks that I wear, the stench of ammonia first thing on a Monday morning is vile. On the plus side we get as many free pregnancy tests as we want, which would have been useful if Marc and I had been planning on starting a family at some stage. But it's a job and it pays the bills, well actually it doesn't with our huge negative equity laden mortgage. Compared to Marc's job, mine is so boring. Although the acting business is tough, and he is out of work a lot, when he does get a job it usually pays well. But it also means that he has to spend a lot when he is working away from home, or buying clothes to wear to the fancy premieres and work dos that he's always going to, so he's even broker than me if that's possible.

Every January my New Year's resolution was to find a new job, something that excited me and that I didn't mind getting up for in the morning, but then life got in the way and before I knew it, January had turned into December and I still hadn't started looking, and I'd another year done. My older sister Clara was always on at me to do something with my life – a call centre supervisor just wasn't impressive enough for her.

I still hadn't been able to contact Marc to find out what had happened. I had left countless messages on his phone all saying the same thing, begging him to come home. *"Marc - it's me, I love you, come home. Pleeeease."* I had lost count of the number of times that I had sobbed hysterically down the phone to his voicemail. I had tried bombarding him with text messages but he still never replied. I couldn't believe he wasn't banging on the door begging for my forgiveness. It was all starting to hit me now; whatever was going on, it was serious. I needed to know *"Why?"* I was tormented with whys. Why did he have to leave? Why wouldn't he come home? Why did he do those awful things? I needed to know what was going on inside his head. And this might sound stupid but I was worried about him too. What if he was going through a mini-breakdown and I wasn't there for him? I was telling myself that it was just a blip, a minor speed bump on the road, and that he was obviously in a difficult place but we could get through it together — if he would ever just turn on his bloody phone. Everyone always says that marriage has to be worked at, but I didn't expect these were the kind of things you had to work at. It was a pity we hadn't covered "What to do when you find your husband in bed with someone else" in our pre-marriage course. I just needed to talk to him and get to the bottom of it all. The longer he was gone, the more the niggling worries inside my head were starting to become real – what would happen if he never came home? It should have been the happiest time of our lives; he should have been so in love with me at that stage. Why would you ask someone to marry you if you're not in love with them? Was he confused? We had been going out since we were seventeen. Was that the problem? That he had never lived his youth? I had thought back over the last few months. Had there been any signs? But I couldn't see them if there were. This had come as a bolt from the blue. Was my marriage over, after only three months? It was just so hard to accept – I didn't want to give up on our marriage and be separated at the age of thirty-two – I wanted to fight for it and to get my husband back. It seemed too cruel. My heart felt as though it was being wrenched in two. I felt an overwhelming lump in my throat, and the panic was rising inside me. I just wanted him back – I didn't care, we had taken our vows for better or worse.

Earlier that day, I had plucked up the courage and decided to ring the film set where he was currently working. I never usually rang him at work, there was never any need because I could always get him on his mobile, but right then I was desperate to talk to him and this seemed like my only option. So with trembling fingers I had dialled the number and held my breath as the phone rang out for an eternity. I was just about to hang up when finally it was answered by a squeaky young girl. I vaguely remembered meeting her at our wedding; I scrambled to remember her name. *Flo.* That was it!

"Flo – how are you? It's Lily – Marc Glover's wife?" I said light-heartedly.

"Oh hi, Lisa."

"It's Lil-y."

"What? Oh sorry, L-*illlll-ly,*" she replied enunciating every syllable of my name.

"Can I speak with Marc please?"

There was silence on the other end.

"Hello?"

"Emmmmm, I think he's busy right now – they're on the twenty-second take." She laughed nervously. I could tell that she knew something.

"Okay well will you tell him I called?" I said trying to mask my disappointment.

"Em . . . sure, Lis - I mean . . . Lily." She didn't sound too convincing, but right then she was my only lifeline so I thanked her profusely and hung up.

I felt sick to the pit of my stomach. I had secretly hoped he would have been too upset to go to work. I couldn't believe he was carrying on with life like all was normal, as if he hadn't just walked out of our home only days earlier, and meanwhile my life was falling apart.

That evening Frankie called again as usual. She had called over after work every day, and I knew she was getting worried about me now because I still hadn't moved off the sofa except to use the toilet. I was still dressed in her uncomfortable MC Hammer pants and vest top and I still hadn't even washed myself. I knew I looked frightful, and she shook her head when she saw me in the same position, with the remote gripped in my left hand and my phone held firmly in my right.

"Lily, how about a shower today, yeah?"

She held me by the two shoulders and steered me into the pokey ensuite, coaching "left foot, right foot, left foot, right foot. Lift your left leg up, step over the curly end of the rug, good girl, now left leg down again, that's it. Now right foot, left foot. . ." until we were in the bathroom. I caught a glimpse of myself in the mirror; my eyes were puffy and my tear-stained cheeks were red and stingy. I was sporting a pair of Susan Boyle pre-fame eyebrows – not a good look. I pulled the string on the light above the mirror to turn it off again. Frankie ordered me to get undressed. She turned on the shower and pushed me into it. I stood underneath the water, just letting it wash over me, I didn't have the strength to even wash myself or shampoo my hair. When I came out, she had heated my towels on the radiator and had my pyjamas and dressing gown waiting for me.

"There now, I bet that feels better?"

I just shook my head. A simple shower was not going to solve my problems.

She had brought me a pile of trashy magazines, a pizza and a selection of my favourite chocolate bars, there was a Kit-Kat Chunky, a Drifter, a Walnut Whip, a Galaxy caramel, one white chocolate Toblerone, and a box of Cadbury's Roses. I couldn't even face opening the pizza box, so I tried to eat some of the Roses, because that's what people are supposed to do in a crisis, isn't it? You're supposed to eat an entire box of chocolates. But they didn't help, and instead I just felt sick afterwards.

"Any word from him?" Frankie probed gently after a while.

"No."

"God I can't believe it – it's been three days now."

"I know."

"Have you tried Facebook?"

"What do you mean?"

"Well Facebook is the twenty-first century equivalent to hiring a private detective. That's the whole point of social media – for stalking people."

It hadn't even crossed my mind to check there but Frankie was right, Marc was always on Facebook updating his status and "checking in" wherever he went.

I waited for ages for the laptop to load up and then I moved over towards the window to try and get an Internet connection, which was dodgy at the best of times in Ballyrobin. Frankie stood behind me looking over my shoulder. I couldn't believe that I had

33

to resort to Facebook to stalk my own husband but needs must.

The usual updates flashed up on the screen before me. My friend Gillian had posted: *"I'm so stuffed from the amazing dinner made by my wonderful hubby."*

Who cares - I wanted to say - my life is falling apart.

There was one from my sister Clara:

"I think we have the makings of a child prodigy - my Jacob who was the youngest child ever to sit a Preliminary Piano exam, has achieved a distinction! Such a clever boy."

Funnily enough, no one had given her status any "Likes".

Marc's profile picture was a photo that I had taken of him on honeymoon, as he had been coming out of the sea. He was running his hands through his wet hair and he looked tanned and ripped in his swim-shorts. I could remember that moment so clearly, I had been proud that I was his wife. I clicked onto Marc's profile but for some reason I couldn't get in. I tried clicking onto the photo again but a message appeared on screen: "You are not friends with this person. Do you want to send a friend request to Marc Glover? "

"A friend request? But we are married!" I shouted at the computer. "He is my husband, don't you know?" And then the awful truth dawned on me - Marc had de-friended me so I could no longer view his profile. Oh God no.

"Why would he do that, Frankie, why would he block me?" I said panicked.

"Lily - I'm sorry - it was a bad idea, I should never have

suggested it," Frankie was apologetic. She took the laptop out of my hands and closed it down.

"Well it's hardly your fault!"

I went back over to the couch and sank back down onto it, feeling even worse than before she had arrived if that was possible. Whatever was going on, it was clear that Marc was avoiding me. It was so hard to take the feeling of rejection from my own husband. I just wanted to grab hold of him and shake him until he saw sense.

"What about his parents?" Frankie asked.

"What about them?"

"You always got on well with them - have you tried asking them where he is?"

"I thought about it but I don't want to worry them, you know what his Mam is like. She'd work herself up into a state if she knew what was going on."

Most people don't get on with their mother-in-law, but I got on great with Marc's Mam. She always welcomed me with open arms, often telling Marc he was lucky to have me.

"Well it's been three days now. Maybe you should ask them if they've heard from him?"

"Yeah you're probably right," I sighed. "I hoped by this stage that Marc would have been home, and we would be sorting it all out without having dragged our families into it."

"I know, honey but maybe they might be able to talk to him for you?" she suggested.

I was filled with a new ray of hope, although he was obviously avoiding me, he might listen to them.

Frankie drove me over to the house of Mr and Mrs G. They lived in an ex-corporation house on the outskirts of the city centre; it was a settled estate where most of the residents were over the age of sixty. They had all lived in the estate for years and their kids had all grown up together and moved on. There was a real sense of community and everyone looked out for everyone else.

It was almost ten o'clock when we pulled up outside their house and I was relieved to see that the living room lights were still on. I got out of the car and knocked softly on their front door so they wouldn't get too startled by callers at that time of night.

Mr G answered and he looked frightened by my appearance.

"Lily, what's wrong? Are you okay, love? Where's Marc? Here come in and sit down."

I let them fluster around me with Mrs G giving Mr G instructions to make me some sweet tea and bring me in a few slices of the Madeira cake that she had made earlier on. They waited until I had drunk some tea and eaten a biscuit.

"Now love, what's wrong?" Mrs G asked.

"Oh, Mrs G, it's Marc. I don't know where he is."

Her forehead creased in confusion and she looked over at Mr G.

"What do you mean? Isn't he at home with you?"

I shook my head. "He left three nights ago, he didn't say

36

where he was going – I had hoped you might know where he is?"

"Well we haven't seen him, have we, Pat?" She looked visibly worried.

Pat shook his head at me.

"Did you have an argument, love, was that it?" Mrs G probed gently.

"No – I wish, I mean it was nothing like that . . ." the tears started again, streaming down my face. "I came home from work and -"

"Go on," they encouraged.

"I found him in bed with Nadia Williams . . ." I said in a whisper.

"I don't believe it!" She hopped up off the sofa. "Marc had someone else – in your bed?" She looked over to Frankie for confirmation. Frankie nodded back grimly.

"Oh come here, love." She sat back down beside me and hugged me.

"Nadia Williams? Isn't that the one from the Oscars?" Mr G asked.

"Well she didn't win, she was only nominated," an ever-loyal Frankie said quickly.

"I presume you've tried ringing him?" Mrs G asked nervously.

"Uh-huh," I sniffed. "I even rang the film set but they said he was busy. I'm just so confused."

They looked embarrassed and shocked by their son's

37

behaviour, so I knew they weren't hiding him in the press under the stairs. His Dad began to get angry and started to phone him from the ancient house phone, but he got the same bloody voicemail that I had been getting.

"Well this is terrible, Lily. I'm so sorry, I'm not sure what is going on with him – he's a grown man, he can't just do that to you and then up and disappear! I'll give that fella a right piece of my mind when I see him!"

I sniffed into the tissue.

It was after midnight, six cups of tea and more than enough slices of Madeira cake later, when Frankie and I said our goodbyes with Mrs G promising she would do her best to get hold of him.

Frankie dropped me off, and as I climbed up the steps to the duplex, I had to pass the gang of hooded teenagers from the bus the other day.

"Would you look who it is?" they roared. I gave them evil dagger eyes, but this just made them laugh even more. I closed the door and shut the world out.

Chapter 4

The next day, as I was setting back up my camp again on the sofa, I was flicking through one of the magazines that Frankie had brought for me. It had the headline **'IS CHERYL HEADING FOR MELTDOWN?'** in pink neon text, and suddenly I had a swell of love for Cheryl. We had a lot in common Cheryl and I - it was her and I crusading through a world of shitty men. She understood what it was like.

Just then I heard the doorbell ring and instantly my heart soared. It was the first time the bell had rung since Marc had left, and a small part of me thought that maybe he was finally coming home. He would have to come home eventually, wouldn't he? Maybe his parents had managed to get through to him. I hopped up from the sofa and ran to the door. I was just about to open it when it dawned on me that Marc obviously had a key, so would hardly ring his own doorbell. My heart fell quickly and heavily, and I was sure I could feel it plunging lower than it had ever been.

"Who is it?" I said, trying to sound normal and not let my tears of disappointment give me way.

"Lily, it's me – Dad."

Dad. The disappointment gripped me and left me reeling. I

really didn't want him to see me like this.

"Is everything alright, Lily?"

"Uh-huh," I said through the door.

"I don't mean to pry but it's just I hadn't heard from you, and you and Marc were meant to come over for your dinner this evening."

God I had totally forgotten about that. We had organised it the week before.

"Sorry, Dad - I'm sorry we forgot." The tears started.

"Lily, can you let me in please?"

"Oh sorry, yes of course." I wiped the tears away quickly with the back of my hand and opened the door to see the small neat frame of my Dad standing there, dressed in his usual slacks and V-neck jumper with a shirt and tie underneath.

"What's wrong, Lily? What's after happening?" he said taking one look at me.

"Oh, Dad," I sobbed and instantly he wrapped me in his familiar arms and rubbed my hair like he used to do to calm me when I was a little girl.

"It's Marc - he's gone," I sobbed.

"What do you mean 'gone'? Has he gone out with his friends?"

"He's left me for someone else," I said in a whisper.

"He couldn't have, Lily! Sure you're only just married!"

"It's true, Dad, I found him in bed with Nadia Williams, and now he is gone."

"Isn't that the one who won the Oscar?" Dad asked open-mouthed.

"She didn't win - she was only nominated," I said, bitterly repeating what Frankie had said to Marc's parents the other evening. "I don't know where he is or what's going on. He won't answer my calls. His parents don't even know where he is."

"Oh, Lily, I'm so sorry - I . . . I . . . I'm speechless - I don't know what to say. Come here, love."

He wrapped me in one of his strong Daddy hugs that have helped to comfort me ever since I was a little girl.

"There, there now. I'm sure there is a perfectly reasonable explanation for all of this."

"Dad how can there be a reasonable explanation for him having sex with someone else?" Just saying the word "sex" to my Dad felt weird. I saw the heat creep up along his face.

"Well you don't think they were acting maybe, y'know for one of them films he's working on?"

"Ah, Dad come on!" I knew he was just trying to reassure me but I wasn't five years old anymore. He was trying his best to be upbeat, but dear God this was above and beyond reasonable.

"Yes, em . . . Lily, I suppose you're right. Had everything been alright between you both before that?"

"As far as I knew we were happy newly-weds but obviously, Marc didn't see it like that."

"Well holy God – I don't know what has come over that fella," Dad said clearly in shock.

***

A short while after Dad had gone home, my phone rang. It was my sister Clara. I had been expecting this call.

"Lily, it's me, Clara – Dad tells me you're having some kind of *crisis* with Marc?"

"Well yes . . . you could say that."

"What on earth could you have possibly done to make him leave so soon, Lily? I mean, God you're only married a wet week! You're hardly Jennifer Lopez!"

"Look, Clara – I'm as shocked by this as anyone. I don't –"

"Well you just have to get him back, Lily – you can't have had a failed marriage after only three months! It's pathetic!"

I was stunned by her reaction. Granted Clara was never one to beat around the bush, but a bit of compassion would have been nice.

"I -"

But she cut me off mid-sentence. "Sorry I have to dash – Joshua is smearing my *Crème de la Mer* all over Jacob's piano – it is probably some jealous reaction to his brother's recent piano success, but it must be nipped in the bud this instant. We'll talk soon –"

"But he's only two!" I was about to say, but she had already hung up on me.

Chapter 5

Somehow the days all joined together, and it turned into two weeks since Marc had left me. His parents had managed to get hold of him, but he wouldn't tell them anything. Mrs Glover had been so upset as she recalled how he had got aggressive with her and warned them not to interfere during their brief phone conversation. He wouldn't even tell them what was going on. So I was still none-the-wiser.

My phone rang. My heart skipped a beat as usual, hoping against hope that it was Marc. But when I looked at the screen, I saw it was just Clara. I would have to stop torturing myself like this every time it rang. The disappointment when I realised that it wasn't him was unbearable. Ever since Dad had told Clara about what had happened she had been calling me constantly, demanding an update and a progress report on the steps I had taken to get him back.

She didn't waste time on pleasantries, and instead cut straight to the point. "Lily – I'm in the area. I had to drop Jacob off to Suzuki violin lessons, there is an excellent teacher out your way believe it or not! Who would have thought it, all the way out in little Ballyrobin? She was the second violinist with the Dublin Philharmonic Orchestra. So myself and Joshua will be over in ten minutes, okay?"

I groaned internally, I was not in the mood for a visit from Clara. She was the last person you would want a visit from when you were going through a shitty time. I would rather poke pins in my eyes than see her. Since Marc had gone, I had managed to avoid seeing her face to face but I knew she would catch up with me eventually.

"Sure," I said. "I'll be here."

I dragged myself off the sofa and picked up an armful of sweet wrappers and the pizza box that Frankie had brought the week before. I opened the window to let some air into the room and then I ran and jumped into the shower. There was nothing like a visit from Clara to snap me back into reality.

Sure enough exactly ten minutes later the doorbell rang. With dread, I summoned the will to open the door.

"Hi, Clara, hi, Joshua," I said wearily.

She was dressed in her Tod's loafers, camel trousers cut off at the ankle and a navy blazer. It was the daytime uniform of all the yummy mummies where she lived.

"Hi, Ni-ni," my two year old nephew greeted me.

I smiled down at him. He was getting so big.

"Look at the state of you!" Clara said.

And this was post-shower. I was glad she hadn't seen me half an hour earlier.

"Thanks, Clara!"

"Sit down," I gestured to the sofa. "Can I get you a coffee?"

"No, no, we won't stay long, it's just a flying visit."

"Beebies, beebies," Joshua kept repeating.

"Pardon, Joshua?" Clara bent down to his level to understand what he was saying.

"I think he wants me to turn on CBeebies," I said. I had babysat Jacob and Joshua the month previously while Clara was at a wedding, and only for CBeebies I don't know how we all would have survived the day.

"But how does he know about it? We have a strict no TV rule in our house," she asked in bewilderment.

"I have no idea – he's obviously a very intelligent child."

This seemed to satisfy her. "Yes, you're right, Lily – he is."

She took out a jigsaw puzzle from her monstrous handbag and put Joshua sitting on the floor with it. "It has eighty pieces," she said proudly before walking over to the sofa, which she inspected closely before sitting down with obvious trepidation.

"So Marc is gone then?" she whispered so Joshua wouldn't hear although I don't know why, he was two years old, he hadn't a notion what we were talking about.

"Uh-huh," I nodded.

"But surely you must have suspected something?"

I shook my head.

"Lily, you can't just arrive home from work and find your husband in bed with someone else. There must have been signs?"

"Clara, believe me, I have thought about this over and over, trying to see if there was anything in hindsight that should have warned me, but it has been a complete bolt from the blue."

"I don't know how you always manage to mess things up so badly for yourself. You were only married a matter of weeks!"

"Clara, this really isn't helping me."

"Well I'm sorry, Lily but you have to face up to this. Someone needs to be the sensible one here."

I stayed quiet.

"Were there problems in the bedroom department?" she probed. "Was that it?"

Dear God, I did not want to have this conversation with her of all people.

"No, Clara. No, there weren't," I sighed wearily.

"Well, Lily you know what men are like, if they're not getting it at home -"

"Clara, can you please stop. There was nothing wrong with our sex life."

"Keep your voice down," she instructed nodding over to Joshua. "Well maybe you weren't being attentive enough?"

"Attentive – that sounds like something from a Mrs Beeton manual!"

"Scoff you may, Lily, but Mrs Beeton wasn't too far off the mark actually. Men are simple creatures really. All it takes is a girl to come and pay them a bit more attention than their wife is giving them and bang – he falls into her arms."

"Wow, you are such an expert!"

"Well I have been happily married for ten years now," she

said proudly fingering her wedding band and not picking up on my sarcasm at all. "Oh dear, look at the time! Poor Jacob likes me to come and sit in on the last five minutes of his lesson, I have to run."

"Yes, you'd better go. You don't want to be late."

She gathered up the jigsaw and Joshua, and was just heading out the door when she turned back to me.

"And by the way, why aren't you in work?"

"Eh, Clara in case you haven't noticed, my husband has just walked out on me!"

"Lily, you need to stop this and pull yourself together, moping around here in this tiny little apartment won't help."

"It's a duplex –" I said defensively. She was forever calling it an apartment and it infuriated me. I knew it was small but it was my home, only I was allowed to say anything negative about it. Just because Clara was older and she and Tom had had enough money to buy their house years before the crash, she was smug and felt she was an expert on the whole property market. She was one of those irritating people who claimed she had seen it coming a mile away and it was nothing at all to do with the benefit of hindsight.

"Apartment/duplex, whatever you want to call it, Lily. Either way, you need to get your life together. Look at the state of you - lolling around here in your tracksuit! Only three months married and your husband walks out, you live in a poky flat in a poorly finished development in the middle of God knows where,

47

and even though you have a degree in marketing you're still working in the same part-time job that you had during college. You're thirty-three years of age for God's-sake!"

"Thirty-two," I said through gritted teeth.

"Honestly, Lily, let's not split hairs here. When I was your age, I had already been married for five years, I had just given birth to Jacob *and* I was next in line to be made a partner in McCann-Bateman-Foy, only that I decided to choose motherhood as the career path for me! You really need to give your life an audit. I have the number of a wonderful life coach. I will business card it to you later."

"Thanks," I muttered, just to get her out the door.

"Okay come along, Joshua"

"Me give Ni-ni kiss"

"No, Joshua, it is 'I-want-to-give-Lily-a-kiss'," she echoed back to him.

He looked up at her in confusion.

I bent down and swooped him up into my arms and planted kisses all over his crown of soft blonde curls.

"Bye, bye, little man."

"Bye, bye, Ni-ni."

I stood and watched them walking back down the steps heading towards Clara's SUV.

As soon as I waved them off, I went back in and closed the door and took a deep breath. I knew what Clara was like, I knew to expect that sort of reaction from her, so why did I let her get to me so much? She was like a whirlwind, she would come in, totally turn my life upside down with her cutting words and then she would breeze back out through the door again, leaving me brooding and upset over all that she had said, whereas I knew she wouldn't give her words a second thought. She didn't need to be so horrible by insinuating that the reason Marc had left me was because I wasn't keeping him happy at home! I knew she had a point about work though; there was only so long more I could get away with being absent. Sooner or later I was going to have to face it. And then it suddenly dawned on me - what if Marc had emailed me in work? Maybe he had sent me an explanation for all of this and it was sitting there in my inbox waiting for me all this time? I decided that the next morning I would have to brave the smell of urine and go back to work.

Chapter 6

My alarm woke me at bang on seven the next morning. I started work at nine, but I had to catch the bus at 7.45 to face the hour-long commute from Ballyrobin into the city centre. Usually I would sleep through my alarm clock and wake in a panic at half past seven and have to sprint to the bus stop, but that day I was determined to be on time.

I dragged myself out of bed and hurried into the shower. After I had dried myself off, I went over to my wardrobe and took out a grey pencil skirt and crisp white shirt. I had just buttoned it up when I noticed there was a stain down the front. I vaguely remembered spilling pasta on it a few weeks ago. Damn it. I took it off again, and found a green silk blouse and put that on instead. I was amazed at how much easier my clothes now fitted me. If there was one upside to this break up, it was that I still didn't have the appetite to eat. I decided to be brave and weigh myself, and I couldn't believe it when the scales said I was a whopping full stone lighter. But it was a hollow victory when I didn't even care about how much easier my skirt zipped up, or that for the first time since I was fourteen how I almost had a flat tummy again. None of it mattered when Marc didn't even get to see it. I managed to find a new pair of tights and my black court shoes. I normally just wore black trousers and a cardigan to work, but I wanted to feel good that day. I needed the confidence boost of knowing I looked my best.

I breathed in the cool morning air as I walked to the bus stop. It felt alien as I walked along listening to the birdsong and watching the spring buds that were starting to sprout on the branches of the trees. I hadn't been outside in daylight since Frankie had brought me home the day after Marc had left. For once I made it to the bus stop in time to grab a coffee-to-go in the café next door to sip while I waited for the bus to come.

Soon the bus pulled up and I climbed on board. I lowered my head when I saw it was the same driver that had brought me to Frankie's the evening I had found Marc and Nadia in bed together. I hoped he wouldn't recognise me as the bedraggled, tear-stained face that had sat on his bus only two weeks ago.

When I got off the bus an hour later, I made my way up the quays to Rapid Response's headquarters. I signed in at the reception desk at a very respectable ten to nine and walked up to my desk.

I quickly switched on my PC and waited the usual ten minutes for it to load up. None of my team was in yet so it gave me a few minutes to get my story together about my severe case of food poisoning. I smelt his sickly aftershave before I saw him; Stephen Swan, the call centre manager and my boss, was standing beside me clutching a travel mug.

"Well good morning, Lily – you're back!"

"I sure am," I tried to sound enthusiastic, but I just wanted him to go away so I could check my emails to see if there was anything from Marc.

"Feeling better?" he asked with a wry smile on his face.

"Much better thank you."

"That was some bout of food poisoning you got. Two weeks?" He raised his eyebrows.

"Yeah, I know it was horrific, I'm never eating shell-fish again."

"Shell-fish, I thought you said it was chicken?"

Oh shit. Everything had been such a blur the day after Marc left that I couldn't remember what excuse I had made up to Stephen.

"Well we weren't sure – I mean I had shell-fish, Marc had chicken and I tried some of his but he was fine so it must have been the shell-fish." I winced having to mention Marc's name like all was normal.

"Hmmh, well Rosie did a great job while you were away, didn't you, Rosie?"

I turned around to see a blushing Rosie Redford, had just arrived in and was taking off her woollen Orla Kiely coat and putting her gorgeous calfskin Prada bag with its soft buttery leather down onto the desk in front of her.

Rosie was beautiful, five foot ten, with long athletic limbs. Her dark hair was always blow-dried to perfection, her nails were always the same length and neatly manicured. She dressed immaculately; her wardrobe was to die for. Today she was wearing a red dress that I was sure I had seen in a magazine as being from Victoria Beckham's new Spring/Summer collection. She was also a champion show-jumper and had competed for Ireland before getting a bad fall, so now she just jumped for fun. She always had somewhere cool to go after work – art exhibitions, charity balls, film premieres or restaurant launches. And she didn't just go to concerts – Rosie always managed to have "Access All Areas backstage passes" for concerts. Unlike most people, Rosie didn't need to work, her Father owned The Savoy, Dublin's swankiest hotel, as well as a huge property portfolio and he would gladly have taken his daughter on board the family empire, but Rosie maintained that she wanted to earn her own money and not to just live off the trust-fund that her Father had set up for her. Even her morals were gorgeous.

"Lily, it's great to have you back – it was so busy without you," she said kindly.

"Thank you, Rosie, and thanks for looking after things while I was away."

"Don't mention it – I'm just glad you're feeling better. It sounds like you had a horrendous bout."

"Yeah, it was terrible," I lied. "I just want to have a quick check through my emails first and then we might sit down together and catch up on things for half an hour if you don't mind?"

"Sure, Lily, let me know when you're free."

Stephen was still standing there with his mouth hanging open, drooling over Rosie.

"Stephen is there anything else you want to talk to me about?" I asked.

"Eh, no – that's it."

"Well I'm going to get stuck in here and make a start on some of this backlog if that's okay?"

"Eh, yes . . . of course." Embarrassed, he took the hint and walked off.

I quickly scanned through the new messages in my inbox but was sorely disappointed to find that not one of them was from Marc. Why had I allowed myself to get my hopes up so much? If he wasn't going to ring me, he was hardly going to email me. All of my excitement and resolve from that morning quickly evaporated and I was starting to feel like shit again. Rosie had typed me up a report outlining all of the calls and complaints she had dealt with for each day during my absence. I had to admire her efficiency; I would never in a million years have thought of doing something like that.

It didn't take long before I was back dealing with all the problem calls. The first was from a woman asking why her test result wasn't positive, I tried to explain to her as nicely as possible that it meant that either she had tested too early or that she actually wasn't pregnant, but she just wouldn't accept it. She listed off all the pregnancy signs that she had had that month, then she just broke down on the phone and started to cry, saying that this was the tenth month that she and her husband had been trying for a baby. I had to do everything in my power not to cry with her. My heart broke for people like her. I tried to be nice and to listen, because I knew she was just looking for someone to talk to. When I had hung up on that woman, I could hear Rosie at the desk beside me consoling a woman who obviously didn't want to be pregnant, and was asking if a positive test could ever be wrong. If only we were able to swop the test results of both women. Sometimes I thought we ought to be trained counsellors.

When lunchtime came, I picked up my bag and strolled outside into the spring sunshine. I had emailed Frankie to see if she was around for lunch. She said she was proud of me for going back to work and we had arranged to meet outside the Merrion deli. We grabbed a sandwich and sat on a park bench as the sound of bright birdsong mixed with the hum of the city. Frankie looked cool as usual, wearing a printed silk tunic, ribbed leggings underneath, black biker boots and a fitted leather blazer with a silk scarf around her neck.

"It's good to see you back, Lily – you look great. I presume you still haven't heard a dicky bird from himself?"

I shook my head.

"He's gone isn't he, Frankie?" I said glumly.

"Don't think like that now, wait until you see him."

"But it's been over two weeks. He's hardly coming home now."

Frankie said nothing.

"I can't believe I've a failed marriage at the age of thirty-two."

"Yeah you're a wild child, Lily McDermott – you would fit in nicely in Hollywood!" She smiled at me.

I nudged her shoulder playfully.

"Dear God, it's such a mess though, isn't it?"

"Just take each day as you find it."

"But everything – my whole life – is a joke. I know I've been saying this for years, but I really need to get out of Rapid Response. You should see how well Rosie managed things while I was away."

"Rosie is gorgeous," Frankie sighed. "I think I fancy her."

Frankie had met Rosie a few times, on some nights out in town and at our wedding.

"Me too," I sighed in agreement.

"What was she wearing today?" Frankie always asked me what Rosie wore to work. Every day.

"A red Victoria Beckham dress, tan Louboutins and her Prada bag – that's my favourite one."

"I love her Hermès Birkin bag," she said wistfully.

"It's amazing," I agreed.

"Look maybe now is a great time to really start thinking about what you want to do with your life, Lily?"

"You sound like Clara."

"No I mean it, you've been saying for years that you need a change, and now is the perfect time to do it."

"Hmmh, maybe you're right. But what could I do?"

"Well something you enjoy and are passionate about! Start thinking about it."

"Shit! What time is it?" I said hopping up off the bench.

"Nearly two."

"Damn, I'm going to be late back, and I was doing so well today!"

"Call over after work and we'll share a bottle of wine," she said.

We said a hasty goodbye and I ran back towards the office. As I tried to sneak back to my desk, Stephen tutted and looked at his watch as I walked quickly past him muttering, "Some things never change".

The conversation with Frankie at lunchtime had got me thinking. She was right, I needed a change, and since my life had already gone tits up, I knew that now might be a good time to try something new. Things couldn't have got much worse than they were right then, I reasoned. When I had a quiet spell in the afternoon, I took out my notebook and started writing a list of things I could do with my life. I love lists. Lists make me happy. There was no better feeling in this life than putting all the little niggly things you have to do down on a sheet of paper and then crossing them off with one fell swoop as soon as you have completed the task. I thought about what I could do and what options were open to me. I knew I could get another job similar to what I was doing in Rapid Response – I had lots of experience after all, and I was sure Stephen would give me an ok-ish reference, but I really didn't want to work in another call centre. It would be like jumping out of the frying pan and into the fire. I knew I could try and do something with my business degree, but I broke out in a cold sweat at the thoughts of doing an interview. I shuddered when I imagined all the questions potential employers would be asking me, wondering why I never bothered doing anything with my degree after college. Plus when I had done my degree the *Celtic Tiger* was alive and roaring – I was sure everything I studied was probably well out of date at this stage.

I could work in a shop I reasoned, maybe a clothes shop or something. I might even get a discount on lots of lovely clothes, but the idea just didn't excite me. If I was going to change career, I wanted to do it properly. I wanted to do something that I loved, that I was really passionate about. I wanted to be like Frankie and to get out of bed every morning and not dread going to work. I brainstormed for a bit longer, but soon found my list changing to a list of reasons why I still loved Marc.

***

That evening I sat back on Frankie's sofa with my feet curled up underneath me while she poured us a large fishbowl shaped glass of wine each.

"I was talking to Joannah earlier, she said she'd been trying to get you," Frankie said.

Frankie, Joannah and I had all been friends in school, although I saw a lot more of Frankie these days, but we still kept in touch with Joannah.

"Yeah, she's left me four messages already. I'm just not ready to talk about it yet though, y'know?"

"Yeah I guessed that. Well you're not going to like this, Lily –" Frankie said.

"What is it, Frankie – my life is a mess, one more little upset won't matter," I sighed wearily.

"Well it's baby Noah's christening on Saturday."

"I know, I'm making the cake for it. " Baking was a hobby of mine - well it was my only hobby really, if you excluded eating and sleeping. I made cakes for family and friends whenever they had a special occasion. I loved the feeling of moulding the sugar-paste between my fingers and crafting it into different shapes.

"She wants us both to come –"

"Well, I can't go. No way. I don't mind doing the cake but I couldn't face the rest if it."

"You have to – I said we'd both be there," Frankie winced.

"Noooo!" I groaned. "Why did you say I'd go? You know what those things are like!" I pleaded to Frankie.

"It might do you good to get out of the house for a while."

"I am out of the house – I'm here aren't I?"

"My place and work don't count. Look we won't stay long and sure we'll lash into the wine when we get back to the house afterwards – it'll be grand."

I said nothing. Just a few weeks ago Marc and I had called over together to Joannah and Noel's house to meet baby Noah, and now here I was with my husband missing in action. It was still so raw. I really didn't want to go and face people. I knew Frankie had told Joannah about Marc and I, but I wasn't ready to talk about it yet and I knew she would have a million questions for me. I was dreading it.

Chapter 7

When Saturday came around, I dragged myself out of bed and into the shower to make myself look somewhat presentable. I had decided that I was going to make an effort with what I wore, because I wanted to look like I was doing okay, even if I really wasn't. I didn't want a barrage of questions or worse still, people to pity me. I put on a simple black and green shift dress that zipped up easily at the side, without me having to lie on the bed and suck in my stomach to get the zip up and then spend the day worrying that it might burst if I moved too suddenly. I put on a pair of grey suede ankle boots and put loose rollers in my hair in an effort to transform my stringy hair into the voluminous tresses of Kate Middleton, but I needn't have bothered as the curls had fallen out before I had even left the house.

I put the cake I had spent all the previous day making into a box. It was a two tier lemon sponge cake covered in white icing. I had cut out miniature bunting from blue icing and draped it along the sides of the cake. I had fashioned four tiny building blocks from the remainder of the blue icing and had piped the letters of baby Noah's name onto each block. I arranged them along the base of the cake. It had turned out well; I just hoped Joannah would like it.

Frankie picked me up and we headed for the church where the christening was to take place.

I swallowed back a lump in my throat as the pointed steeple came into view in the distance; it was St. Columba's church – the same church where Marc and I had got married.

"This is going to be hell," I muttered to Frankie.

"C'mon," she said putting her arm around my shoulder and steering me inside. I hadn't been back in the church since our wedding day – yes I know I am a hypocrite. As I walked up the aisle, I couldn't help thinking over everything that had happened during the last few weeks. When we said our vows up there at the altar, there was no way I had seen this coming.

We sat in a pew midway down the church.

"Are you okay?" Frankie asked, looking concerned.

"I'll be fine – I'm just a bit sad."

She gave my hand a quick squeeze.

Some priests enjoy a full bells and whistles ceremony, no matter how many times they do a mass they still get a kick from it, and unfortunately Fr Furey fell into this category.

To make matters worse, baby Noah wasn't the only baby being christened that day. No, there were seven other babies to get through too. I took a deep breath in – it was going to be a long one. Frankie and I obeyed the ceremony, we stood when everyone else stood, we knelt when everyone else knelt down, except for the bit where some people knelt and some stayed standing, neither of us was too sure which group were right or what to do, so we kind of half knelt, half stood. We prayed along with everyone else, and we reamed off a list of Saints, most of whom I had never even heard of when finally, two hours later, it was over and we headed back to Joannah and Noel's place.

"I need a stiff one after that," Frankie sighed.

"Me too."

Back in the house I set up the cake, while Joannah settled baby Noah. Frankie made chitchat with the various aunties and uncles. When I was finished I went to the toilet, and came back to find Frankie deep in conversation with Noel's elderly grandaunt. She was singing the praises of Fr Furey saying how he always did a good mass, and that some of the younger priests these days didn't put the time in but Fr Furey always enjoyed a good sermon. I needed to rescue Frankie so I called her over and pretended that I wanted her for something.

Myself and Frankie looked odd among all the friends and relations. All of Joannah and Noel's other friends were coupled up and had babies, so they had something in common. They automatically gravitated towards each other and sat together, taking over the sitting room. Two women beside us were deep in conversation, practically competing about how many times they had been up with their teething babies the night before. Then when the sleep deprivation conversation had been exhausted, they moved on to discussing the number of cubes their little ones were taking belonging to some lady called Annabel Caramel or something that sounded like a toffee apple.

I could feel Frankie getting restless beside me.

"Here, where is the wine?" Frankie asked looking around her but there was no sign of it.

Eventually we spotted Noel making his way over to us with a tray with two bottles.

"Now, ladies, sorry it's taking me so long to get over here, you're both probably parched, what would you two like to drink?"

"I'll have a glass of red please, Noel," Frankie said.

"Eh, I only have sparkling water or apple juice I'm afraid, girls." He was apologetic.

Frankie and I took another look at the tray where sure enough, instead of red and white wine, the bottles were actually sparkling water and some fancy-dan apple juice. We both looked at his hands to make sure he wasn't hiding it somewhere else.

"Eh, have you any wine at all, Noel?" Frankie asked panicked. "Even rosé?"

"'Fraid not. Sorry, Frankie, we're not serving any alcohol today. It is baby Noah's day after all," he reminded her gently.

"What? No alcohol?" Frankie shouted loudly so some of the relations turned to look at her.

"No worries, Noel – I'll have a sparkling water and Frankie will have the same won't you?" I said giving her a look.

"Sure," she said sulkily.

"I can't believe there is no alcohol - that was the only reason

I came to this bloody thing!" Frankie hissed through gritted teeth as soon as Noel had gone.

Soon they were doing the obligatory passing the baby around and I could see baby Noah was getting closer as he made his way towards us. Don't get me wrong, I loved baby Noah, he was the most gorgeous little pudding making o-shapes with his small mouth and bashing his arms about over his head, but I knew I was going to get upset when it was my turn to hold him and I was terrified I might not be able to keep my emotions in check. The last time I had held him was with Marc, and we had cooed over how cute he was the whole way home in the car. We had talked about when we had our own babies and how if we had a little boy, he would be dressed like a mini-Marc, or if it were a girl how protective Marc would be over her. We hadn't decided on when we were going to start a family, we hadn't had *that* conversation but we both knew we wanted children at some point in the future.

When it was Frankie's turn to hold him. I could feel my palms beginning to get clammy – it would be my turn next. Frankie freely admitted she was uncomfortable with babies, she was the youngest child in her family and she never babysat as a teenager, plus they always cried as soon as they were in her care. Her awkward arms were held stiffly at just the wrong angle. Sure enough two seconds later, baby Noah began to scrunch up his face before letting out a wailing cry. I could see the panic in Frankie's face begging for someone to take the baby off her.

Joannah came rushing over, laughing at Frankie's awkwardness as she promptly removed Noah from her arms, and without warning offered him to me to hold while she went to fetch the prawn parcels from the oven. I took baby Noah into my arms and watched his eyelids get heavy again as he settled back to sleep. I sniffed his milky head. He was just so pudgy and gorgeous; I wanted to squeeze him so tight against my chest. I felt my eyes filling with tears so I wiped them away quickly.

"He likes you," Joannah said when she had returned and was offering us a tray of hors d'oeuvres.

"He is just gorgeous, Joannah, you and Noel are very lucky." I meant it.

"Thank you, Lily, and thank you so much for the cake, you did an amazing job as usual. Everyone has been asking me about it. Honestly, you're just like a professional."

"Don't mention it," I mumbled feeling embarrassed.

She paused before continuing. "I heard about Marc . . . how are you doing?"

"Well . . . I . . . em . . . well I'm not going to lie, it's tough."

"Uh-huh, uh-huh." She was nodding her head quickly so I could tell she wasn't really listening.

"But you're doing good, aren't you?" She was doing that awkward head tilted to the side thing.

"Well yeah, I'm just taking each day as it comes, y'know?"

"But you're okay, aren't you?"

There was only one answer she wanted to hear.

"Yeah I'm doing fine, Joannah."

"Great!" She let out a huge sigh of relief. I could almost hear the 'phew – thank God she's not going to ruin my baby's christening' at the end of it.

"Now, I'll take him off you and put him down for a nap. Would you mind serving these for a few minutes?"

"Not at all." She handed me the tray and scooped up her newborn son from my arms, smiling down on his sleepy face. I felt the wrench tighten once again around my heart.

As I walked around the room, politely offering appetisers to the guests, I felt an arm pulling me out into the hall. It was Frankie.

"Leave that there." She lifted the tray from my hands and plonked it down on the console table. "C'mon, quick." She pulled me into the downstairs loo and bolted the door behind us.

"What are you doing? You scared the bejaysus out of me!"

"Here, I found some alcohol," she sang giddily as she produced a bottle of wine from underneath her cardigan. "An excellent bouquet if I do say so myself," she said mimicking a wine connoisseur.

"Where did you find that?" I asked in a mixture of horror and gratefulness.

"In a press in the kitchen."

"You went snooping around her cupboards? What if she notices it's missing?"

"She won't. There's a load more where that came from –

they have a right little wine bar going on in there, pity the stingy gits wouldn't serve it!"

"Frankie!" But I couldn't hold back a smile. "How are we going to open it?"

"Screw-cap!"

She promptly opened the bottle before putting it up to her lips and knocking it back before handing it over to me.

"This is dead classy, I must say – we're both over thirty years of age and drinking wine from the bottle while squashed into a downstairs toilet."

We continued swigging from the bottle until there was a knock at the door from someone who wished to use the bathroom. We polished off the rest very quickly and I hid the empty bottle in Frankie's bag. When we emerged from the toilet we got a strange look from one of the women who had been having the sleep deprivation contest and was waiting to go in.

We weren't out two minutes when I was starting to feel a bit light-headed from the speed we had drunk the wine at. Noel had started to give a little speech thanking everyone for coming to share the day with them and how baby Noah had completely changed their lives. He revealed that they had actually come up with his name from amalgamating both of their names No-ah. I had never copped that before. I watched Joannah who was smiling up lovingly at him as he spoke. I would be lying if I said I didn't feel just a tinge of jealousy while looking at the two of them – not in a bad way, but I used to have that. Marc and I used to be like that. How had it come to this? Don't get me wrong, I was happy for Joannah and Noel - baby Noah was gorgeous, and the transformation that had overcome the two of them had been nothing short of astounding, but I had thought that that was what was in the plan for Mark and I too – not a runaway husband. I must have stared for just a second too long, because they instantly pulled away from each other when they saw me looking at them. Joannah flashed me a sympathetic look, and it just made everything worse. I didn't want their pity - I just wanted my husband back.

Chapter 8

The next day, Clara had invited Dad and I over for Sunday lunch, she took these figaries now and again. They were normally quite a formal affair, the two boys would be dressed in their Sunday best of chinos and shirts - her husband Tom too, and woe betide anyone who turned up wearing jeans. Clara would serve up a three-course meal, and then after dessert Jacob would perform a little recital of what he had learnt in piano lessons that week before we were excused from the table.

My first mistake was that I had arrived majorly hungover. After baby Noah's christening, Frankie and I had hit town and had a fairly wild night culminating in a bar in Leeson Street. I dared not tell Clara that I had only been in bed for four hours, but I'm sure she could smell the vodka fumes on my breath.

I took my designated seat around the oval mahogany table that Clara had bought at an auction. The table was set with the heavy silver canteen that Mum and Dad had received as a wedding present, but Dad had no use for them now and I *certainly* didn't, so he had passed them onto Clara. The candles were lit in the silver candelabras, and classical music was playing gently in the background.

"How's work, Tom?" Dad asked politely. Tom was a barrister, and had made a fortune in the nineties from tribunals that had pretty much set him and Clara up for life. He had made a name for himself as being able to find a loophole in even the most black and white of arguments, and now was in demand by the top companies and individuals in Ireland when they needed a strong case made.

Clara cut in, "Tom is very busy working for some high profile clients at the moment," she lowered her voice to a whisper, "I'm not meant to say it but it's the Butler case." She sat back against the chair with a triumphant smile on her face. For a man used to holding his own in the courtroom, Clara never let him speak for himself. Tom glared at her but she was oblivious.

Clara was referring to the sinister court-case that was all over the news whereby a prominent businessman had been accused of murdering his wife to cash in on the huge fortune she had recently inherited from her wealthy family to help him repay some of his debts. We listened as Clara divulged far too much information about Mr Butler while Tom squirmed uncomfortably in his chair, but he was afraid to tell her to shut-up at the same time.

"So, Lily, any word from Marc?" Clara turned to me when she had finished spilling the beans about Tom's confidential work.

I knew we'd have to address the elephant in the room sooner or later.

"Ermm . . . no actually, not a word," I said quietly.

Dad reached for my hand under the table and squeezed it tightly inside his own.

"I presume you're still trying to make contact with him?" she continued.

"Of course, I'm ringing him every day - he's even avoiding his own parents right now though."

"Oh dear. It's not looking good then is it? I was just saying to Tom before you came in the door that it's all very odd isn't it, Lily? I mean you must have seen it coming? You must have seen *some* signs?"

"I didn't honestly, Clara, it's been as big a shock for me, as anyone," I said quietly.

"Yes well being separated after only a few months of marriage is pretty shocking alright. It really doesn't bear thinking about - being separated before you are even thirty-five years of age. It's not really something to be proud of now, is it?"

There she was again, twisting the knife in a little deeper.

"Now, Clara, go easy –" Tom went to speak but before he could finish, Clara had cut him off; she always had to have the last word.

"Jacob would you play the piece you learnt this week please?"

And we all sat brooding in angry silence while Jacob played his piece note-perfectly.

"Good boy, Jacob!" Clara declared when he was finished

while we all clapped exaggeratedly. "Of course you will need to practice the second movement again but a good effort all in all."

Clara was like Simon Cowell on the X-factor. Poor Jacob, how I wished she could just say well done and leave it at that instead of always pushing him for more.

When we could finally go, Dad dropped me home.

"So how are you doing, pet?" he asked kindly as we drove along from the leafy streets of Ballsbridge where Clara lived to the backs of beyond of Ballyrobin.

"I'm okay, Dad, good days and bad days."

"Of course – it's all still very fresh."

"Why did he do this, Dad?"

"Well it's beyond me, because you're such a beautiful, intelligent woman and I think he was very lucky to have you."

"You would say that!"

"I'm very proud of you, Lily, you know that."

"I wish Marc thought the same way," I sighed wearily.

"Well more fool him if doesn't realise how special you are!" He was uncharacteristically sharp.

"Do you think it's my fault, Dad? Maybe if . . . I don't know, if I had done things differently – looked different – I don't know maybe, lost some weight?"

"Will you stop that nonsense talk, aren't you the most beautiful young woman?"

"But Clara always says –"

"Don't mind your sister. You know what she's like. She

doesn't mean to be so . . . well –" he paused for the right word, "thoughtless."

"Well tact and Clara were never very friendly."

He flashed me a smile and reached across the gearstick with his left hand and put it over mine.

"I know it hurts now, Lily and to be honest none of us know what way it's going to pan out, but keep your chin up. Keep that head of yours held high do you hear me? No man is worth your tears, Lily. I'm one myself so I should know." He smiled at me.

"I love him so much, Dad – I would do anything for him. I just don't think I'll ever get over it." My voice started to quiver.

"You will, my dear, and this might be a hard thing to hear right now but I'm a firm believer that everything happens for a reason."

I knew he meant well, but I really hoped he was wrong on this one.

Chapter 9

It had been almost four weeks since Marc had left. Four weeks since I had found him in bed with that woman, and four weeks since I had last seen or heard from him. It had finally sunk in that he wasn't coming back. I had stopped trying to get hold of him. It was hard to believe that he didn't want to talk to me, but he had changed his number, blocked me on Facebook and avoided the many attempts that I had made to contact him in work, so I was finally getting the message. I went through the motions every day – I got up and went to work, and dealt with horrible Stephen as he continuously leered over poor Rosie. She always managed to remain composed, even though I could tell she would love to stick pins in his eyes. Weekends were usually a hungover blur, spent with Frankie so I didn't have to face being on my own.

One morning while I was in the middle of sorting out a new batch of returned pregnancy tests, wearing two pairs of latex gloves as well as a facemask while trying to avert my nose away from the stench of wee, my phone rang. My ringtone was One Direction's *What makes you beautiful*. I loved that song. Was it wrong to fancy them when they were almost half my age, I wondered? I checked to see who it was, but I didn't recognise the number. My curiosity got the better of me, so I peeled off the two pairs of gloves. I was just about to press the answer button when it stopped. I had just put on another two fresh pairs of gloves and was about to pick up another urine-ridden stick when it started ringing again. I got them off quicker this time and pressed answer. When I heard Marc's voice on the other end, I was nearly sick. My stomach somersaulted three hundred and sixty degrees. The conversation had pretty much gone like this:

"Hi, Lily, it's me –"

"Marc – I, well, I–" I had waited for four weeks for this moment, and now that it had come, I had turned into a gibbering wreck, incapable of forming any rational speech. I could see the heads of my team rising from behind their desks, wondering why I was acting weird on the phone to my own husband – they knew nothing about what had happened over the last few weeks. "Just um - just hang on a minute, I just want to go outside."

I went out of the lab where we separated the sticks, and into the corridor. "Sorry about that, y'know what this place is like . . ." I gave a small nervous laugh.

"Look, Lily, I'm sorry for everything that has happened over the last few weeks, I know I've been a complete asshole, actually that's probably even being kind . . . but I just needed some space."

"Uh-huh." My mind had gone blank. I couldn't think of what to say.

"Look, we need to talk. Can I come over – maybe this

evening? If you're free that is? I mean, if you've plans well . . . I can call tomorrow instead?"

The relief coursed through my body. Finally. Finally I was going to see him. Finally I might get to understand what had happened and why.

"No, no this evening is fine," I said quickly. I knew I sounded eager, but there was no way I was waiting another day to see him. "What time were you thinking?"

"Well how about eight. Would that be okay with you?"

"Sure. Eight is good with me."

When I hung up the phone my hands were shaking. Dear God I couldn't believe a brief phone call with my own husband could have this effect on me. Oh my God, oh my God, I was finally going to see him. My mind was racing with all kinds of possible scenarios as I tried to analyse every piece of our conversation. He had said he was sorry, and that he had needed space. Did that mean that he had finally come to his senses? I really didn't want to get my hopes up, but that was what it had sounded like. I rang Frankie straight away.

"You'll never guess what?"

"What?"

"Marc just phoned!"

"He did not!"

"Uh-huh."

"And did he say where he'd been hiding his skanky, asshole, cheating self for the last few weeks?"

"No, we didn't get into it, he just said that he was sorry and he needed some space. That sounds good, right?"

"Well, em –"

"He's coming over later, Frankie. To talk. God I'm so nervous just thinking about it. I know he's my husband and it's silly, but I'm a bundle of jitters."

"And what else did he say?"

"Well he said he was a complete asshole, but it sounds like he has finally copped himself on, doesn't it?"

"I know you're excited, but try not to get your hopes up, Lily," she cautioned.

"I thought you'd be happy for me?"

"Of course I am but well, I don't want you to be disappointed. Just don't raise your hopes too high that's all I'm saying."

"I'm not, Frankie." I knew I sounded defensive but I hoped she would have at least been excited for me.

Just then Stephen came out through the swinging double doors that led back into the lab.

"Lily – there are tests to be sorted in there. Maybe when you're finished your *personal* call, you could go back in and lend Rosie and the team some support?"

"Sure. Sorry, I'm coming now," I said to Stephen.

"Look, I've got to go here –" I said to Frankie.

"Okay well, good luck and make sure you let him know just how badly he's treated you. And ring me straight away as soon as

82

you can, no matter what time, okay?"

When I had hung up and went back in to my desk, I must say I was a bit miffed by Frankie's reaction. I knew she was just looking out for me and warning me to be cautious, but didn't she realise how monumental this was? I had been a devastated mess for the last few weeks, and now I finally was getting a chance to see my husband again and get some answers. I had just wanted her to be happy for me, but instead she had stripped the gloss off and made me seem silly for getting excited at all.

After the faulty tests had all been categorised, I headed back into the call centre. As I answered calls for the rest of the afternoon, I couldn't keep my head straight. My mind just kept wandering to all the possible scenarios that could happen that evening. I imagined us having a tearful heart to heart where Marc apologised over and over again, saying that he didn't know what had got into him and begged me to take him back if I could ever find room in my heart to forgive him. I wouldn't make it easy for him though – there was no doubt about that. He had hurt me very badly, but I just wanted to start over and move on from this awful mess.

***

Although it was long anyway, the journey home from work on the bus that evening felt longer than ever. Eight o'clock couldn't come quick enough. The traffic tailed back more than usual, and every set of lights that we came up against seemed to be red. I had hoped to have time to get myself ready before he called, and this was eating up valuable minutes.

I wanted to look good when Marc saw me, and I had planned exactly what I was going to wear on the bus journey home. I had decided on my favourite red polka dot tea-dress. I had worn it the day after our wedding. It was dressy but not formal, because I didn't want to look like I made *too* much of an effort. Luckily my fake tan was done from the weekend before, so I just needed to put a few rollers in my hair. Then I would touch up my make-up so it looked subtle, not like I was going out or anything. The only upshot of Marc leaving me for the last four weeks was that I had lost weight. I was always a curvy size fourteen, and no matter how many times I had tried to lose weight, I never had the will power to stick to a diet. I would always start full of good intentions on a Monday morning and by three o'clock I would be reaching for the Starbars again. Marc was always playing with my "jelly-belly" as he called it. He would make little remarks about how I should join the gym to get fit, or cut back on the salt and vinegar flavoured Hula Hoops – well wait until he saw me now – comfortably fitting into size twelve jeans! I was thinner now than when we had first met. I knew it was silly, but I really hoped that when he saw me looking good that he would remember what we used to have and realise how much he still loved me.

When I got in the door, I hurried down to the bedroom and quickly got changed. Once I had myself ready, I came out to the kitchen and threw some eggs, flour, butter, sugar and lemon zest together into a large mixing bowl to make some cupcakes – nothing too fancy, just some Madeira ones so I had something to offer him with a cup of coffee. I spooned the mixture into a muffin tin and "popped them in the oven," as Rachel Allen was so fond of saying. I put on the Paulo Nutini CD that we used to listen to together softly in the background in the hope that it would evoke some good memories for him.

When the cupcakes were finished I took them out of the oven to cool. The house had a lovely smell of baking. Didn't they always say that houses sold better when there was a smell of fresh baking? Well maybe the same trick would work for abandoned wives. Then I sat down and waited. And waited.

At eight on the button, I walked over to window to peer down into the car park to see if there was any sign of his Mazda MX-5 sports car down below, but he wasn't there yet. I kept hopping up every few minutes to check if he had arrived, and finally after I had checked the car park for the nineteenth time, I heard the bell ring. My stomach somersaulted, and my heart instantly started racing so loudly that I was sure Marc would be able to hear it through the door. I told myself that I was being ridiculous - he was my *husband* for God's sake but the word husband now seemed strange, it implied an automatic togetherness, or a righteousness, but we hadn't even got out of the starting blocks of our marriage. I cursed my thumping heart inwardly and told myself to calm down but to no effect, so I took a deep breath and pulled back the door.

"Marc!" I could hear myself crying out like this was all a lovely surprise instead of a pre-arranged visit. "Here, come in, come in." I knew my voice had a slightly hysterical edge to it. *Calm down, play it cool*, I warned myself.

I noticed he had new clothes – clothes that he didn't have before. There was a leather jacket for a start that didn't exist when he was with me and he was wearing skinny jeans. *Skinny jeans!* I had never seen him in anything remotely like that before. His hair was longer now too and he had it styled up high, at least two inches high on top of his head. And even though he never wore his hair like that when he was with me, I had to admit that it suited him like that – I wasn't too sure about the clothes though.

"Lily," he said nervously.

"Here sit down, well you don't need me to invite you to sit down . . . I mean it's your house too, so I shouldn't be telling you where you can and can't sit . . ." There it was again, the hysterical little laugh. "Would you like tea or coffee?"

"It's okay, look I can't stay long, Lily." He lowered his eyes to the floor. "Nadia is waiting in the car for me."

I felt as though he had taken a knife from the set that we were given as a wedding present and stabbed me in the centre of my being.

"Oh I see." My heart plummeted. All my excitement and anticipation at seeing him that evening was wiped away in an instant and replaced with a feeling of despair. "So are you two . . . *together* . . . then?" I found myself asking in a small voice that didn't sound like it came from me.

He nodded sheepishly.

The pain was unbearable, it wasn't just a spur of the moment thing where he had had an affair with another woman for a few weeks and was now regretting it. This was a lot worse. He was leaving me for her.

"That's why I called over – I feel it's only fair that I tell you in person that it's over between us, Lily. I'm sorry –"

"I -I -I -" I could feel my lip quiver. This wasn't happening. This wasn't happening. This really wasn't happening. Do not cry, I warned myself. Don't you dare cry, Lily McDermott!

"You look great, Lily, by the way," he smiled kindly at me. Did he really think that this compliment would soften the blow of the devastating news he had just told me? I knew all about this technique. The human resources department in work used it all the time - it was called sandwich feedback, where you *sandwich* some bad news in between two positive things, but it was for situations where things like your sales figures were down or "we've no wine left, but we do have beer" – not that your husband was leaving you for someone else. It was that same charming smile that he always used to get his way. That familiar smile that would always make me melt into his arms, no matter how hard I tried to be mad at him – all he had to do was flash me that smile and I was his, but did he really think that it would work here? That a compliment would ease the pain of what he was telling me?

"I just don't understand, Marc –" My voice was croaking and I knew it was going to break into tears. "I thought we were good, I just don't understand what I did to make you leave me?"

Then the tears started and I could feel my carefully applied mascara and eyeliner run in streams down my face. Then my nose began to run and drip. Don't be so desperate, have some pride, Lily, a voice warned inside my head but I shut it out.

"Look, Lily – I'm sorry. Really I am – it's just, well -" he broke off without finishing.

"Please, Marc, you owe me an explanation. You can't just up and leave me for someone else, we were only three months married!" I tried to wipe my snotty nose with the back of my hand. "You can't just move out!" I started to feel a bit light-headed. The ground felt like it was rising to meet me. I had to steady myself using the wall as a support.

"I'm sorry, Lily, my head is wrecked from it all. . ."

"Wrecked from all of what? I don't understand, Marc. It doesn't have to be wrecked – you can come home, we can work it out," I pleaded. I knew I sounded desperate.

"Look, Lily, please don't cry - I hate seeing you like this –"

"But, Marc – we're only just married. We're newly-weds for God's sake – you can't just leave!" I spluttered.

"Please don't make this any harder than it needs to be." He hung his head. "Lily, I love Nadia."

Another blow rained down upon me, I didn't think I could take it anymore.

"No, no you don't. You *think* you love her, but can't you see, Marc? She's just a fling! You can't just marry someone and then meet somebody new a few weeks later – that's not how it works! This is your home!"

He looked sheepishly at me.

"It's not just a fling, Lily – look can't you just try to be strong?"

"Please don't do this, Marc. Please, Marc, " I begged. "I can change - I promise things will be different."

"I'm sorry, Lily, I truly am, but I think it's the best thing for both of us. It frees us up to move on again."

Frees us up? I didn't want to be free. I wanted my husband back. Where did he get this shit from? I bet it was all her! Had they sat in the car before he came up here concocting their little story and practising exactly what he was going to say like they were both rehearsing their lines for a scene? These were her words all right – there was no doubt about it. What was he doing? *It's me*, I wanted to scream, *me, Lily – your wife!* Only three months ago we had skipped down the aisle together to the tune of the bloody Queen of Sheba's march; we were married for fuck sake! We were good together, we were Marc and Lily, Lily and Marc; people like us didn't separate! We were interrupted by the noise of someone sitting on a horn coming from the car park.

"Look, that's probably Nadia, we're meeting friends for dinner – I have to go."

I watched my husband's back as he walked out of our

duplex without so much as a second glance back at me. I couldn't get my head around what had just happened. Well I wasn't letting him go. I ran out after him.

"Marc!" I croaked from the top of the concrete steps outside the door. "Come back, Marc. Marc! Please, *come back*." I knew I sounded like Rose in Titanic when she was calling Jack to wake up, but I didn't care. The curtains next door appeared to move by themselves. *"Marc!"* I pleaded desperately. He broke into a run and sprinted across the car park to where Nadia was waiting for him. Dear God, he was actually running away from me. I watched as he had to bend down to lower himself into the white convertible Audi. I tried to catch a glimpse of this woman who was causing all this pain and anguish, stealing my husband, *my* husband, but I couldn't see her through the tinted windows. Then the car sped off out of the estate. I imagined the two of them together, tossing their heads back having a great laugh about it all.

It hurt so bad, the pain seared through me so that it felt like every cell in my body was crying. For the last few weeks since I had discovered them in bed together, I had been able to blame it on so many things from Marc suffering from amnesia to him having a midlife crisis, they were all reasons I could accept, but the one reason I didn't want it to be was because he was in love with her and not me. How did you marry someone and then a few weeks later fall in love with someone else? It just didn't make any sense to me. One minute I was a fresh out of the box, loved-up newly-wed and the next – well the next I was a potential divorcée, rambling around alone in our negative equity laden duplex. I didn't want to be a divorcée. It was an odious word, meant for older people – grown-ups – not someone who was barely in her thirties for God's sake. It was a hideous, embarrassing word to have to use about oneself. And besides how did someone who you might consider to be well-educated and to have a modicum of intelligence manage to rack up such an epic fail by the ripe old age of thirty-two? I was still trying to work that one out myself. In my head divorcées were sun-aged with wrinkly, leathery skin and filler plumped lips. They were normally poured into dresses that were too tight as they tried to relive their youth, and they almost always had unresolved "issues". They were the people who cornered you at a party, that you tried desperately to get away from while they poured their heart out to you, launching into a bitter tirade of abuse about their ex. And before you knew it, they were tipping a gin and tonic all over your new shoes. They weren't people like me; I wasn't like that. And as for her - she knew we were married! I actually think we even sent her an invitation to the bloody wedding, but she had been off flaunting her bits in the Caribbean or something if I remembered correctly.

In my desperation, I briefly thought about faking a pregnancy like they always did in Coronation Street but it would never work because (a) in Coronation Street the characters never get pregnant then when they need to and (b) my good old

91

Catholic guilt from years of being educated by the nuns meant that I was a crap liar.

All I knew was that I didn't want this. I wanted to still be married to my husband, but it was only now that it was starting to hit me that he was gone for good. I felt powerless and out of control. Why didn't I get a say in any of it? How come he got to be the one to make a decision that affected both of our lives irreparably? It wasn't fair. I had to face up to the fact he wasn't coming back, no matter how much I wished he was going to change his mind or how many rom-coms I watched where the man came running back and the whole thing was a big misunderstanding, there was no way back from here for Marc and I.

My hands started to tremble, my mouth started to water; I could feel the nausea rising up my throat. I ran back inside and somehow found the toilet before I puked and collapsed into a tear-sodden heap on the tiles.

Chapter 10

Frankie's number flashed up on my phone. I knew she was probably looking for an update on how things went with Marc, but I couldn't face talking to her. I let it ring out to my voicemail. She had been right the whole time. She had only been looking out for me and I had been ratty with her. I didn't deserve her as a friend. This just made me feel even shittier. Twenty minutes later her number came up again, and again I let it ring out.

I went into the kitchen to find something to drink – something strong to numb the pain. I opened back the red shiny laminate presses one after the other. God how I hated those presses – they had looked so cool in the show-house, but now they were already looking a bit dated. I had to open the doors carefully because they were starting to hang off at the hinges, due to the shoddy workmanship. I was searching for alcohol, but as I opened them one by one there was none to be found in any of them.

"Dear God if you are listening could you not give me a break? Just a small one," I begged aloud. Then I remembered, the bottle of Jameson whiskey that Marc had won at some charity fundraiser that he had gone to a few months back. He was always going to events like that, not because he was particularly charitable but because he wanted to raise his profile. He wanted to be seen by the "right" people, and there were always important people, and of course the press, at these events. I could remember Marc banging on about it being a single malt and how he reckoned it would be valuable in a few years, so he had kept it up on the top shelf in his wardrobe. I went into the bedroom and opened up the doors where I saw his treasured bottle teasing me from up high. I got a chair from the kitchen, climbed up and lifted it down.

"Aha! You might just have ruined my life, Marc Glover but I will have this, thank you very much!"

The thing was that I didn't even like whiskey but I would have drunk paint stripper at that stage to numb the pain. I went back out to the living room and poured myself a generous glass, letting the golden liquid fill up the crystal tumbler (another wedding present). I raised it to my lips and sipped it back. It tasted bloody awful, it burned my mouth on the way down, but I didn't care. I poured myself another glass and did the same thing again. It wasn't long before I felt warm and fuzzy and detached, exactly how I had wanted to feel. Soon after I heard the doorbell and I wasn't sure if it really was the bell or not. I could hear someone calling my name. I listened again, and there definitely someone knocking too. Wearily I pulled myself up off the sofa and made my way across the living room to answer it. I stumbled over the footstool and realised that I was drunker than I thought I was. I eventually managed to pull back the door and saw Frankie standing there.

"Frankie, pleased to see you," I slurred as I held out my hand to shake hers.

"Are you drunk, Lily?"

"Yes indeedy, my friend, yes indeedy, and it feels marvellous. Come on into my humble abode." I gestured roundly with my arm.

"I take it things didn't go too well with Marc then?" Frankie said closing the door behind her before walking over to the sofa and picking up the bottle of Jameson. "Jesus, whiskey, Lily? Since when did you drink whiskey?"

"Oh no, Frankie – it's not just any whiskey. It is a Jameson 1980 single malt. It might actually be worth something in a few years, but oops we'll never know now will we?" I sang.

"Want to talk about it?"

"About what?"

"What happened with Marc – I've been trying to ring you! I guessed when you didn't answer that it didn't go well."

"Well spot on Sherlock, because Marc, my *husband,* wants a formal separation!"

"He wants to separate?" For once Frankie sounded completely shocked, it took a lot to shock her but I think this had done it. "So it really is over then. God, Lily I'm sorry."

"He reckons by formally separating it will 'free us both up to move on again' and then sure down the line we can apply for a divorce. Isn't that awfully considerate of him?"

"Yeah, you got really lucky when you met him!"

"I want to go out and get drunk. So drunk that I can't even remember his name. Actually no, I want to get so drunk that I can't even remember my own name."

"But it's almost eleven o'clock, on a Wednesday night, there won't be many places still open."

"We'll make last orders in one of the pubs down the village. Come on, quick!"

***

The next day I groaned when the alarm went off at seven a.m. I peeled my eyes open to find that I was back in the bedroom. I looked across to see a sleeping Frankie with her mouth wide open drooling onto the pillow beside me. I pressed snooze and next thing I knew the red LED display told me it was after eight o'clock, and bearing in mind I was due to start work in Dublin city centre in less than an hour's time, I was in trouble. I was dying with the hangover from hell. My head was pounding, and my hands were shaking. It was bad. I vaguely remembered getting into bed after three. The pub had given us a lock-in. It had seemed like a great idea at the time – now, not so good.

I tried shaking Frankie to wake her but she told me to get lost so I left her alone. I hopped out of bed and stubbed my toe on the end of the bed frame as I tried to run into the bathroom and jump into the shower.

I am not a morning person, even as a child I would surround myself with a wall of cereal boxes at the kitchen table so Dad or

Clara wouldn't talk to me. I'm convinced humans are not designed to get up at that time of day. Why couldn't we just have a working day that started off at ten or eleven o'clock? Whoever invented early starts should be taken out and shot. My resolution of making an effort with my work wardrobe was fast put to one side as I grabbed a tracksuit and trainers from the wardrobe. I dressed quickly and sprinted to the bus stop.

The bus finally arrived twenty minutes later. There were no seats free, so I had to stand the whole way for the hour-long journey. My legs felt weak and beads of sweat were running down my back. My hand was clammy and kept slipping down along the chrome pole that I was holding onto. When we went over a ramp I could feel the vomit making its way up my throat. I put my hand over my mouth and thank God it went back down. I wished the journey was over so I could get some fresh air. Of course we hit every red light in the city and the traffic was awful.

It was after ten when I finally rocked up to the office. My heart was beating furiously because I knew I would have to deal with Stephen. There was no way he would let this go. I tried to walk subtly past his desk, but the man must have psychic powers because he peeped his head up from the paperwork he was supposedly busy looking at, just at the very moment that I walked past.

"Lily?"

"Stephen?"

"Late again I see," he tapped his watch as if I was an

imbecile.

"Yeah sorry about that I was –"

"The meeting room – in five minutes, yeah?" He looked me up and down taking in my get up of a hoodie and tracksuit bottoms. Then I remembered I had forgotten to brush my hair. I reached my right hand up to my head and tried to smooth it down without making it too obvious, but I could feel bits sticking out and long strands hanging loose from the ponytail.

Oh dear this was not good. I was not in the mood for another verbal dressing down from Sleazy Stephen. I went and put my bag down on my desk and gave my team a weak smile. They had heard the whole conversation with Stephen.

"Are you feeling okay, Lily? You look very pale?" Rosie asked concerned. She was of course immaculately dressed, wearing a wine leather pencil skirt and a sheer white silk blouse, which I'm sure Stephen was enjoying immensely.

I was only able to shake my head at her because I had to run to the bathroom to be sick.

I felt much better when I stood up again after having heaved my guts up into the toilet bowl. I went out to the sink and rinsed my mouth out, and then washed my hands. I looked at my appearance in the mirror, my face was the colour of the white wall tiles and my skin was all red and blotchy – alcohol really was a poison.

"Are you sure you're alright, Lily?" It was Rosie. "Sorry to follow you into the bathroom, but Stephen sent me to get you," she said with an apologetic smile.

"I'm okay thanks, Rosie, just one of those stupid stomach bug things. I'd better run – I don't want to keep him waiting on me."

"Sure – well I'll get started on those weekly reports for you while you're in with him then."

Christ I had forgotten all about my weekly reports! They were just routine reports about the volume of calls, the general nature of the problems – I did them every Thursday for Stephen to present to the directors in their weekly meeting. If I wasn't there I usually briefed one of my team on what to write, but I had completely forgotten this time.

"God, Rosie, I'm so sorry – that would be great if you could start them for me. Thank you."

"Not at all, I'll just use one of your templates and update it."

We walked back out together, and I could see Stephen standing up now and walking towards the meeting room in his machine washable pinstripe suit and plastic loafers. "Okay, I won't be long so we'll catch up when I'm out?"

"Great!" Rosie smiled. Her perfect gnashers could have featured in a Colgate advert. Why did she have to be so beautiful and lovely? She was the kind of girl that you really, *really* wanted to hate, but you couldn't because she was just too damn nice. I went into the meeting room and my heart started racing.

"Stephen?" I tried to sound cheery, "What's the matter?"

"Take a seat, Lily" He gestured to the high-backed swing

chair before walking over to close the door shut behind me. It was just me and him. Him and me. In a three-metre square room and I started to break out in a sweat. I was *never* drinking again.

He sat down on the other chair opposite me, but we were so close that I could smell the garlic that he must have eaten for dinner last night off his breath. I'm sure he could smell the whiskey on mine, so we were even on that score.

"Well, Lily, I suppose we'll get straight down to business then shall we?" He was stroking his ginger goatee. "Your behaviour over these last few weeks has been well – nothing short of –," he paused for the right word, "disappointing," he said solemnly.

"Look, Stephen – I'm sorry, I just have a few –" I was starting to feel claustrophobic in the room. Sweat was breaking out across my back.

"This company needs team players, and as you well know, Lily, there is no "i" in team! We need someone who is reliable, who lives and breathes the company's values – someone who wants to reap the rewards of picking the low hanging fruit. Especially someone in a senior role like yourself."

"I do – I do all of that but I –"

He raised his hand to tell me to stop.

"Lily, I'm afraid we're going to have to let you go."

"What?" I said in shock. "But you can't – I'm sorry, I've just had a lot on my mind but I'll change. I promise."

"It's too late, Lily. Too late for that now. I never know in the morning if you're going to show or not. I need somebody who I can rely on."

"Hang on, Stephen – I was absent for two weeks due to illness, and I was late this morning, but before that I hadn't had a sick day in I don't know how long."

"We've warned you about your tardiness before, so I'm afraid there can be no more chances."

It was true Stephen had hauled me into this same room a few months back to give me a verbal warning about my timekeeping, but I had never thought that he would actually fire me. "Even your presentation, Lily – this is an office and you turn up here wearing tracksuit bottoms with the word *'teaser'* printed across the behind. And trainers? It's hardly very professional now is it? And please don't take this the wrong way, but did you even brush your hair today?"

I suddenly wished I had rethought my choice of outfit that morning.

"I mean look at Rosie. She always manages to look professional. She always turns up well-groomed."

There he goes again, I thought, banging on about perfect Rosie.

"Look, Stephen, you fuck-face I know you're in love with Rosie, and you think that by giving her my job she'll sleep with you, but Rosie has far better taste than a two bit wanker like you."

Of course I didn't actually say this – I wish I had though. Instead I begged: "Look, Stephen, I completely see your point –

I've let my standards slip but I will change, I promise."

I spent a few more minutes pleading desperately for my job back, but he wouldn't back down. I asked if I could return to my desk to gather up my stuff, but he said that as I was no longer an employee of the company, for insurance purposes they couldn't allow me to stay on the premises anymore so my "effects" would be sent on to me. Then he frog-marched me on the walk of shame back through the office where everyone knew by my demeanour that I was a goner. A few brave folk peeped up from their work and gave me sympathetic smiles but most people chose to look the other way, fearing they would be next in line if they showed me any solidarity. Before I knew it I was standing outside on the street without my coat or bag in total shock at what was after happening. I didn't even have money for the bus fare home. I pressed the buzzer to reception to get back in.

"Hi, Rachel, sorry it's me, Lily – I forg –"

I heard the click of the receiver being hung up. So I pressed it again hoping that she had just got cut off. This time it rang for ages but nobody answered. I tried again and again, and it was the same thing. She was purposely ignoring me. I started to bang on the door but still no one answered. I'm normally pretty easy-going but I was really starting to get angry. I was entitled to my coat and bag at least.

"Let me in," I started to shout at the door as I pounded on the glass. Soon I began to draw attention from some passers-by.

"They just fired me," I said by way of explanation pointing

a finger angrily towards the door of Rapid Response, but they just looked down at the ground and hurried on past my one-woman picket.

Eventually I heard the click of the door being opened, but instead of seeing Rachel the receptionist, it was Kevin, the burly security guard who looked after the office block.

"Okay, Lily – now enough is enough." Kevin grabbed my arm and steered me away from the door. "You're making a scene, so we can do this the nice way or the hard way, whichever way you'd prefer – it's up to you."

"But I just want to get my coat and bag –" I protested.

"You no longer work here, you're trespassing not to mind damaging Rapid Response's property. You have sixty seconds to leave the premises before I call the Gardaí."

"But, Kevin – it's *me!*" We had shared a cigarette in the smoking area at last year's Christmas party.

"I'm sorry but members of the public cannot be here. You will have to leave."

"But I'm only standing on the doorstep!"

"One, two, three . . ." he started to count.

It was like he had been brainwashed by the Rapid Response way. What was wrong with everyone? Days earlier they were happy to have the craic but now they acted like they didn't know me.

"But I have no money for the bus -" I protested.

And with that, he started digging around in his pocket, and

fished out a two-euro coin and flung it at me. I ducked my head out of the way just in time, and watched as it landed on the pavement behind me.

"It costs four euro thirty-five -" I said but he had already gone back inside the door.

I felt anger course through my veins, and I knew I had reached my tipping point. I picked the two-euro coin up off the ground and fired it back against the door. I watched in horror as a crack instantly appeared across the glass and spread out along the pane before it started to shatter, falling into millions of tiny pieces on the ground. Oh my God, I hadn't meant for that to happen. Suddenly the door opened up again, but I didn't stay to see who it was this time. Instead I just ran.

***

I walked from the offices of Rapid Response, across the broad swell of the Liffey and up to Frankie's apartment, which was about half an hour away. I didn't know where else to go. My phone was in my handbag so I couldn't call anybody to come and get me. I had never been so humiliated in my life. The anger quickly subsided and was replaced by tears. What on earth was I going to do now with no job? How would I pay the mortgage or the bills? Things had been bad enough without having Marc to share the load, but now I was in trouble. I was so glad when Frankie answered her buzzer. Luckily she had no shoots scheduled for that day, so she had just gone straight home to bed after she had left my place. I told her what had happened, and she sat me down and put a cup of warm, sugary tea in my hand. She couldn't believe it as I recounted the awful events of that morning but she burst out laughing when I told her about the door.

"Oh, Lily," she laughed as tears streamed down her face. "I'm sorry, I know I shouldn't laugh, but that could only happen to someone like you."

After I had finished my tea and the shock had begun to sink in, I asked her to drop me home to Ballyrobin. Stephen had said that my "effects" would be delivered to me, and I wanted to get home before they arrived because there would be no one there to take them in. All my belongings; my keys, my wallet, my bag, my coat and not to mention all my other stuff, had been left behind in Rapid Response. But when I climbed the steps to my duplex, I found my "effects" were already waiting for me on my doorstep, sitting outside in the rain for all and sundry to see. All the bits and pieces that had littered my desk for the last ten years, now stood in a large cardboard box that had once held boxes of photocopier paper. I instantly looked inside to find the photo of my Mum and Dad, and Clara and I, which was taken at the zoo. It was one of the only photos I had of all of us together, and was one of my most prized possessions. I was relieved to find it lying at the bottom of the box, shoved under a pair of old trainers and some gym leggings that I couldn't remember ever having worn. I felt angry that they had treated it with such disregard. I lifted it out delicately, held it in both hands and stared at it. Mum and Dad stood behind Clara and I, in front of the sea-lion enclosure. We

105

were dressed in matching navy and white sailor dresses with knee-high white socks. Clara must have been about five because I was only two. Dad had his arms on Clara's shoulders and Mum had her arms on mine. It was at times like this that I missed her desperately. This was where I needed a reassuring hug, and for her to tell me that everything was going to be okay. My eyes started to fill with tears, so I put the photo back down again. Frankie rooted out my keys from my handbag and opened the door. We tried pulling the box inside, but the cardboard ripped at the sides, having disintegrated from the rain, so we manually lifted the items out and carried them inside, one by one. Luckily my wallet still remained inside my bag, but my coat and everything else were soaking wet with rain. There were three books that I had borrowed from Rosie but I had never actually got around to reading. They were all literary tomes with Pulitzer and Booker accolades, but now they were looking quite pitiful in their soggy, wavy paged state. Oh well, I was sure she wouldn't want them back at that stage. There were a couple of A4 notepads. I flicked through them - there were lots of doodles and lots of lists of things from the wedding that I had needed to organise. They all started the same with the heading "List" underlined with two thick biro strokes and then bullet points the whole way down. And just to add salt to the wound, there was also a large photo in black and white of Marc and I standing outside the church on our wedding day, both smiling happily. It was still so fresh and I could remember every detail. How had it all gone so wrong? How had I become this pathetic mess in the space of a few short months?

I plonked myself wearily down on the sofa. The combination of the day's events and the hangover from the night before had left me exhausted. I didn't even have the energy to talk to poor Frankie who was sitting beside me.

"You head on," I said to her after a while.

"Are you sure you don't want me to stay? I have a shoot with some actors in town first thing in the morning, but I can just get up a bit earlier?"

I shook my head. "I'm just going to have a bath and go to bed."

She nodded. "Well, I'll call you in the morning. Try not to worry, it's all going to be okay."

"But how will I pay the mortgage and bills?"

"Don't worry about that now, I can help you out if needs be."

"But I can't borrow money from you!"

"Of course you can, sure you'd do the same for me if the shoe was on the other foot. Look, Lily, it's all going to be okay, I promise," she said soothingly.

"I hope so, Frankie. I really do."

After Frankie had gone, I had just turned on the taps, letting the water cascade into the tub when I heard my phone ring in the living room. I ran out to get it and saw that it was Rosie.

"Lily, I am so sorry for what happened today –" she said

straightaway.

You see? She was just the loveliest person – even when everyone else in the office was pretending not to know me, Rosie had picked up the phone and called to see how I was doing.

"Thanks, Rosie."

"I just wanted to say that I think you were treated appallingly." She stretched out the word "appallingly" in her lovely posh accent. "After you left, Stephen offered me your job, but I declined. I told him that there was no way I could do that to you, it wouldn't be right."

"Really? You did that for me?" I asked incredulously.

"Of course I did."

"No, Rosie, you should take it, you deserve it." I didn't want her to put her career advancement prospects on hold because of me.

"Are you sure you wouldn't mind?" she said eagerly.

I couldn't believe it! She hadn't taken much convincing. I thought she was in solidarity with me! She could have at least played the charade out for a bit longer. I knew she was too good to be true. I just knew it all along.

"You're welcome to it, Rosie," I said wearily. I just wanted this whole thing to be over.

"Well thank you, Lily for being such a good sport about it all," she gushed. Although it had never bothered me before, her accent was now starting to grate on my nerves. Who used the word "sport" in this day and age anyway?

"Okay, well I've got to dash – I have dinner plans." It was a lie but I just wanted to get her off the phone.

"Okay well, toodles!"

"Yeah toodles to you too."

I mean who says "*toodles*"? I'm sure in Rosie's clique they had their own unique language consisting of air kisses and words that no one else outside the postcode had even heard of.

Chapter 11

"You are not going to believe this, Lily," Frankie said as soon as I answered the phone.

"What?"

"Well you know that shoot I told you I was working on?"

"Yeah the one with the actors –"

"Well the actors were Marc and Nadia."

"Marc as in my *Marc*?"

"I'm so sorry, Lily if I had of known there was no way I would have accepted the job, but I literally went along to the address I was given and I nearly got sick when I saw who it was. There was no way I could have walked away leaving everyone in the lurch like that – I could say goodbye to ever working again. I feel desperate. I've been worried sick all day about how I was going to tell you."

"It's not your fault. Did he say anything to you?" God I was pathetic clinging to any nugget of new information.

"He blanked me, Lily!"

"What do you mean?"

"He pretended that he didn't know me."

"But how – you were a bridesmaid at our wedding!"

"I know – I was raging, but obviously I couldn't say anything because I had to remain professional. But he wouldn't look me in the eyes. I gave him dagger eyes at every opportunity though. Nadia hadn't a clue who I was because she kept saying that the clothes were amazing and you could see that he just wanted to curl up and die."

"She's gorgeous, isn't she?"

"No she's not."

"Oh come on, Frankie – she's a ride."

"Well I saw her without her make-up."

"And?"

"She has some premature skin-damage - too much sun exposure."

"That's it?"

"Well . . . one of her nipples is inverted."

"How do you know that?" I was aghast.

"Because she was practically naked during all the different outfit changes – there was only a thong between me and her lady garden. I saw it all."

"I can't believe everyone I love in this world keeps seeing this woman naked."

"Well I could hardly avoid it – she was practically whipping off her clothes as soon as I came in the door."

"Did you check out her bum?"

"Uh-huh."

"And?"

"Even though it kills me to admit it – it's a good one."

"Isn't it? I still can't get over it. So soft and peachy . . ."

"Yeah," she said wistfully.

"What magazine will it be in?"

"*Social Importance* – it's the cover story in next week's issue, but don't you dare buy it. Do not do that to yourself!" she warned.

"Where are they living?"

"You promise you're not going to rock up there and stalk them?"

"Frankie – what do you take me for?"

"Well she lives in one of those Georgian townhouses just off Fitzwilliam Square."

"Nice."

"Are they all loved-up?"

"It's hard to know – Nadia knows how to turn it on for the cameras and she knows all the right things to say – years of being prepped by her publicist, I'm sure. But he's like her little lap dog. I can see he's revelling in all of this – the free clothes, the photo-shoots and magazine spreads. You should have seen him posing in front of the camera and talking about the 'projects' he's working on at the moment - how he got himself into character for his new role and how the whole process was so 'cathartic'. He is so far up his own arse it's not funny."

"Eh . . . role? It was a five-second walk on part."

"Exactly! But of course I had to nod and smile and fawn

113

over him like he was the next Michael Fucking Fassbender. And he fired all the clothes on the floor when he was finished with them leaving them for me to pick up. Not cool. Then he went ballistic when the caterers brought curry for lunch shouting 'didn't they know what the carbs would do to him?' so the poor assistant had to run off and find him some sushi! He was a complete diva. I could see the magazine staff biting their tongues, but they couldn't say anything because Nadia is the lady of the moment. He won't get far in that business let me tell you, Lily."

It hurt. There he was getting the A-list treatment while I was left jobless and picking up the pieces of our broken marriage. It was very hard not to feel bitter and angry and even though Frankie had warned me not to buy the magazine, a twisted part of me desperately wanted to see what it was that they had together. What did she have that I didn't? Okay so I already knew the answer to that one; a body to die for, a glamorous career and millions in the bank trumped my life hands down, but still it was so hard to believe how much my life had been turned upside-down in just a few weeks.

"Promise me you won't buy the magazine?" Frankie said.

"I promise," I lied.

Chapter 12

It was always the same - whenever I was in work, I couldn't wait until I was off again but when I had no work to go to, the novelty had quickly worn off and I was already lonely and dying for someone to talk to. The trouble with being off midweek was that everyone else was busy. Frankie was on an all-day shoot, so I couldn't hang out with her. The only people I knew that didn't work were Dad and Clara. I knew Dad had his computer course, run by the local secondary school to try and integrate him into the modern age that morning. The only other person who wasn't doing anything was Clara, and even I wasn't that desperate. Plus that would involve telling her that I had been fired, and God only knew how she would react to that bombshell. She had taken news of the separation pretty hard, and I couldn't begin to imagine how she would cope with that as well. It was bad enough having a sister whose marriage broke down after a mere three months, but an unemployed divorcée sister was in another league altogether.

I watched a bit of *Jeremy Kyle* titled *Can I smell another woman on my man?* and another called *Could my twins have different Dads?* I waited for the best bit where Jeremy says "Dean, –" *cue collective holding of breath,* "you are not the father." When Jeremy was over there was only *Cash in the Attic* on, or a repeat of *Country File,* so I chose *Cash in the Attic* and wished something like that would happen to me, except that we didn't have an attic because our house had a flat roof.

My phone had rung then just as we were getting to the best bit and annoyingly my heart skipped a beat thinking it might be Marc. When was I going to stop doing that? He had already made his feelings pretty clear, and I was getting annoyed that my heart didn't seem to be taking this into account. But it was just Marc's mother checking to see how I was. She still didn't know that Marc had asked me for a formal separation and she had reacted angrily when I told her, saying she felt she didn't know her own son anymore, and asking what had she done wrong raising him. I knew her heart was almost as broken as mine.

By lunchtime I was going spare. I realised I had no food, so I went to the supermarket to stock up on a few essentials like wine, chocolate and ready meals before the last of my money ran out.

I saw Piotr the homeless man who sat begging outside the supermarket most days sitting in his usual spot beside the trolley bay. He had a piece of cardboard folded underneath him, and a well-worn sleeping bag covered his legs. He had come over from Poland during the *Celtic Tiger* to work in Ireland's booming construction trade but, after the work had dried up during the recession, now found himself homeless. I usually bought him a cup of tea from the deli whenever he was there.

"How are you doing, Piotr?"

"Not too bad, Lily."

I looked down at his weathered hands, which were a pinkish-orange colour. He looked cold. "I'll get you a tea to warm you up."

"Thank you, Lily, you are very kind lady."

I smiled and went inside. I made my way through the aisles, picking up the things that I needed. I had just reached the frozen food aisle and was busy looking at a two for one deal on pizzas when I heard a voice.

"Lily – Lily McDermott, is that you?"

It was high pitched and shrieking like it always had been. I swung around and sure enough it was the unmistakable voice of Wendy Murphy. Wendy had been in my class in school, and was as annoying then as she is now.

"Wendy – good to see you!" I forced myself to smile even though it felt like I was pulling my cheeks back with vice grips.

"How are you, Lily?"

"I'm good. How are you, Wendy?"

"No really, Lily how *are* you?" It was the way she said "are" that I knew that she knew. "I mean since Marc, –" she cocked her ear to her shoulder, "you know?"

"Well I'm okay –" I said feeling a bit unnerved. I hadn't seen Wendy in years, how did she know about Marc and I?

"What a terrible thing to do. Really it was the lowest of the low. When Janice told me what had happened, I was so shocked. Especially to you - you're just such a *nice* person." She sounded so condescending. Describing someone as "nice" was akin to saying they were harmless, and was possibly the biggest insult you could give someone.

"Erm . . . thanks Wendy," I muttered.

"He always was a bit of a jack-the-lad, wasn't he?"

"What do you mean?"

"Come on, Lily – everyone could see it?" She laughed nervously.

"See what?"

"Lily, *y'know*. That you and Marc . . ." She was starting to get flustered now.

"*What*?" I demanded.

"Oh God, Lily, I'm sorry I feel like I'm digging a hole here . . . he always had an eye for the ladies . . ."

"What are you saying?"

"I don't know – I well . . . now don't take this the wrong way, but I don't think you two were ever really suited. I mean when we were in school, he was so . . . so . . . good-looking . . . y'know? He was the one boy everyone wanted to go out with. And he was trendy too, and into his keeping fit and clothes and you – well you're . . . well you're different . . . y'know?"

"No, I don't know actually," I said through gritted teeth.

"Well you're more . . ." she paused for the right word, "homely." She plastered a saccharine smile on to her face.

"Homely?"

"What I mean is that you're both very different people. You

118

must be able to see that?"

"Eh no, I don't think I can."

"Aw sorry, honey, I've offended you now, haven't I?"

"No – not at all, Wendy. How would you have done that?" I said sarcastically.

"Oh good – look, I read a really good book after I broke up with Darren Fielding in sixth year. It's called *He's just not that into you.* I can't remember who wrote it but it really helped me move on after him."

"*He's just not that into you?* I repeated. "We were *married,* Wendy, he must have been into me at some point."

I wanted to grab one of the bags of potato croquettes that were in the freezer beside me and batter her over the head with it.

"Of course, Lily – look I'm sorry, I'm only trying to help you but I'm probably making everything worse. I know how devastating a break up can be, especially when you're the last one to know."

How did she know all this? Did everyone know something that I didn't?

"Last to know what?"

"Sorry, Lily – I'm digging a hole here, me and my big mouth. Look I have to run and get the kids from school."

And before I even had a chance to ask her what she was talking about, she was gone straight past the frozen waffles, down the aisle where the pasta and sauces were before turning around the corner into the fruit and veg section and out of my sight, leaving me standing there spitting chips.

Stunned, I made my way towards the checkout. What had Wendy meant when she said that I was the last to know – how long had it been going on? It couldn't have been that long, because we had only got married three months before and why would he have married me if he had been having an affair? But still her words had rattled me. And what had she meant when she said that we were very different people? She had made it out as though I was batting above my league being with Marc in the first place. At least that was what she seemed to be hinting at. I knew Marc was good looking, and if I was *really* honest he's probably the better looking one in our relationship – if we were on *Your face or mine?* we'd probably both pick his face, but at the same time, I'm not a minger. I knew I could do with losing a few pounds – I was a bit curvy, but curvy women were in – you just had to look at Kim Kardashian or Beyoncé. But had everyone else known what I had secretly feared – that Marc was too good for me?

I had just reached the queue to pay when I saw it on the magazine stand beside me: **"'*The Recluse*' – hottest young stars, secret romance revealed - see full story on page 10."** Below it was a picture of Marc kissing Nadia on the lips like love's young dream. So this was the shoot Frankie had been working on. Even though she had warned me not to read it, I quickly picked up a copy off the stand and flicked to page ten. I knew I was only torturing myself by looking at the pictures but I couldn't help it.

The headline at the top of the page screamed: ***"Exclusive Interview with 'The Recluse' stars Nadia Williams and Marc Glover as they welcome us into their beautiful city centre home - the beautiful actress talks films, her charity work and the rock that helps her through it all."*** The photo on the opposite page was of Marc sitting perched on the edge of a sofa while Nadia lay along the length of it, leaning back in to his arms. She was wearing a delicate white lace dress sewn with tiny gold beads, which looked amazing on her dark skin. Marc was wearing a white shirt to compliment Nadia's dress, grey skinny jeans and a black skinny tie. His hair was styled up into a quiff. He was barely recognisable – I had to admit it, he looked well. Could Frankie at least not have picked something a bit uglier for him to wear, I wondered?

There were five full pages dedicated to them in various poses and outfits. Their smiling faces taunted me from the pages – it was the salt in the wound. It hurt. I had to admit they looked well together, like they were meant for each other. They were both glamorous with their Hollywood white teeth and cool hair. How could I have thought that Marc would ever be happy with the likes of me? They were in a different league altogether. This must be how Jennifer Anniston feels when she sees Brangelina on the cover of every magazine, I thought.

Nadia Williams has plenty to smile about – not only is she the critically acclaimed star of The Recluse, and a successful business woman with the launch of her own perfume the

eponymous named Nadia last year, but now she is loved-up with her new man Marc Glover. Nadia – tell me how you and Marc met?

Nadia: *"We met on the set of The Recluse. Marc just walked into the shoot one day and I noticed him straight away. I couldn't concentrate for the rest of the scene – I kept forgetting my lines and my heart was beating wildly. I said to Charlie (co-star Charlie Woodward) who is this man? I knew instantly that there was going to be something special between us."*

Marc: *"Well obviously I knew who Nadia was. I have always been such a big fan of her work, so when she asked me out for coffee – I jumped at the chance. I was so nervous because I was in awe of her, and I almost cancelled, but I needn't have been as we just clicked straight away."*

Nadia: *"We ended up spending the rest of the day together – neither of us could bear to say goodbye and we've been together since."*

I couldn't believe it – Marc had started working on that film just before we got married. Was it going on before then? It would kill me altogether to know he had been having an affair and still had gone ahead with our wedding because he didn't have the balls to call it off.

So Marc how do you balance working together and living together?

Marc: *"Nadia and I just work – from the day we met, we just clicked. We love being around each other, and I am* *happiest when I am in Nadia's company. I feel very lucky that I get to both live and work with this amazing lady."*

The up-and-coming actor is clearly smitten with the beautiful actress. It is obvious this couple can't keep their hands off each other, as Nadia lovingly reaches across and gives her boyfriend's hand a reassuring squeeze.

Nadia – what is it about Marc that you love most?

Nadia*: "Well Marc is hugely supportive, and never lets me get stressed. He is my rock during all the madness," smiles a radiant Nadia, her brown eyes sparkling with happiness."*

Marc: *"We make a good team." An adoring Marc smiles back at his other half.*

Then there were some pictures of Nadia posing in the various rooms of her apartment. There wasn't an IKEA flat-pack wardrobe in sight.

Every item in their stylish apartment has been carefully chosen from Nadia's travels.

Nadia: *"I found these vintage fabrics at a flea market in L.A. and I had them made into cushion covers, and the artwork came from a tribal community, which I visited when I was filming in Marrakech last year."*

Blah, blah, blah. Look at me – I'm so worldly and exotic, I thought bitterly. On the next page there was a full-page photo of them standing on the balcony staring into each other's eyes with the caption, **"***Love's young dream.***"** Nadia was wearing a flowing silk maxi-dress with a string of daisy chains in her hair, and Marc was wearing a cream linen shirt with cut-off khaki pants.

When asked about the charity Children First, of which she is patron, an emotional Nadia tells us how close the work is to her heart.

Nadia: *"These children have no one to care for them – no one at all, and I am honoured if I can use my profile to help highlight their plight. Even if I'm exhausted from travelling halfway around the world and staying in faceless hotel rooms, when I think of these poor children then I feel very grateful indeed."*

A modest Nadia laughed off the question when asked about the secret to maintaining her beautiful looks with such a hectic schedule. But it is clear that there is one obvious reason for the actress's glow - and that is her boyfriend Marc.

I wanted to scream at the page – that's my husband. They are not 'love's young dream'! There they were lolling about at photo-shoots and acting like they were just destined to be together. It wasn't fair. She had everything a girl could dream of – a cool job, gorgeous home, she looked beautiful, she had magazines fawning all over her and designers begging her to wear their clothes – she had all of that but it still wasn't enough, she had to go and take Marc too.

"Eh . . . this isn't a shoe shop, love – there's no try before you buy here." The girl behind the checkout shouted over to me.

"Sorry, it's just this is my husband – I pointed at a picture of

Marc looking deep in thought sitting backwards on a chair."

"Do I look like I give one?"

"Well . . . no, I suppose not . . ." I made my way up to her till and rooted around in my purse for the change to pay for the magazine and the few groceries that I had managed to pick up.

I went back out through the automatic doors and saw Piotr looking up at me expectantly. *Shit!* I'd forgotten the tea I'd promised him. I couldn't very well leave him without it so I trudged back around the store and got a cup of tea at the deli-counter. I quickly added one sugar and a splash of milk, which was the way he liked it best and hurried back to the checkouts to pay.

"There you go," I bent down and handed the polystyrene cup to him when I got back outside.

"Ah thank you, Lily – you're very kind lady you know that. When I get enough money I take you out on date to dinner," he said in his funny Polish-Dublin accent.

"I'd like that, Piotr. Now you wrap up warm, do you hear me? I saw on the forecast that it's going to be wet tonight."

I hauled my bags of shopping home thinking over everything. I walked past children playing chasing, and I wished I could join them – not to play chasing, I'm far too unfit – but just to be that innocent and carefree again, and to have none of the pressures and worries that come with adulthood. I wanted to go over and tell them to enjoy it now while they could because it wouldn't last, and soon they'd be old like me with a property in negative equity and a broken marriage. But I knew I'd probably just scare them away and then I'd feel really bad.

Chapter 13

When I reached my duplex, I climbed the steps and opened the door. It was only then that I realised that I had just bought butter and had forgotten to buy the really important things like alcohol and chocolate that I had gone to the shop for in the first place. I sank wearily into the sofa and sighed. I knew I was feeling sorry for myself, but I figured I was allowed to wallow given the recent events in my life. I was unemployed in a recession, with a husband who had left me after only three months of marriage and was now gracing magazine covers with Ireland's leading actress. And I had managed to achieve all of this by the ripe old age of thirty-two. My phone rang and I didn't recognise the number so I pressed the answer button and put on my polite phone voice.

"Is that Lily McDermott?"

"Speaking."

"Hi, Lily this is Greg O'Connor calling from Irish Bank Mortgages."

Uh-oh. "Hi, Greg, what can I do for you?"

"Well, Lily, your mortgage payment bounced yesterday and I was just calling to find out when we may expect to receive June's payment?"

"What?"

"There weren't enough funds in your account to meet the direct debit."

Even though I had just been fired, I had been paid last month so I knew that that wasn't the problem and then it suddenly dawned on me. Marc.

"Sorry, Greg I wasn't aware of this. Can I call you back? I just want to have a look at the account."

When I hung up from Greg, I opened up the laptop and logged onto the Internet to check our bank balance. I knew the mortgage went out on the first of every month, and to be honest I hadn't even thought about discussing our finances with Marc. It wasn't really up there on my list of priorities the evening he had called over telling me he wanted a separation.

I quickly scrolled down the screen and saw our balance was dangerously low. I checked through the recent transactions, and saw that Marc hadn't put any money into our joint account like he normally did at the end of the month. I looked down through all the recent activity on the account. The standing orders for his gym membership and his subscription to *Social Importance* magazine (he liked to check if he had managed to get photographed at any of the many charity events that he went to) had already left the account for that month. Funny how he hadn't thought to cancel those! I took a look at our credit card account next and noticed recent transactions for the last few weeks that we hadn't been together. There was one for 1 St Martin Lane, the new restaurant in the city centre that was getting rave reviews in the press and that I could never afford to go to in a million years. There was a transaction for Hamill & Forrester jewellers, and another for the Apollo cinema. Then there were recent ones for different bars and restaurants in Puerto Banus. Well, Marc Glover had another thing coming if he thought I was going to be subsidising his wining and dining of Nadia. I was seething with rage. It was bad enough that he had walked out on me for another woman like that – but if he expected me pay his share of the mortgage, while he was living a high fallutin' life, he had another thing coming. How could he be so selfish? He knew I would be struggling to meet the mortgage on my measly pay packet, and that wasn't even taking into account all the direct debits for electricity, gas, insurance and God knew what else came out of the account. We were in the midst of one of the worst recessions in living memory, as the economists were keen to tell us, so it wasn't as if I could even put the place up for sale; it was worth half of what we paid for it, and there were at least ten identical duplexes in the estate for sale for over a year now, and all were showing no sign of budging. We had bought our house in Ballyrobin because it was all we could afford. Even though it was miles away from all our friends and families and where we both grew up, it was okay because we were together and it was *our* home. But now that Marc and I were no longer together, I was stuck out here in the middle of nowhere on my own. I knew I could probably ask Dad to help me out, but what would happen the following month? I needed to get another job quickly. God it was all such a mess. I would have to ring the bank first thing in the morning and cancel all of his standing orders and the credit card too. A smile came over my face at the thoughts of him bringing Nadia out for a fancy meal, but then not being able to pay because his credit card was declined.

I felt a gnawing hunger grow in my tummy. I needed something sweet but I had forgotten to buy chocolate in the shop. There was only one thing for it, I decided to bake myself a cake, and I was going to eat it all by myself and not feel an ounce of guilt.

I raided my baking cupboard and thankfully I found all the ingredients to make a sponge cake. I had flour, butter, sugar and eggs. I measured them out using my trusty four, four, four and two recipe; then I mixed them all together until the mixture was a creamy yellow colour. I rooted around my presses to find a heart shaped cake tin, because I thought things always tasted better when they were heart shaped. I poured the batter into the tin and put it in the oven. Then, while it was baking, I made a large bowl of butter cream icing.

After the cake had risen, I removed it from the oven and when it had cooled, spread the icing generously over its golden top. Then I cut myself a slice and fought off any guilty thoughts about the magnitude of calories that I was about to consume – I deserved this. My life was shit. I ate another slice, then another one, until finally half way through the fourth slice I started to feel slightly queasy.

Frankie called over with a bottle of wine, while I filled her in on my woes. I had phoned her to tell her that the magazine was out, but she told me she had already seen it. Even though she was cross with me for buying it, we analysed every detail of the photos while we finished off the rest of the cake.

"That is one hell of a cake, Lily," Frankie said, helping herself to another slice. My God it should be illegal, it tastes so good."

"I know." I stopped to feed myself another forkful. "There are probably that many calories in it that it should actually be illegal. You're not allowed any guilty thoughts when you eat it, that's the rule."

"Great rule." Frankie said through a stuffed mouth.

"Here – wipe your face," I said pointing to a blob of icing Frankie had managed to get on her cheek.

"What do you think Wendy was talking about?" I said looking up at her meekly.

"Who knows – you know what she's like. She's a mouth almighty, take no notice of her."

"But I can't help it – she was making out that he was too good for me."

"Well let me tell you, she is waaaaay wrong on that one. *You're* the catch not that bollox."

"But what do you think she meant when she said I was the last to know. Did you know something, Frankie?"

"Lily you're my bestest friend in the whole world – I was a

bridesmaid at your wedding. If I had known something I would have told you. She was just stirring it, trying to push your buttons to get a reaction. Honestly just forget about it, you've bigger worries right now than Wendy Murphy trying to fish for a bit of gossip."

"Yeah I suppose you're right . . ." I sighed. "God, Frankie my life is a mess. What am I going to do?" I suddenly felt the cake stick in my throat.

"Okay, well first things first, I think you're going to have to get a job ASAP."

"But I don't even know where to begin, I don't even have a CV. I've never even done an interview!" I got the job in Rapid Response through an agency. They had been so desperate for staff to man their call centre at the time and deal with all the pee-filled sticks that I had started the same day, without ever having to do an interview. "And it's a recession," I sighed.

"Well if you can't get a job, you can always make this cake."

"I can hardly pay the mortgage with cake."

"Well no but you're good at this stuff. You make fantastic cakes and buns. Why don't you open a bakery?"

"I could never do that, Frankie, imagine me responsible for a business?" I was shuddering at the thoughts.

"Well it doesn't have to be a bricks and mortar place, but what about doing it from your own kitchen, making cakes for birthday parties, christenings, weddings - all that kind of thing."

"But who would buy them?"

"People would!" she laughed. "You start small, and then hopefully through word of mouth you might get a bit more business."

"Do you really think I could?" I was starting to get excited now at the prospect of being able to lick icing from the bowl every day.

"Of course you could – your cakes taste fab, you're great at decorating them. Why don't you do up some business cards and I'll hand them out to a few people on shoots, and you never know what might come out of it. Look, there are no start-up costs, a few business cards won't cost you much and if it doesn't work out then you're no worse off than you are now."

"Yeah I suppose . . . oh God, Frankie, are you sure?"

"Yes!"

"But what will I call it?"

"How about *Lily's Sexual Cakes*?"

"Hmmh. I've visions of men ringing me up with odd requests. How about *Hot Buns*?" I offered.

"That's even worse than what I suggested. I know, what about *Baked with Love*? Every bite is a little piece of love."

"Oooh I like it. *Baked with Love*. Wow imagine a job where you get to eat cake every day?"

"That's the spirit!"

"Okay now I just need to get some business."

Frankie laughed, "Well yeah, that tends to be the idea."

***

The next day I tried phoning Marc to ask him to put money into the account for the mortgage but he never phoned me back. I texted him next but he just responded with:

"Sorry babe - pretty broke right now," with a smiley face on the end as if that made it all okay. I was normally pretty patient, but that time I felt my blood boil. Even if he did have the money, I wondered would he have paid it? Was this all part of his plan – to leave me with a shit-load of negative equity?

Even though I would never admit it to anyone else, I always knew that Marc was a tight arse. He never seemed to have a problem splurging money on himself – designer shoes and clothes were *de rigueur* for him, but when it came to other people he hated splashing the cash. Like for his Mum's birthday he would just give her a bunch of flowers from Tesco, or the time when we got engaged in New York and my battery was dead but he wouldn't let me call my Dad from his mobile because of the roaming charges. I had to wait until we got back to the hotel room and had charged my phone again before I could call him. Of course by the time I had enough battery in my phone it was the middle of the night in Ireland so I had to wait until the next morning before I could share my news. Well this time, Marc Glover, you are going to have to stump up the cash, I thought to myself.

Chapter 14

After my conversation with Frankie that night, I started to get a little bit excited at the prospect of starting my own business. She was right; I could do it from my own kitchen without going to too much expense. Frankie had worked me up a logo using a graphic design program that she had on her computer. It was a cupcake with pastel pink icing and blue cherry on top. The fonts were coloured shocking pink and I couldn't believe how smart and professional the whole thing looked.

I did a lot of research on the Internet and had managed to find a website running deals for small businesses to print their own stationary, so with Frankie's encouragement I had taken the plunge and ordered some business cards and fliers.

When they arrived in the post a few days later, I tore off the brown paper wrapping, it had been an incredible feeling seeing my name there in ink on the business cards just above the words "Company Owner".

It had been two weeks since I had been fired, but I still hadn't been able to tell my Dad and Clara about it. I knew their reactions would be poles apart – Clara would probably go for the disgusted and disapproving reaction, whereas Dad would probably just be worried about me. I decided to start by telling

Dad because he would know best how to handle Clara.

***

I rang Dad on Tuesday morning to check if he would be at home. Since his retirement he liked to fill his days playing golf, visiting Clara or doing his computer course. It made me kind of sad that he had to do this. I was glad he was busy, but I had to wonder would things have been different if he wasn't on his own? Somehow I don't think he would be so keen to always have plans made just in case he ended up at a loose end. I knew he was surprised to hear from me when I should have been in work. He told me he would be at home and I got ready to get the bus over to his house.

A while later I was walking up the street to my childhood home. Dad let me in to the small red-brick house, and I followed him into the kitchen and sat down on the battered settee that ran along one wall while he made us a pot of tea. Sunlight streamed in through the windows, announcing that summer had arrived.

"So to what do I owe the pleasure of a visit on a Tuesday morning?" Dad asked handing me a mug of tea a minute later.

I took a deep breath, and started by telling him the whole story from the start about the evening Marc had called over, and about work firing me the next day. Dad listened patiently to every word I said without butting in or showing any reaction on his weathered face. When I had finished, he still remained quiet until I finally asked him was he going to say something?

"I'm just disappointed, Lily."

It was awful to hear him say that to me. I would way have preferred him to roar and shout at me rather than face his disappointment. "I'm so sorry, Dad."

"No, no, not disappointed *in* you but *for* you – you deserve more than all of this. And I can't help wondering if I've failed you in some way."

"Dad how can any of this be your fault?"

"Well with Marc – I don't like saying this because he is your husband –"

"Was –"

"Okay is/was it doesn't really matter, but sometimes I felt like he just didn't truly appreciate how lucky he was to have you."

"Oh, Dad – I hope this isn't a 'no one is good enough for my daughter' spiel?" I groaned.

"No, I'll be the first person to admit that you're certainly not perfect, Lily – but there were just a few little things down through the years, just small things really, but things all the same that I didn't like."

"Like what?" I said with a tinge of defensiveness.

"Well like the time, when you were both supposed to be saving up for your house and he went off travelling for a year, and you stayed behind here to save. Or on your wedding day and he was nowhere to be found for the first dance."

As if I could I ever forget it. I could still hear the drums beginning the familiar strains of Jennifer Rush's the *Power of*

137

Love. We had chosen that song because – well I had chosen it – Marc maintained it was corny, but I had always loved that song, and it had been playing on the night we first kissed, so he finally relented after I had begged him for the hundredth time. But as I had stood on the edge of the dance floor ready to dance with my new husband, Marc was nowhere to be seen.

Frankie and Clara had run off in opposite directions to try to find him, while I stood at the edge of the dance floor, with all the eyes of our guests on me, willing him to hurry on.

"Has anyone seen the groom?" The DJ began calling out over the microphone. "We appear to have a groom missing in action. Going once, going twice . . . Anyone?"

The humiliation was desperate.

"Has he enough of you already, ha-ha-ha?" the DJ roared into the microphone laughing heartily at his own joke.

Frankie and Clara returned soon after, both shaking their heads; they couldn't find him anywhere. Richie his best man and Clive his groomsman were also nonplussed as to his whereabouts. By that stage the song had reached the climax as Jennifer Rush belted out *Cos I'm your lady . . .* Marc was supposed to be twirling me around the floor like we had practised.

When it became clear that the song was nearly over and Marc wasn't coming, my Aunt Julie pushed my cousin Nigel who was standing on the edge of the dance floor over towards me. Although he was my first cousin, I barely knew him – I had met him about twice in my life, once at Christmas about ten years ago and the other time at my Granny's ninetieth birthday. He was only about eighteen, and I could tell he was clearly mortified at being forced into doing this by his mother. I had no choice but to have my first dance with my own cousin. We kept each other at arms distance and shuffled awkwardly around in a circle, neither of us knowing where to put our hands. After all the time I had spent begging Marc to let this be our first dance song, I was now willing for the song to end. We were moving too fast to keep in time with the music, while Clara and Rich and Frankie and Clive danced alongside us, trying to keep up with the speed that Nigel and I were going at to make everything seem normal. The shame was fierce, but I forced a smile onto my face and tried to laugh along with everyone else like it wasn't bothering me.

When my humiliation was finally over and I could escape the dance floor, I went off to look for Marc myself. After searching the rooms of Kilbritten House high and low, I finally found him sitting outside at a patio table, even though it was December. He was sitting with some guys I vaguely remembered meeting at a wrap party that I had gone to with him one time.

"Hey, Lily where have you been?" he asked me. "Sit down here for a minute – I've barely seen you all day!" He pulled me down onto his lap. The table in front of him was littered with empty shot glasses. He had a glass of whiskey in one hand and a cigar in the other. His eyes were glassy, and I could tell he was already well on.

"Where were you? You missed our first dance!"

"Did I? God I'm sorry, love – why didn't the lads come and get me? I told Rich I'd be outside."

"Well he said he couldn't find you –"

"You know Rich – he wouldn't find his way out of a cardboard box." The group of lads started to laugh.

The wintery air was cold on my bare shoulders. I began to shiver. "Well I'm going to go back inside, it's freezing out here." I stood up to leave hoping he'd come with me.

"Okay, love, I'll just finish this and I'll be right in after you – here would you mind doing me a big favour and run over to say thanks to my Auntie Liz for that vase she gave us?"

"Sure," I said giving him a weak smile. This was our wedding day and I didn't want anything to blight it by getting annoyed with him.

Now as I thought back on it all, maybe the signs had been there all along that he didn't really love me but I hadn't wanted to see them? I knew Dad was right. Deep down I had always known it.

"I shouldn't have said anything," Dad was now saying. "I've gone and upset you, haven't I?"

"No, Dad, sorry look I appreciate your honesty – it's just hard to hear that's all. I'm learning a lot in these last few weeks," I said.

"Look, Lily these things happen – yes it breaks my heart to have to watch you go through it, but you will come out the other side of it."

"But what about the separation and potential *divorce,*" God I hated saying that word, it almost got stuck in my throat every time. "I'm scared, Dad –" I said in a small voice.

"Whatever happens, we'll get through it." He squeezed my hand and smiled kindly at me. "I'll be with you every step of the way." Just the way he said the word "we" made me instantly feel better. I rested my head against his shoulder. I was glad now that I had told him. I knew he would help me through it.

"And my job?"

"Well you were wasted in that company anyway – maybe I should have pushed you to do something else with your life before it came to this. But I didn't want to be an interfering parent, you see?"

"Dad, it's my own fault, I got lazy. It was handy and paid the bills – but look at this." I handed him one of my new business cards.

"What's this, Lily?" he asked puzzled.

"Read it."

I watched him read the card in confusion.

"It's my new business venture *Baked with Love* – I'm setting up a cake making business. I'll be starting small, just birthday cakes, christening cakes, all that kind of thing – initially I'll just be doing it from home but if it takes off . . . well who knows . . . I might one day have my name over the front door!" I couldn't contain the excitement in my voice.

"Well would you look at that!" he studied the business card

141

again. "Well done, Lily – and 'Company Owner' if you don't mind!" Tears pricked his eyes. "I'm so proud of you."

"Thanks, Dad," I said trying to keep my voice level.

"What am I going to tell Clara?"

"You leave Clara to me."

"I can't, Dad – no I'm thirty-two years of age, it's about time I stopped being scared of my older sister."

Dad smiled at me. "Well I can go with you for the moral support whenever you're feeling up to it, if you want?" he offered.

"That'd be great, thanks, Dad."

I went home that evening feeling as though a huge weight had been lifted off my shoulders. It didn't seem like the end of the world after all. Yes I was still facing a messy separation, and I had no reliable source of income for the next while until hopefully things took off with *Baked with Love,* but just talking things out with Dad had really helped. I didn't feel so alone and the future didn't seem so bleak any more.

Chapter 15

I had decided to delay telling Clara my news for a while longer. I knew I couldn't put it off forever, but Dad wouldn't say anything until I was ready to tell her. I just wanted to get *Baked with Love* off the ground first, and then at least I would have a bit of good news to help cushion the blow. I had already handed out some fliers to the businesses around Ballyrobin, and I had booked a stand at a local craft fair, which was taking place the following Sunday. I spent the whole week getting ready for it and buying ingredients using my last pay cheque from Rapid Response. I spent my days measuring and mixing. Tasting my batters and adding ingredients as necessary where I felt they needed tweaking. I practised my icing on some dummy cakes before making a five-tiered wedding cake with alternating tiers of ivory roses. Then I made a stand of tiered cupcakes with lemon butter cream icing in blue paper cases. I also did a cake in the shape of Thomas the Tank Engine and another one of Peppa Pig. I made multi-coloured macaroons, and I ended up having to make a second batch because I ate most of the first batch. I then did mini crown cakes decorated with pink and blue ribbons and little pairs of bootees on top, which I thought would be really cute for a christening. I hoped I had something to appeal to everyone, and that I had covered all areas of my business.

On the day of the fair, Frankie picked me up in the morning and helped me load the cakes into her car, and I sat in the front seat with the five-tiered wedding cake on my knee. She was going to give me a hand on the stand because I was so nervous. By the time we arrived the cake was beginning to resemble the Leaning Tower of Pisa, but luckily I was able to reassemble the tiers to straighten it up. I set up my table, and covered it with a blue and white gingham tablecloth, while Frankie hung some navy and pink spotted bunting that she had robbed from a shoot over our heads. In the meantime, I cut up samples of lemon Madeira cake, chocolate biscuit, fruit cake and what I hoped would be my speciality, orange cake, into small rectangular pieces and put them into baskets for people to taste. I was so nervous about what people would think and how they would react to my cakes, but Frankie assured me that everything looked great, and more importantly tasted great and to relax and enjoy my unofficial launch party.

The day flew by talking to people. There were couples, families and elderly people visiting the fair - it was a real mix of young and old. I received great feedback when people took a bite of my cakes – everyone loved their buttery texture. Frankie was on fire, she enthusiastically walked around the fair getting people to try my cakes, and she talked about my baking using superlatives that I had never even heard of before. By the end of the day I had an order for three birthday cakes and one christening cake. I spoke with an engaged couple who were interested in my wedding cakes. I was impressed with how enthusiastic the groom was about the whole thing, he listened patiently as I explained how I made the cakes, and he was genuinely interested when I showed him a book with some designs. There was no way Marc would have shown that level of interest if I had brought him to look at wedding cakes, or even any aspect of the wedding planning. In fact his standard reply whenever people asked him was he all set for the wedding was "Of course. Sure all I have to do is to turn up on the day". I didn't mind planning our wedding by myself, but looking back on it all now, I suppose I would have liked him to have taken more of an interest in the whole thing like the man before me, instead of leaving me to my own devices. I knew for a fact that the couple in front of me wouldn't come a cropper like Marc and I - you could see the love between them.

I was on such a high as we drove home that evening. I was nervous too, I hoped I was able to do it, and that I hadn't gone in over my head, but Frankie assured me that I needed to start believing in myself a bit more. I knew those orders would keep me busy for a while – it was just the right level of business to allow me to give the cakes the right attention without completely swamping me, resulting in me turning out shoddy cakes. I had deliberately kept my prices low so that I was competitive. I wouldn't be earning a huge amount of profit, but it would be enough to keep me going and I would worry about the mortgage and other bills down the line.

After my success at the craft fair, I finally felt ready to tell Clara. Dad picked me up, and we drove over there in silence as I thought about how I was going to break the news to her that once again her little sister had made a complete and utter fuck-up of her life.

We drove along passing the manicured lawns fronting the mansions of Clara's neighbours. Houses that most people could only ever dream of owning. Dad turned his Nissan Micra into Clara's gateway. I had to hop out of the car to buzz us in through the electric gates. I briefly thought about making a run for it, but Dad gave me a warning look that told me to get back into the car. The gates parted and we continued on over the crunchy gravel of her meandering driveway before finally the red-brick house came into view. Dad drove around the fountain before pulling up outside. His yellow Micra always looked like a little dinky car parked beside Clara's monstrous Range Rover SUV. I took a deep breath and got out.

We let ourselves in the back door, and found Clara sitting at her kitchen table surrounded by colouring pencils and a small pile of shavings. The place was spotless as usual – even though Clara could easily afford a cleaner, she refused because she didn't trust anyone enough to do as good a job at cleaning her house as she would herself. Her issues were numerous, including the type of cloths they would use, the use of own-brand bleach, and whether or not they would pull out the sofa when they were hoovering.

"Dad, Lily!" she exclaimed. "Well this is a nice surprise!" She stood up to greet us.

"Where are the boys?" Dad asked.

"Oh their French tutor is in the living room going through some *articles définis* with them."

"Oh right . . ." Dad muttered obviously not having a clue what Clara was talking about either.

"Whatchya doing?" I asked plonking myself down at the table.

"Just sharpening these colouring pencils for the boys – I hate it when they go all short and stubby," she said as she picked up a blue Crayola one from the pile on her left and twisted it around inside the pencil sharpener before putting it into a pile of already sharpened pencils on her right.

"Well it's important to have sharp pencils," Dad said with a nervous laugh. I think sometimes he worried for Clara's sanity.

"Exactly, Dad! As I always say *'fail to prepare, then prepare to fail'*." And she continued on with her little sharpening exercise as if it was perfectly normal behaviour. I always wondered how Clara found the time, or even the inclination to do all of these things, but she was a perfectionist.

"Now would you like a herbal tea?" she asked as she tidied up her pile of sharpenings and disposed of them in the organic bin, before sanitising the table.

"Just regular tea for me thanks, Clara," Dad said.

"Sorry, Dad – I've stopped drinking regular tea because of

the caffeine – it tended to make me wired but I do have green tea, peppermint, lemon and ginger or dandelion root tea – it's great for the digestive system."

"Ah sure, I'm grand – I had a cup before I left the house anyway," Dad said.

"Suit yourself, what about you, Lily?"

"Erm, I'm okay thanks – we probably won't be staying long anyway." *Not when I've told you my news,* I thought grimly to myself.

Clara made herself a peppermint tea before joining us back at the table.

"So to what do I owe the pleasure of this social call?" she asked in her annoyingly over-formal voice. "Any sign of that errant husband of yours?"

"Well, em, that's partly why we're here. Lily wanted to talk to you about something. Didn't you, love?" Dad said looking at me.

"Well, you see, Clara – there have been a few things going on my life lately, and I suppose I haven't really told you about them because I was worried about how you might react."

"Why would you worry about how I would react? I have always been a supportive and loving sister."

"God yes of course you have – I know, but well –"

"Come on, Lily – I'm not going to bite you."

"Well it seems as though Marc has left me for good. He's not coming back."

"What?"

I nodded to confirm it was true.

"He can't have – I mean you're only married a few months."

"No, Clara – he wants us to separate formally."

"But this is ludicrous – you can't just marry someone and then change your mind a few weeks later!" she spat.

"Tell me about it," I mumbled.

"So what you're saying is that you're going to be separated – as in next step divorce!"

"Well yes, I suppose I am."

"It's just a mishap, Lily – it has to be. I mean these things don't just happen, especially to our family!"

I took another deep breath. Why was she having such a hard time accepting this – after all it didn't directly concern her. She was almost finding the whole thing harder to accept than I was.

"I know it's a shock, Clara but how do you think I feel? Marc has made up his mind and well, I don't think he's going to change it – no matter how much I wish he would."

"Well, Lily – *that* kind of defeatist attitude is exactly the reason why you're in this mess in the first place!"

"Now hang on, Clara –" Dad interrupted.

"But Dad, she *needs* to get him back."

"But why? Why does she?" Dad asked exasperated. "Maybe she might be better off on her own."

"But she can't be separated by the age of thirty-two!" she spluttered. "No, it's just a mishap, that's all it is. I know these things!" She was shaking her head defiantly, and I knew there was no point arguing with her. This had come as a shock to her – she needed time to let it settle in. "And who is she? Who is this brazen hussy that goes around having affairs with married men. She is an embarrassment to the female race."

I was secretly pleased with this.

"It's that actress one, you know her, Nadia Williams - the one who won the Oscar," Dad said.

"She didn't actually win," I said through gritted teeth. "She was only nominated!"

Clara clearly didn't read *Social Importance* magazine. "Oh God, he has really done it in style, hasn't he?"

I nodded weakly. "Look, Clara – there is something else I've been meaning to tell you." I knew I might as well get it all over with there and then, in for a penny, in for a pound.

"What now, Lily?" she sighed wearily from where she was massaging her temples with both her hands. "What on earth can you have possibly done now?"

"Well it's my job –"

"Go on, I'm listening–"

"I've been fired."

"You've been what?"

"Fired," I repeated glumly.

She took her head out from her hands and looked at me.

"I bloody well heard you the first time!"

Oh dear, this was bad. Clara *never* swore.

"Well it wasn't my fault – my boss has always been a dick and he fancied one of my team, so really it was just an excuse to fire me."

"It never is your fault though, is it, Lily?" she said bitchily.

"I can't believe how much of a mess you have made of everything – it's like you manage to attract trouble to yourself."

"I'm really sorry, Clara."

Silence.

"But the good news is that Lily has set up her own business, haven't you?" Dad said looking at me to take up his lead.

"Yes I've set up my own cake making business – it's called *Baked with Love*."

"*Baked with Love*?" she spluttered. "I don't think I've heard anything more preposterous in my life! I mean working in a call centre to help people who don't have the brain cells to know how to use a pregnancy test was bad enough, but now you're suddenly a baker! Can you even cook, Lily?"

"Well, Clara, you should see the stuff she makes – it's amazing. She really does have a talent for it. Lily show her one of your brochures," Dad urged.

Reluctantly I pulled out one of the brochures that I carried around with me from my bag and gave it to her.

She studied it carefully. "Well I've seen it all now."

"She's already had lots of orders – haven't you, Lily?"

I nodded my head.

"Well I suppose it's better than scrounging off the dole," she said but her tone wasn't as bitchy as before. "But knowing you, it'll turn out to be a disaster as usual."

"Clara, you should have more faith in your sister," Dad chastised.

We were interrupted then by the boys and Ms Dubois, the French tutor.

"Granddad! Lily!" They ran towards us excitedly.

"How did the boys do this week?" she asked Ms Dubois without introducing Dad and I.

"Much better, clearly you 'av being doing a lot of extra work with them this week," Ms Dubois said in her French accent.

Clara smiled, proud that her efforts had been acknowledged.

"I will go 'ome now but I will see the boys next week, à bientôt!"

"Lily and I better head on before the traffic," Dad said, excusing us after she had left.

"Of course," Clara said walking us to the door, clearly relieved that we were leaving. "I have to attend to the boys now anyway."

We said awkward goodbyes before climbing back into Dad's small car.

Chapter 16

A few weeks later, I had enough work to keep me going for the next month. The fliers that Frankie had designed seemed to have worked. I had a few calls from people looking for cakes, one for a retirement party, and another for a thirtieth birthday. I was so excited – I wanted to put my best into each and every cake, and hopefully word of mouth would ensure I got repeat business. I even had to turn down a wedding cake because I already had two booked in for the same week. Frankie was my one-woman PR machine – I had lost count of the number of people who had placed an order because they said that Frankie had recommended me to them.

I had never worked harder – I got up every morning at seven and went into my kitchen to put on my apron and got straight to work. I worked all day until late in the evening, by which stage I was a sweaty and sticky mess from being covered in icing sugar. I was exhausted when I rolled into bed every evening, but I had never felt better. I loved what I was doing, it felt as though each cake I was making was a little piece of love – and I loved being able to help people with their special occasions. I had also borrowed some cake decorating books from the library and had got loads of great ideas, which I was currently experimenting with. Frankie was helping me to put together a website too, with photos of some of my recent baking and contact details. She had pulled in a favour from a friend who was a web designer, and all he wanted in return was a batch of my lemon meringue cupcakes!

I re-named a deep filled apple pie *humble pie* in honour of Clara, after she tasted some and finally admitted that my cakes tasted good. I had found some really cute heart shaped moulds, and I was going to make chocolate heart shaped lollipops. I set the chocolate hearts onto long thin wooden handles, and then I covered the chocolate in cellophane and tied it in place with a red bow around each one. I got some labels printed with my logo, that I tied around the sticks. Even I had to admit they looked gorgeous. As I didn't have much money to spend on marketing, I was going to send them into all the Dublin radio stations, tied in a box saying "Happy Friday from *Baked with Love,*" and hopefully get a bit of free publicity out of it. I had also set up a stall with my treats every Friday at lunchtime in the IFSC. I figured it was the best day, as people didn't mind treating themselves on a Friday, whereas other weekdays might be a harder sell. Word of mouth was spreading, and soon I had a constant queue in front of my stand from twelve o'clock until I finished up at two.

I was busy baking all day, and in the evenings I would call over to Frankie or go out for a walk to try and burn off some of the evil calories that were the one downside of my new job. At weekends Frankie and I would head out in town. Because of Frankie's work, she was forever getting invitations to launch parties so we would go to these first and get tanked up on the free drink before heading on to a club.

For the first time since Marc had left, I wasn't constantly thinking about him and wondering what he and Nadia might be up to now. I was too busy. Things were going well. I had just enough money to keep on top of the mortgage every month. I knew I shouldn't be paying the mortgage on my own – I knew this was a no-no because legally Marc could demand half of the house even if I had been paying the mortgage all along, but I just didn't want the hassle of it. The bank would be onto me if they were only receiving half of the money every month, so it was just easier to pay it all. I knew I would have to sort it out with Marc sooner rather than later, but for the moment - I didn't need the extra stress. Once the mortgage was paid I had very little left over, but somehow I managed. And Dad had helped me out a bit whenever I was stuck.

One day I was just putting a vanilla sponge into the oven, when my phone beeped with a text message. I wiped my hands on a tea towel and went over to the table where I had left it. I picked it up and when I read it, saw it was from Marc. My heart skipped a beat. Since that evening when he had called over to tell me that things were over for good, I had barely heard from him except for messages to say that he couldn't afford to pay the mortgage yet again, with the ever present smiley face stuck on the end. If it was another one, I swore I was going to fashion a Voodoo doll and use it to stick pins in his eyes. I opened up the message but instead of the usual excuses, it actually just said;

"We need to talk – can I come over?"

I read and re-read the message. What was that meant to mean? I had been asking him to talk for weeks, why did he suddenly want to talk now? Maybe he was finally going to try and sort out our finances, God knew it needed to be done, I couldn't stick my head in the sand forever – there was our joint account for a start, the mortgage, all the bills that were in both our names. I took a deep breath. I knew sooner or later I needed to face up to it all, so I waited for a minute before texting him back so I didn't look like I was sitting watching my phone constantly – which I wasn't anyway because I was too busy with *Baked with Love*, but Marc didn't know that did he? I wanted the message to be breezy too, and not like I was worried or desperate. So I typed:

"Sure – when suits you?"

I restrained myself from putting kisses on the end. It was a habit at this stage, and I really had to resist. I had a hierarchy for kisses – usually I put three kisses on the end of messages to Marc, two to Frankie and my family and one to people that I liked but didn't know quite well enough to elevate them to two-kiss-status. Yet again it reminded me of just how awful the last few months had been. If you had told me this time last year, in the run up to our wedding that Marc and I would in fact now be separated I would have laughed at you, but you just never knew what was around the corner. A few minutes later my phone bleeped again;

"How about tonight? I can call over - 8 ok with you?"

I wanted to appear cool, calm and collected so I typed:

"Okay, see you then." No kisses.

Oh dear God my heart was thumping manically once I put down the phone – why did he still have this effect on me? I told myself to calm down. It was only to sort out our finances – so it wasn't going to be pleasant. I hated confrontation, but I knew I would need to stand my ground on this. I was going to have to make Marc start paying half the mortgage again, or else the house would be repossessed. I loved our home, yes it was poky and small and you could hear next door flushing their toilet (yes, really) but I had put so much into decorating it. I had painted all the walls myself when Marc had been filming down in West Cork. I had chosen the carpets for the bedrooms, the tiles in the kitchen and bathrooms. I had spent practically all my spare time for months in IKEA choosing the furnishings – I had nearly fallen asleep in those lovely display beds on several occasions during the long days I spent in the place. It would kill me to lose my home.

I tried to keep busy for the rest of the day. I had to make a cake in the shape of a golf ball for a friend of Dad's in the club. I had bought two semi-spherical shaped moulds and a mottling tool that I hoped would give it a golf ball effect. But my head was all over the place, and I forgot to set my timer on the oven. When I finally remembered and hurriedly opened the oven door to check them, it was too late - the tops of the cakes were charred. I would have to do the whole thing again. I was annoyed with myself for being so easily distracted, so even though it was only three o'clock, I decided to call it a day and I spent the rest of the afternoon getting ready for my big meeting with Marc.

I knew it was ridiculous to be putting so much effort in, when we would only be talking through our finances, but I wanted him to see me at my best. I wasn't going to give him the satisfaction of seeing me looking broken. I needed any confidence boost I could get. I put a conditioning treatment into my hair and lay soaking in some Jo Malone bubble bath that Frankie had given me for my birthday. It was the kind of thing I would never dream of buying for myself – it was far too posh and expensive. I was almost afraid to use it; I kept keeping it for very special occasions, which meant I had only used it twice before – once on my wedding day and then last Valentine's Day. When I got out I smoothed baby oil all over my skin and put on my dressing gown. I put some large rollers in my hair as usual trying to curl hair that just didn't want to be curled, but I was persistent. I put on my red jersey wrap dress – it was dressy without looking like I'd gone to too much trouble – I debated whether or not to wear heels, but Marc knew that I barely wore them going out, let alone around the house, so I put on a pair of cream pumps instead. I took the rollers out of my hair and looked at my reflection in the mirror in dismay; my hair appeared more bendy than curly. When would I ever learn? I put some cupcakes that I had made yesterday onto a plate and casually left them on the living room table. Then all I had to do was wait. And wait. By 8.15 he still hadn't come, I checked my phone for the billionth time in case he had been trying to get hold of me but he hadn't. Finally at twenty-five to nine, the bell went. "Marc," I said opening back the door. "Come in."

"Lily- how are you?"

"I'm good thanks –"

He came in the door and briefly looked around the room.

"Sit down. Would you like a cupcake?" I offered him the plate. We were both being overly polite and formal, and we knew it. I sat back against the sofa with one arm placed on the arm of it in what I hoped was an elegant pose. I had seen Kate Middleton do it in *Hello* magazine.

"These are nice – where did you get them?" he asked through a mouthful of cake.

"Oh I made them myself," I said trying to sound nonchalant.

"Really – wow they taste just like the M&S ones."

This grated on me – they tasted a hell of a lot better, but I let it go.

We sat eating our buns, neither one wanting to be the first to raise the subject.

"You look great, Lily."

"Do I?" I was secretly chuffed.

"You've lost weight."

"Thanks."

"So do you," I lied. If I was completely honest with myself, as much as I loved him – he looked ridiculous. Nadia had

159

obviously taken to styling him, but it just didn't work. He was too big a build to suit the blue skinny jeans and grey cardigan that he was wearing. It was a look best left to Harry Styles.

"So what have you been doing with yourself?" he asked.

"Oh this and that."

"How's work?"

"I got fired actually."

"What?"

"Well it's not as bad as it sounds – you knew I was fed up in the place for years, I've been meaning to find something else, so it just gave me the kick up the backside that I needed."

"But how are you managing financially?" He sounded panicked.

"Well I've set up my own business."

"You? You have your own business?" He was looking at me sceptically.

"Yes, Marc – me. I'm making cakes, buns and all kinds of sweet treats. It's called *Baked with Love*," I said proudly. "I've had a lot of changes over the last few months."

"I see. . ."

Was I mistaken or did he seem a bit peeved?

"Look, Marc – I hate to bring it up because you know me, I hate talking about money but I'm really worried about the mortgage. I can barely cover it each month, and I already have Dad helping me out -"

"Yeah, I know sorry, Lily – I'm pretty broke at the

160

moment."

"That is why you called over, isn't it? To talk about the icky money stuff?"

"What? Oh no . . . I know we need to talk about it but can we do it again sometime? I couldn't face that now . . ." He didn't seem himself. He was distracted.

"Oh I see . . . look is everything okay with you, Marc?"

"Ah yeah –"

I could tell by his tone, he wanted me to ask him more.

"How's Nadia?" I tried to keep the contempt out of my voice.

"Yeah she's okay - y'know yourself . . ."

"No I don't know actually."

He smiled at me. "Look, Lily if I'm honest – I miss you. I miss this -" He gestured around the room. "I miss us," he said lowering his gaze to the floor.

I was speechless. Had I heard him correctly? What was going on with him?

"But, Marc – this was your choice, I was happy with us," I said softly.

"I know, Lily and I'm sorry. For everything." He paused for a minute. "Look, this was a bad idea – I'd better go . . ." He stood up and before I could say anything else, he had walked back out through the door again. I ran out after him watching him take the concrete steps two at a time before quickly making his way over to where his car was parked. He got inside and soon he had drove

161

off out of sight.

I hurried back inside and rang Frankie straight away to analyse.

"So what do you think? Should I ring him?" I asked her biting down on my lip.

"Do not ring him, Lily – I repeat, Do. Not. Ring. Him."

"But it sounds like he has regrets, doesn't it?"

"Well, it's hard to say, Lily – he has an awful lot of making up to do. He can't just waltz back into your life that easily."

"I know but it sounds like he wants me back doesn't it?" I just wanted her to confirm what I hoped was true.

"Be careful, Lily – he has already hurt you badly. You need to be sure before you do anything else."

I knew she had my best interests at heart, but sometimes I just wished she would jump up and down with me.

"I'm a big girl, Frankie, I'm not naïve. Of course I'm not going to roll-over and welcome him back with open arms but I think he is finally coming to his senses!" I couldn't keep the excitement from my voice.

"Look, Lily – just wait and see, yeah? If he really is sorry and wants you back – he will do anything to show you how he feels."

"Yeah you're right, I suppose."

I spent the whole night tossing and turning, wondering what was going on in his head. Was he having second thoughts about leaving me? He had looked lost and confused and instead of being angry like I should have been, I actually felt pity for him. A small part of me wanted to ring him and tell him to come home, that all was forgiven. But I knew I needed to be careful, even if he begged me to take him back, things could never go back to the way they were before. And how could I ever begin to trust him again after that level of betrayal? My head was swimming with questions that I didn't have an answer for. All I could do was to wait and see, but God waiting was so hard.

Chapter 17

I tried to put my head down over the next few days and keep myself busy, but I could not stop thinking and obsessing over Marc. The thoughts were a constant loop inside my head. It was like he had been about to tell me something the other evening, but had lost his nerve and then he had left. It was so hard not to pick up the phone but whenever I felt the urge to call him, I rang Frankie instead and wrecked her head by going over it all again.

I had received the most romantic request from a man who wanted to propose to his girlfriend using cupcakes, each with a letter iced on top spelling out "J-E-S-S-I-C-A–W-I-L-L–Y-O-U–M-A-R-R-Y–M-E-?" I was nearly in tears as he explained how wonderful and special she was and he couldn't keep the excitement out of his voice when he spoke about her. This was one of the best parts of my new job – I was honoured to be able to help him out. I had made and iced all the buns, and was just boxing them up, when I noticed that I had spelled out "J-E-S-S-I-M-A–W-I-L-L-Y-O-U–C-A-R-R-Y–M-E-?" That would not go down well – I could potentially ruin the most important moment in this couple's life. I needed to pull myself together. I gave myself a stern talking to, but inevitably I would concentrate for five minutes before my mind would start to wander again.

Just then my phone rang, startling me out of my thoughts. I groaned when I saw it was Clara. I held the phone in place between my shoulder and ear while I continued on with my cupcakes. She didn't mention anything about Marc or my job as I expected her to, so I knew she wanted something. Sure enough, a minute later she was asking me if I would babysit for her because her long-suffering au pair, Tatiana, had let her down. Clara was furious as she recounted how they were meant to be going to a partner's dinner for Tom's law firm, but when she had said it to Tatiana she had refused point blank to reschedule her date with her boyfriend. I had to stifle a laugh – I was glad to see that Tatiana was finally standing up for herself. As I had nothing better to do, I offered to do it – plus I liked having the boys to myself for a while. I always felt it did them good to let loose a bit. I loved seeing their excited little faces when they watched in amazement as I took out sweets from my bag and turned on Sponge Bob Square Pants. Treats and TV were such a rarity for them, let alone having both together.

"Now, Lily there is to be no sweets or television!" Clara reprimanded me as if she could read my mind.

"Of course not!" I lied.

***

I arrived over to Clara's just in time to see Tatiana heading out the door in a teeny tiny purple bodycon dress that only an eighteen-year old Russian girl could get away with. I eyed her slim body and never-ending tanned legs enviously. Clara looked Tatiana up and down before giving her dagger eyes, but thankfully Tatiana was oblivious as she skipped out the door to have wild sex with her lover.

After Clara and Tom had left, I had just teed the boys up in front of the TV with bowls of popcorn and Maltesers mixed in through it as a double treat when my phone rang. When I saw it was Marc, I immediately jumped up and went outside the room to answer it so the boys couldn't hear me.

"Marc, hi –" I was breathless after my quick exit from the room. I really was going to have to go to the gym, especially with all my baking. All my weight loss from my heartbreak diet was rapidly starting to go back on.

"Hi, Lily."

He sounded depressed.

"Is everything okay, Marc?"

"Yeah – I just wanted to talk to you that's all."

"Oh sure, how're things?"

"Yeah – okay." He sounded like a sulky teenager.

"Right."

"Are you at home?" he asked suddenly.

"No I'm babysitting for Clara."

"Oh I see," he said sadly.

"Auntie Lily –" Jacob was pulling at my leg.

"Just one minute, my love, I'm on the phone."

"Auntie Lily –" He was persistent.

"Just one sec, Jacob – this is *really* important, just go back in for one minute and I'll get us some Curly Wurlys from my bag. How about that?"

"But, Auntie Lily, Joshua is getting sick."

"*What?*" Did these children not understand? *Dear God, why oh why now?* It was possibly one of the most important phone calls of my entire life and then this had to happen. They had a brilliant sense of timing.

"I'll have to ring you back, Marc, sorry."

"Sure, Lily, okay. . ." He sounded so down.

As I went back into Tweedledum and Tweedledee, the stench of vomit greeted me. I wanted to gag.

"Me eat too much, Auntie Ni-ni," Joshua sobbed.

"There, there, it's okay now." I stood in front of the mess and wondered where I would even start. Brown and orange lumpy puke trailed down the front of Joshua's pyjamas right down to the floor where it covered Clara's cream wool carpet. They had obviously eaten spaghetti bolognese for dinner. Did I clean up the child first or the carpet? Child or carpet? Obviously the child was more important, but this was Clara's cream carpet we were talking about here.

"Ni-ni, I sorry," he convulsed into tears.

I felt awful then. I wanted to cry with him. I'm bad with other people's sick.

"It's okay, baby, here let's get you out of these clothes." I went to lift him up, but it was impossible to find anywhere on his

168

clothing that wasn't covered in vomit, so eventually I lifted him up underneath his armpits, held him out from my body and carried him out to the bathroom. I placed him straight into the bathtub and took off his clothes as carefully as I could, so the sick wouldn't touch me. When I had him undressed, I ran the bath for him. While Joshua played with his bath-time ABCs, I sat on the toilet with the lid down, thinking over everything with Marc. He was definitely having second thoughts now – there was no doubt about it. It had sounded like he wanted to call over if I had been at home, but of course I wasn't so now I would never know what he wanted. A while later Jacob came into the bathroom.

"Lily the carpet is turning brown."

"Shit!" I had completely forgotten about it.

"What does 'shit' mean, Lily?"

"Never mind!" I lifted Joshua from the bath and wrapped him in a fluffy towel before carrying him back to the kitchen.

I found an assortment of carpet cleaning products in Clara's utility room and read the instructions but as soon as I started scrubbing I knew it wasn't going to come out. The stain had already dried in. I spent another thirty minutes scrubbing but it was useless. I tossed the sponge down in defeat and a cold sweat, broke out across the back of my neck. Clara would kill me. Not just because her carpet was destroyed, but also because I had given the boys sweets. The only thing I could do was to drag the coffee table across the room to cover the stain. It looked bonkers, because instead of being perfectly centred in the room, it was now in the southwest quadrant. I knew Clara would spot it straight away but I hoped I would be safely home first.

After all that drama, I finally got the kids into bed. Jacob blackmailed me into reading them two stories each by threatening to tell Clara exactly what had happened. I was tempted to ring Marc back, but I knew I needed to play it cool so instead I decided to paint my nails using Clara's fancy Chanel nail polish in *Particulière*. That was a tip from Frankie, because she knew I wouldn't be able to ring him with wet nail polish.

Clara and Tom came home after eleven, and I greeted them in the hallway with my coat on and bag in my hand.

"Aren't you going to stay over, Lily?" Clara asked.

"I think I'll head home to my own bed actually." I wanted to be gone before Clara noticed the stain on the carpet.

"You can't expect Tom to drive you home at this time of night, surely?"

"I'll get a taxi."

"But that will cost a fortune!" Clara protested.

"If she wants to go home, she wants to go home, Clara, it's the least we can do after she babysat for us." He turned to me. "I'll call you a taxi."

"And I suppose there has been no sign of Tatiana yet?"

I shook my head.

"I've a good mind to lock her out."

"Now, Clara, she's entitled to a night out. You go on upstairs to bed and I'll wait with Lily until her taxi arrives," Tom cajoled.

Ten minutes later, I had escaped Clara's house and was sitting in the backseat of a taxi heading home.

It was just after seven the next morning when Clara rang. But instead of thanking me for helping her out by babysitting at the last minute, she launched straight in to demanding that I tell her exactly what had happened to the carpet? She told me that she had asked the boys, but they had refused to tell her, so she wanted answers from me. I had to give it to the boys – they were loyal even in the firing line of Clara's wrath. I'm not sure I could have withstood the pressure so well.

"Clara, sorry – I was going to tell you. I was painting with the boys and I accidently knocked over the muddy water."

"Mmmh," she said dubiously. "There is an awful stench of vomit in that room."

"Really? Well maybe Tatiana had a few too many last night. . ." I felt awful landing the blame on to her.

"You're probably right – I'll have to have a word with her about the dangers of excessive drinking. Honestly I sometimes wonder who needs minding more, the *au pair* or the children!"

After she had hung up, I thought about Marc again. I still hadn't heard from him since the night before, and it was eating me up inside. I needed to know what was going on with him. I decided I was going to ring him, but it wasn't even half past seven yet so I couldn't do it that early. Finally just after nine, I decided it would be safe enough then. I just hoped he would be nowhere near Nadia. With shaking hands, I dialled his number and waited while the phone rang. Finally he answered on the sixth ring.

"Lily?" I was relieved when he sounded pleased to hear from me.

"Sorry about last night – you know what the boys are like, they never give me a second."

"Of course – how are they, Lily?"

"They're good, same as usual. Clara thinks butter wouldn't melt in their mouth, but they can buy and sell her already."

"I miss them."

"You do?" I tried to keep the shock from my voice. I knew Marc couldn't stand them. They drove him insane. It was a gripe Marc always had, that whenever Clara wasn't around the boys went wild. I think when they threw Marc's brand new iPad into the bath it had been the last straw. And no matter how many times Clara tried to defend them by saying that they had been trying to demonstrate the Archimedes' principle, Marc just wasn't buying it.

"Yeah – they're great kids." He sounded wistful.

"Is em . . . everything alright, Marc?"

"With me? Yeah, I'm doing alright."

"You just don't sound yourself?"

"I'm cool and the gang."

"Okay, well I'd better go then." I had read countless books on relationships and they all agreed that the person who ended the phone conversation first had the upper hand.

"Oh okay . . . well, Lily, it was good to talk to you. Really good."

"Yeah you too, Marc," I said hanging up.

There was definitely something wrong with him. I wasn't just imagining it.

Chapter 18

That evening Frankie and I had arranged to meet Joannah for dinner in Café Le Monde. It was Jo's first night leaving baby Noah, and I could tell she was nervous, but three phone calls home and two glasses of wine later she was finally starting to relax.

The waiter had just cleared the plates from our main course away, and we were waiting for our desserts.

"Sorry, ladies, but I have to go pump and dump," Joannah said standing up from the table.

"What?" Frankie asked.

"Y'know because she's breastfeeding, Noah," I said.

"But where have you put the pump?" Frankie asked looking around the room. I think she was expecting to see a bicycle pump somewhere.

"It's in my bag," she said giving it a tap and laughing at Frankie's horrified face as she walked off towards the toilets.

Frankie might have been horrified, but I was in awe that she was such a good mother, doing her best for baby Noah. I really hoped that would be me one day.

I took my phone out from my clutch bag to check it and I saw there was a message from Marc:

"It was really good to talk to you earlier, Lily. Goodnight xxx"

He had even used my kisses hierarchy. OMG.

I handed the phone to Frankie.

"Well?" I asked, after she still had said nothing.

"Well, I think you're right. It does seem as though he is having second thoughts alright."

"Really? So I'm not just imagining it?" I asked giddily.

"But, Lily after everything he's done, do you really want him back?" She placed both her hands on the table and leaned forward to me.

"Well it's not that simple. . .," I said defensively.

"Really? Isn't it?" Frankie seemed disappointed in me, but she didn't understand. Frankie's longest relationship had lasted a whopping six months, and that was because she got bored. She had finished it because Anton wanted to get more serious, so she had run a mile. When they had first started seeing each other, he would stay over in hers one or two nights a week, but soon he was looking for more. After a weekend together, he would call in on his way home from work on a Monday, and then again on a Tuesday evening. So Frankie had quickly put a stop to that. Poor Anton had been devastated – he was a lovely guy but he was just looking for more than Frankie was able to give. Frankie had heard that he had met another girl soon after they broke up and they were now engaged. She was happy for him. She wasn't like me, she loved her independence but I hated being on my own. Plus Marc was my husband after all.

"We were married, Frankie – are married – it's not that simple," I said miffed. She had never been married. It wasn't black and white.

"Look you know I'll support you either way – it's your decision, but I just don't want you to get hurt again. Look how far you've come? I'd hate for you to go back to that broken woman that you were when he first walked out on you."

"What's going on?" Joannah asked, sitting back down at the table.

"Lily has received a text from Marc."

"I didn't realise you were back in contact?"

"We weren't until the other day. He just phoned me up out of the blue and we've been talking a few times since."

I handed her the phone and she read the text.

"Wow, Lily – it sounds like he wants you back!"

She was happy for me, I could tell.

"Do you not think though, Jo after all he has done, there's no going back?" Frankie turned towards her.

"Well, it's not that simple, Frankie – they were married after all. He deserves a second chance," Joannah said, echoing me.

"Exactly!" I said. She understood because she was also married.

"Well not if he was my husband," Frankie retorted.

"Can you not just be happy for me?"

"Lily, if that's what you want, then I am happy for you. Of course I am. Just be careful is all I'm saying."

"Of course I will." I took another sip of wine. I couldn't escape the giddy feeling in my head. I began to text him back.

"You're not texting him back already?" Frankie asked looking at the message I was in the middle of typing.

"Well yeah, why not?"

"God at least wait a while. You don't want him to think you're just sitting there watching your phone the whole time."

"But I am."

"Look, give it an hour and then just say something like 'Night Marc,' no kisses."

"No kisses?"

"What do you think?" I turned to Joannah.

"Frankie's right – you have him where you want him, now you just have to play it cool."

"But I hate playing it cool – I'm the uncoolest person I know."

"Don't we know it," Frankie started to laugh. "Seriously, Lily, just be careful."

Chapter 19

Later that night as I slept in deep, wine-induced sleep, I dreamed a strange dream where Frankie had invented a new-fangled breast pump that also doubled up as a bicycle pump, and was doing door-to-door sales targeting it at sporty mothers.

I thought I heard the doorbell, but I wasn't sure if it was Frankie ringing another doorbell in my dream. I opened my eyes and looked at my clock – it was 9.54 a.m. Then I heard it again, there was no mistaking it – it was definitely real. I began to panic. Who on earth would be calling to me so early on a Saturday morning? Everyone I knew lived in town, Ballyrobin was miles away for anyone to be just passing. Then I started to worry – I hoped nothing was wrong. I jumped out of bed and wrapped my humongous dressing gown around me and hurried out to the door. My heart was thumping. Nervously I looked through the peephole to make sure it wasn't an axe-murderer trying to kill me, but instead I saw Frankie standing there, her face looking strangely round through the glass.

I took off the chain to let her in.

"Frankie? I was just dreaming about you!"

"You were?"

"You had invented a breast pump that doubled as a bicycle

pump – I'd patent it if I were you."

She looked at me quizzically. "Sit down, Lily, I have something I need to show you." Her voice was serious.

"What is it?" I asked suddenly feeling panicked. I made my way over to the sofa and sat down. She took off her khaki parka jacket to reveal a yellow and blue silk tunic over grey skinny jeans and her Isabel Marant trainers. The same outfit on me would look like I was just a lazy scruff, but on Frankie it looked cool and effortless.

"Here." She handed me the latest issue of *Social Importance* magazine. "You had better read this." I saw the headline instantly: ***"Nadia and Marc's Baby Joy – Read Their Exclusive Interview Inside!"*** I couldn't believe it. The two of them were on the front cover again, with Marc sitting behind Nadia on the sofa and both their hands protectively holding her non-existent bump. It felt like a kick to the stomach.

The magazine practically fell open at the centre-page spread, as I quickly read through it to see what wonderful PR spin Marc and Nadia were spouting out of them now.

Actress Nadia Williams and her partner Marc Glover will soon be hearing the patter of little feet after her announcement that they are expecting a baby together. Congratulations, Nadia, can you tell us how you felt when you first found out that you were expecting a baby?

Nadia: *"When the test first turned positive it was such a shock – but a good one. We hadn't sat down and planned to* *have a baby, but it was the best surprise I could have asked for. I couldn't wait to tell Marc, and when he came home that evening I handed him the stick, of course he didn't know what it was," Nadia explains as she laughs good-naturedly. "When we had the first scan, I cried. I couldn't believe there was an actual baby kicking away inside me, and yet I couldn't feel a thing. Having a baby really is one of life's miracles."*

And Dad-to-be, Marc, can you tell us about the moment you found out you were going to be a father?

Marc: *"I was in complete shock – I still am. I am in awe of the whole thing. I've always loved children, so to find out I'm having one of my own is such a blessing. I can't believe a little person will be calling us Mummy and Daddy. This baby is going to be the biggest responsibility of my life, and I'm ready for that,"* said the actor, who is clearly besotted with the nation's sweetheart.

My blood was boiling – he didn't "love" children. He tolerated them. This was such bullshit, especially after all the text messages he had sent me this week.

Nadia, pregnancy obviously suits you – tell us how have you been feeling?

Nadia: *"Well I was very sick for the first three months, but I've had a real burst of energy in the last few weeks. Marc has been great – just the other night he scoured Dublin at midnight to find a shop that was open because I was desperately craving Hula Hoops. He's really minding me."*

"I feel so protective over her now," Marc adds as he gazes adoringly at the glowing Mum-to-be.

Nadia: *"I've just started to feel the first kicks, and it's a fantastic, wonderful feeling. The baby kicks me when I'm rushing around and stressing out – it's as if it's saying to me, 'slow down, Mummy'."*

Admirably Nadia isn't going to go down the birthing route favoured by most celebrity mums:

Nadia: *"I want to have as natural a birth as possible – I'm in training for the birth at the moment. I'm reading up on everything I can. I'm doing pilates and yoga and lots of walking and swimming. I'm also practising visualising my baby's entrance into this world to make it a calm and enriching experience for all three of us."*

I flicked to the next page, where there was a picture of them both holding hands and standing beside an empty cot.

The couple has decided on an animal theme for the nursery after Nadia's love of animals. They have already commissioned Kip St Clement, who counts Kate Moss and Victoria Beckham among her clients, to custom design furniture.

And will you be present at the birth, Marc?

Marc: *"Absolutely. This is one of the most important moments of our lives and I want to be there to welcome our little one into the world."*

"I don't know, we'll see," he laughs when asked if he will

cut the cord?

Was this the same Marc who fainted when he got a verruca removed last year?

The last page in the spread had a photo of a serene Nadia standing to the side with her head bowed in thought. She was barefoot on grass, and her hands cupped the underside of her bump. The caption underneath was *"My life feels complete now – it's me, Marc and our little baby"*.

I was raging after reading it. Here he was playing happy families with Nadia and acting like he was Mr Nice, whereas in reality nothing could be further from the truth. It should have been me. It should be Marc and I having a baby not her. Why did all the good things have to happen for them, after he had treated me so badly? Where was my happy ending?

"Oh, Frankie," I sobbed. "I've been such a fool." I knew she wasn't the kind of friend to say "I told you so," but still, she had been right all along and I hadn't wanted to listen to her advice. She had been able to see what I couldn't. "You were right," I mumbled eating a large slice of humble pie. "He's such a dick."

"I really wish I wasn't right though," she said kindly. "This is one time I had hoped you'd prove me wrong." She sighed. "Try not to let it get to you – they have publicists and PRs putting the words into their mouths and telling them all the right things to say. I've been on shoots where they spout such lovey dovey nonsense and then as soon as the interview is over they literally start killing each other. It's just the way the industry works."

"But if they only knew he was texting me last night!"

"You could sell your story – get revenge and solve your money worries in one go?"

"Nah – I'd be too chicken shit. It just hurts. People go through break-ups and separations every day, but they don't have to watch their husband splashed across glossy magazines with his now pregnant girlfriend."

"You're doing so well, Lily, look how far you've come. It won't always hurt this much. And aren't you glad that you aren't Nadia? Imagine bringing a baby into the world with someone like him?"

I knew Frankie was right, but it still was painful. It was hard to accept the mistake I had made in marrying Marc, and to let go of my romantic image of our relationship, which Marc had clearly proven hadn't been like that at all.

Frankie and I had spent the rest of the day lounging around talking it over and over. She had hugged me as I had sobbed my heart out at the unjustness of it all.

"Come on, we're going out tonight," she said eventually.

"I'm sorry, do you mind if we don't, Frankie? I couldn't face it –" All I wanted to do was curl up into a self-pitying ball.

"Come on, get out of those pyjamas. Go into your room and get changed," she ordered.

"You're so bossy, you know I have some pretty big problems in my life right now in case you hadn't noticed!" I said sulkily.

"So why make saggy pyjama bottoms another one? Go on, off you go now!"

I did as I was told and changed into a cream shift dress and black heels. I didn't even bother trying to curl my wispy hair.

Frankie drove us back into town, and we left her car in her car park before walking to the wine bar around the corner.

There were a few trendy looking couples sharing cheese boards and sipping wine as we entered the dimly lit bar.

"You choose something, Lily, I need to use the loo," Frankie said.

"But what if I choose something awful? I don't know anything about wine."

"I trust you," Frankie said with a wink, leaving me to sit down at a cosy table and quickly scan the wine menu that the sommelier handed to me. I pretended that I knew what I was ordering by picking the second cheapest red wine on the list. I sat back into the leather tub chair and eyed up the little bowl of olives that he had left on the table. I hated olives – they were evil little green things.

The sommelier returned, and made a big display of presenting the bottle to me to check it was correct before opening it with his corkscrew. Then he folded his left arm behind his back before using his right hand to pour a small glass for me to sample. I always hated this bit – I felt he was watching me for my complete lack of wine knowledge to be exposed. I swirled the glass a bit like I had seen people do somewhere once, and then took a little sip. It tasted good to me, so he poured the glass fully and left me to get stuck into my vino.

I instantly started to relax as I breathed in the heady aromas of whatever fancy grapes went into making the wine.

Two bottles later, and we were the last ones left in the bar. The staff were starting to clean up around our feet, so we finally took the hint and left. The wine had made us giddy, and we were in the mood for more. As we went out into the night air the effect of the alcohol hit me hard, and suddenly I was feeling drunk. We walked up and down South William Street, but most places had stopped serving and were busy folding up tables and stacking chairs to get ready for the next day.

"This is shite, our capital city and I can't get a drink after midnight!" Frankie complained loudly.

Just then we saw a gang of men making their way down tiny metal steps leading to a basement. They were all dressed in suits, with the top button open and loosened ties. They were obviously work colleagues celebrating something. Their laughter was loud, and they were all well on.

"That's where we'll go," I said pointing towards them.

We made our way down to the basement, our heels clanging off the metal steps. We entered the tiny room where there were only four small tables. The place was practically in darkness except for a small lamp sitting on the bar. I could see that the walls were painted a deep red, and a purple tasselled curtain hung on the back wall. Beside it was a handwritten sign, which said, "toilet." I made up my mind there and then that no matter how badly I needed to go, I would cross my legs and hold it.

Frankie looked around warily. "I don't like the look of this place. What if it's a sex-den?" she whispered.

My eyes scanned the darkness of the room and I suddenly realised where we were. "It's a karaoke bar!" I cheered giddily.

"Are you sure?" Frankie said as she took in the dodgy surroundings.

"Of course – I love karaoke." If I could ever wish to be blessed with a talent, well then singing would be it. If I had even a hint of a note in my head I would audition for the X-factor. I'd probably even be able to coast through to Judge's Houses on the back of my sob story with Marc.

One of the men from the group got up straight away to sing Queen's *We are the Champions* while I went to the bar and ordered two double vodkas for Frankie and myself. Another sang ACDC *Thunderstruck,* complete with air guitar accompaniment and knee skids, and before I knew it he threw the mic at me and all eyes were waiting on me expectantly. I was well tanked up at that stage so I gladly claimed the mic and hopped up on the stage. I chose Madonna's *Like a Prayer* and Frankie came up beside me to do the Gospel choir bit. The lads cheered us on. Next we did Wilson Philip's *Hold On,* before we passed the mic back to another of the lads who did Nirvana's *Smells like Teen Spirit* while we all clapped wildly. It had been so long since I had had this much fun. One of them came back with a tray of shots for all

187

of us and we knocked them back. Frankie had caught up with me, and she got up to do Lady GaGa's *Poker Face*. Frankie then did a duet of *Islands in the Stream* with one of the lads. As I watched them I started to think of Marc and all that had happened. I started to feel a bit morose. I went up and requested Tammy Wynette's *D-I-V-O-R-C-E*. As I took to the stage and sang the first few lines, I could see the lads looking at me as they tried to place the song. I kept going until I got to the chorus *"Our D-I-V-O-R-C-E becomes final today/Me and little J-O-E will be goin' away"* and belted my heart out with real emotion. I started thinking about poor little Joe, and felt awful for the poor child, and then I remembered that I didn't have a little Joe or any children for that matter. And then that made me even sadder. I know people always say "at least there are no children involved," but the truth was, as selfish as it may seem, I sometimes wished there *were* kids involved. I wished I still had a part of him, any part, and maybe if we had had children together he wouldn't have done that to me. If we had kids he would have to call to see them. I would get to see him. I would know what he was doing, what his plans were. Hell the little buggers could be like mini-spies into his life with Nadia for me. I don't remember much after that, because the next thing I knew I was lying in Frankie's clashing pink and orange spare room, the same one I had stayed in the night Marc had left and I thought I was going to die. Why did I always end up in that room when I was hungover? It was the worst possible place you could be with a hangover. Every nerve ending, every synapse was in a heightened sense of pain and my entire body ached. I tried to open my eyelids, but it was too painful and my brain felt as though it was pounding against my skull. There was an awful taste in my mouth of stale alcohol. I fell back asleep for a while longer and when I woke again I still felt no better. Soon after I began to feel sick, and stumbled out of Frankie's bed and ran into the bathroom just in time to vomit.

"You better not puke on my carpet!" Frankie roared at me from her bedroom.

When I had finished being sick, I brushed my teeth with the spare toothbrush I left in her place, went into her room and climbed into her bed beside her. "What were you thinking decorating the room in those colours, it's killing my eyes."

"How are you feeling?"

"I am dying."

"No you're not, you're hungover."

"No – I am pretty sure I'm dying."

"I'm not surprised."

"How bad was I?"

"On a scale of 1-10?"

"Uh-huh."

"I'd say 9.5."

"Oh no," I squealed putting my hands over my eyes. "I can remember singing D-I-V-O-R-C-E and then I go blank."

"So you don't remember the tears then?"

"Noooooh . . ."

189

"Or falling off the stage on top of the poor karaoke man?"

"Noooooooooh - okay you can stop, I don't want to hear anymore. I'd say those lads thought I was a right mentaller."

"No they didn't - they loved you, they thought the tears were all part of your karaoke act!"

I cringed. "I am so embarrassed." I grabbed a cushion off the bed and used it to cover my face.

"Don't be. It was a great night, and you'll never see them again."

"Thankfully."

Frankie dropped me home later on, and I was still in bits. I had no food in the house, so I phoned the Chinese and ordered a chicken curry with chips, prawn crackers and Coca-Cola to help ease my hangover. As I walked past the hallway to get cutlery from the kitchen, the photo of Mam and all of us in the zoo beamed down on me from where I had hung it up. She was so youthful in it, but then again she was around the same age as I was now – by the age of thirty-two she was already married with two kids. Although the picture was black and white you could still see how flawless her porcelain skin was and the shine of her dark hair, which was neatly turned out just below her shoulders. I wondered what Mam would think of the way I had turned out. I knew she would never approve of the state I had got myself into last night – she was such a lady from what Dad told me. Here I was a hungover mess, separated and trying to scrape a living by baking because I had been fired from my last job. Would she be disappointed in me for the way my life seemed to have plummeted over the last few months? I wanted so desperately to make her proud of me, but I think I had managed to do everything but that over the last few months.

"I'm sorry, Mam," I whispered.

Chapter 20

I spent the next few weeks in a dark place. Never, ever, ever in my life had I been so angry. Never. The stupid, fuckedy fuck. The wanker, symbiotic bollox – I wasn't sure what that even meant but it sounded impressive, and Marc was such a thick that he wouldn't even understand it. How could he raise my hopes that perhaps he was having second thoughts about leaving me and meanwhile he and Nadia were announcing their "baby joy" for the whole world to read? I felt like such an idiot. He had tried calling me a few times since but when I didn't return his calls, he finally seemed to get the message and I hadn't heard from him in a while. That was it, I thought. There was no going back. I had finally woken up to the fact that Marc was no good. We were done. I was separated by the ripe old age of thirty-two. I would have to wait the obligatory four years and then when that was done, I supposed we would have to get a divorce. To be separated and potentially divorced by that stage of my life was embarrassing. Then there was "The Fear". What was going to happen to me? Would I be left on the shelf now? The thoughts of meeting someone new, getting to know them, moving in together, pottering around B&Q early on Saturday mornings buying sensible things like decking and radiator cabinets. Maybe getting a cat or a pot plant – well I was running out of time to do all of that all over again. Most of my friends bar Frankie were going out with people or getting married, and some even had babies now to show for their time together, but I was back in the starting blocks.

I couldn't even bring myself to bake, that's how bad it was. I knew I needed to concentrate on *Baked with Love* – I had lots of orders coming in. My cousin Tina was getting married and she had asked me to do two hundred mini cakes all iced with her and her grooms initials with navy ribbon trimming to match the invitations and the bridesmaids' dresses. Then Frankie had phoned me to say that she had recommended me to a male client of hers who happened to be the CEO of First Ireland Bank, and they wanted me to do a tower of two hundred and fifty cupcakes to celebrate the opening of their 250th branch. I was really excited about this – the corporate market was huge, but notoriously hard to break into. There were so many bakeries doing what I was doing, all competing for the weddings, christenings and birthday parties, but the corporate market really was untapped. I just knew if I did this job well, then it could lead on to more. I had a meeting with his P.A. and she briefed me on what was required. It sounded like it was a really big deal – they were going all out, no expense spared. They had already ordered three custom made steel framed cake stands, made in the shape of the numbers, 2, 5 and 0 and then it was my job to make the cupcakes to put onto the stand. I was busier than ever, and I knew that if I didn't get my act together soon, I wouldn't be able to fulfil all my orders, but I just couldn't get myself in the right headspace.

I had wanted every trace of Marc gone from the house so I set off on a blizzard of cleaning. I took a black sack from underneath the kitchen sink and went into the bedroom. I opened the doors of his wardrobes. He had taken a lot of his stuff already when he had left, but there were still some of his clothes in there. I took cashmere jumpers off their hangers. There were Paul Smith shirts. I lifted out a tailored Tom Ford suit – how in the name of God had Marc been able to afford that on what he earned? I stuffed them all into a black sack. On the floor there was a stack of vinyl records that he had been collecting – including an original Led Zeppelin one. I didn't care if they were priceless – one by one I snapped them in two. "Whoopsie!" He had left his lotions and potions on the bathroom shelf – the man had more anti-ageing creams than I had. I poured his aftershave down the drain – the smell of it, of him, made me gag.

Next I went around the house and gathered up every photo that had Marc in it, then I took a copy of *VIP* Magazine from the coffee table and cut out photos of all the good looking men. There was a photo of the Irish rugby team so I cut out Tommy Bowe and Rob Kearney's faces. I flicked on a few pages and there was a photo of Bressie at an awards ceremony, so I cut the face off him as well. There was some guy who I didn't know, but he was a gorgeous chunk of hunk so I cut him out too. Then I dismantled all the photo frames and stuck the faces on top of Marc's. And for the *pièce the résistance* – our wedding photo – I stuck Ryan

195

Reynolds's photo over Marc's. I put the photo back inside the frame and sat back on the couch and surveyed my new husband. Ryan and I looked quite good together actually - we were both beaming smiles at the camera, looking very happy together in fact.

After I had de-Marc'ed the house, I had gone to Tesco with the black bag of Marc's effects and given them to Piotr.

"Hi, Lily."

"How are you today, Piotr?"

"Good thanks." He smiled up at me.

"Here, I have something for you." I handed him a huge bag of designer clothes. "There's some stuff that might keep you warm, you can sell the rest of it. "

There was a NorthFace jacket that Marc usually wore whenever they were shooting outside. There were also fleeces and sweatshirts in the bag that might come in handy for Piotr. The Tom Ford suit was in there too. To be honest I wasn't sure what he would do with a Tom Ford suit – with its ruffled lapels, it would look a bit fancy for begging, and might even stop people giving him money and I didn't want that to happen, but still I hoped he could sell it on and get a bit of cash for it.

"Thank you, Lily that is very kind of you."

"Don't mention it. It's a bit dull today - do you want a cuppa?"

"That'd be great thanks, Lily."

When I came home, I suddenly felt hungry so I decided to

make myself some French toast for breakfast. I was just mixing up the eggs when I saw I had a message from Dad:

"I'll pick you up at 12, Dad."

He always signed his name at the end of his text messages.

I groaned, I had totally forgotten that we were going to Clara's house for Sunday lunch. The thoughts of enduring her criticisms did nothing to help my mood. Plus I knew I would have to tell her about Marc and Nadia having a baby together.

That afternoon Dad and I trudged over to Clara's house for our dinner. Even though Tatiana should be off, Clara had her in the study preparing lesson plans for the boys for the week ahead. When she was finished, Clara would review the lesson plan and tweak if necessary. Even playtime had to have a learning element. As I walked down the hallway to the dining room, I stuck my head around the living room door, and miraculously the table was back in the centre of the room and the stain had disappeared. Either Clara had had the stain professionally removed or she had replaced the entire carpet with an identical one. Either way the room was restored to its perfect glory once again.

The boys came in soon after wearing matching sailing jumpers with white polo shirts underneath, navy cords and deck shoes. They looked ridiculous – even Dad was dressed younger than them. I don't think the boys even owned a pair of jeans. We all took our seats, and when Clara had finished serving out the starters of foie gras we began eating. Well everyone else did – I hated foie gras. I thought it was cruel. Clara gave me a lecture about being too fussy, and not opening my horizons to the range of flavours out there waiting to be discovered . . . blah, blah, blah . . . She was banging on about how the boys had eaten sushi since they were one year old, and now had the most rounded palates of all their friends. I wanted to tell her to get lost.

Just then Joshua piped up, "I no like this."

"Yes you do," Clara chided. "Come on, eat up now!"

"But it's yucky, Mummy," Jacob chimed in.

"Now, Lily, see what you've done?"

"Me? What did I do?"

"You and your faddiness are prejudicing my children's tastes!"

The dinner had started as it meant to go on. Clara had just served the duck à l'orange for our main course when I dropped the clanger that Marc had got Nadia pregnant, and that our marriage was definitely over. I thought Clara might just cry. Dad rubbed my shoulder hard, and told me it would all be okay, but Clara was stunned. "I can't believe Lily is going to be a divorcée!" She kept repeating over and over again. There it was again, the d-word – I hated it. Dad and I decided to skip dessert, claiming we were too full.

"I think Clara nearly took that worse than me," I sighed on the way home.

"She just needs time," Dad soothed.

"But she's not the one who actually has to get the divorce!" I wailed. Every time I uttered that horrible word, I was filled with a dread so strong that my stomach did a loop, and I would feel like getting sick.

"You know what she's like, Lily. She's just worried about you."

"Well she has a funny way of showing it," I muttered.

Chapter 21

The wedding for my cousin Tina came around quickly. It felt as though it was all engagements, weddings and babies these days. I suppose I was a bit more sensitive to it after everything that had happened with Marc, and working in *Baked with Love* didn't help with all the cakes I seemed to be making for loved-up couples or for tiny babies on their christening day. Don't get me wrong, I wasn't jealous of these people. I was so happy for everyone and felt honoured to be playing a small part in their special occasions – I just wished I had had a happy ending too.

Tina's mother, Joan, was Dad's sister, and Dad was looking forward to catching up with all his family again even though I knew that he found occasions like this hard on his own without having Mam at his side.

I had been up until all hours baking the mini cakes because I had left it until the last minute and my blasted oven could only fit twenty-four in at a time. The panic I had felt at the thoughts of letting Tina down on her wedding day had been enough for me to wake up and realise that I needed to pull myself together. I had spent the last while crusading around in a sea of misery, and I had had enough. I wasn't going to spend any more of my life getting wasted over Marc Glover. He had taken up enough of my life already and I needed to move on.

By the time I had finally removed the last tray from the oven, I had only had two hours sleep before I heard my doorbell go at 7.30 a.m. I opened my eyes and groaned. Clara was driving Tom, Dad and myself to the hotel where the reception was on, and I was going to set up the mini cakes on the stand and then get ready in the hotel. She wasn't supposed to be picking me up until eight, but of course she had to be ridiculously early and was now depriving me of a valuable half hour's sleep. I pulled back the duvet, put on my fluffy dressing gown and went out to answer the door.

"Morning!" she sang brightly as she bustled in past me. "Are we ready for the day of weddingness ahead?"

"Come in," I grunted to them all. "You're early!"

"Oh you know me – I don't like sleeping in late," she sang. "It's not a good example for the boys."

At least she was in a good mood, I thought. Maybe I'd be spared one of her talks.

"Hi, Lily," Tom said with an apologetic smile coming in the door behind her. He seemed to be feeling like I was.

"Morning, love," Dad said giving me a kiss on the cheek. "I hope we didn't wake you?"

I told them to help themselves to tea and coffee while I jumped into the shower.

"Hurry on, Lily," I heard Clara call into me as I was towelling myself off ten minutes later. I threw on a tracksuit and started gathering my stuff together to pack my bag.

After I had boxed up the mini cakes, we set off in Clara's SUV. Clara was driving – she never let Tom drive. The wedding was a two-hour drive away in the Tipperary countryside. She dutifully obeyed each and every speed limit sign that we encountered.

If I was completely honest, I was dreading the day because the last time I had seen all my relations was at my own wedding. But what was worse was that I hadn't told them about what had happened between Marc and I since then. I didn't think they'd be big *Social Importance* magazine readers, but you never knew. I knew people would be asking where Marc was, and I wasn't sure what I was going to say. Even though it was over for good, I wasn't ready yet to admit to all and sundry that Marc and I were *finito* – it was hard to even admit it to myself.

After I had set my cakes up, I had to admit that they looked impressive on the stand. The white icing was decorated with navy ribbon and each mini-cake had the initials of the bride and groom piped in silver on the top of it.

"Wow, Lily," Dad said, standing back to take a look at them. "You really have a talent, do you know that? I'm so proud of you. These last few months have been awful for you, but you still came here today and put on a brave face and look at what you created!"

"Thanks, Dad," I mumbled, feeling embarrassed. "I just hope Tina likes them."

"Of course she will."

I started to turn and tweak them slightly, making sure they looked perfect.

"Leave them alone now, they look amazing," Dad said.

When I was finally happy with the cakes, I ran upstairs to my room to get changed. I was wearing an old silk dress that I had bought for a wedding last year. It was sage green in colour and I was pleased to find that it fitted me better now than when I had last worn it. I put on a necklace and a shawl to cover my shoulders, and then we headed to the church.

The wedding itself was wonderful. As Tina and Oliver said their vows, their words weren't lost on me – Marc and I had said those words too. Admittedly, I shed a few tears during the ceremony – tears of happiness for Tina and her groom Oliver, and tears of sadness for Marc and I. No one said anything about my strange behaviour, they were used to my weepy eye.

Back at the reception, the mini cakes went down a treat and I had three other couples book me on the spot to do their weddings.

"Lily, how are you dear?" My aunt Flor said coming up beside me.

"I'm good, Auntie Flor," I said leaning in to give her a kiss on the cheek.

"And where's the lovely Marc?" she asked. There it was, the question I had been dreading since I had opened the invitation. I grabbed a glass of champagne off the tray of a passing waiter and gulped it back.

"Well he . . . mmh . . . well, he's –"

She was looking at me expectantly.

"He's working," I finally finished as I fixed a smile on my face. I knew she wouldn't be one for the gossip magazines, and I just wasn't ready to tell people and answer all the questions that would inevitably come. I wasn't ready yet to look like the world's biggest disaster, having failed at marriage after only three months in. I knew it would all come out eventually, but for now I was prepared to lie.

"Ah the poor guy – but at least he has a job. Better to be working on a Saturday rather than be an out of work actor."

"True," I agreed taking another gulp from the glass.

The rest of the day continued in much the same way with relatives asking me where Marc was, and me replying that he was working. I also had to endure countless people telling me what a great day they had had at our wedding, and what a great couple Marc and I were. It was horrendous. Dad was beside me on one occasion, but in fairness he gave nothing away as he listened to me lying through my teeth.

Finally dinner was called and as we tucked into the meal, I could tell Clara was well on. She had been knocking back the champagne during the reception, and now she was lashing into the wine. She did this sometimes when she had a rare night away from her children. She had refused to drink the table wine being served with the meal because she claimed it wasn't "paired" properly, so had ordered her own bottle from the menu and was drinking it all by herself. Nobody else was able to get a word in. She was starting to talk louder than her usual level, which was already very loud. Her hands were waving all over the place as she regaled poor Tom with some story.

After the meal was finished I went to the bar to get a round of drinks. I was taking it easy myself - I still hadn't got over the whole karaoke debacle. The bar was packed with everyone getting up after the meal ordering drinks. A guy squeezed in beside me. I had seen him in the church, he was very good looking, his blonde hair was styled and he wore a pink open necked shirt under a slim-fitting grey suit and brown leather brogues.

"Bride or groom?" he asked me while we waited on the barman to serve us.

"Sorry?"

"Which side are you on – the bride's or the groom's?"

"Oh right –" I said realising what he was talking about. He must have thought I was a complete imbecile. "Bride – Tina is my first cousin. How about you?"

"Groom – I work with Oliver."

"Oh I see." I couldn't think of anything else to say. I always got nervous around really good looking men, whether I fancied them or not.

"What's your name?" he continued.

Damn it why hadn't I thought of that question.

"I'm Lily."

"Matthew. Nice to meet you, Lily." He held out his hand to shake mine. He had nice hands, big and manly, with just the right amount of roughness, not too soft.

"So where are you from?"

"Well originally from Dublin but living in Ballyrobin now," I smiled.

"What brought a Dublin girl all the way out there?"

"It's a long story . . ."

"I've got time."

I felt my cheeks flush. Was he flirting with me? I wasn't sure how people flirted anymore; it had been so long since I was in the game. Actually, I don't think I was ever really in the game to be honest, because I had been with Marc since I was seventeen years old.

I gave a nervous laugh and I was pretty sure he thought I was a loon. I willed the barmen to hurry up and serve me, but the bar was deep with people. I felt someone tip my shoulder then and I turned around to see Clara.

"Can you get Dad a brandy instead? He needs an aperitif to help him digest the meal."

"Sure."

She eyed up Matthew waiting for an introduction. Her eyes were glassy and I knew she was tipsy.

"Sorry, Matthew – this is my sister, Clara," I said. "Matthew works with Oliver."

207

"I see," Clara said looking at Matthew disapprovingly. She didn't make any move to go. It was awkward as the two of us stood there with Clara eyeballing us.

"Well, Matthew, did Lily tell you about her little *mishap*?" Clara looked at me and then back to him again. *What was she doing?*

Matthew looked at me to see if I could shed some light on what the hell she was talking about.

"Clara, I –"

But she interrupted me again before I could finish. "Yes, our Lily is getting *divorced?* Aren't you, Lily?" She practically hissed the word "divorced". A few heads turned around – thank God they weren't any of our relations.

Then she turned and left the bar as quickly as she arrived. What was wrong with her? I was just making polite conversation with the guy and she had turned the whole thing ugly. I watched his eyes widen to see if he had heard her right over the music and when I nodded to confirm his doubt, his face twisted up. Any minute now the excuses would come pouring out.

"Oooh, I just remembered I'm supposed to be getting in a group photo with the lads. Yeah, sorry I have to go. But nice to meet you, Lily."

"Yeah you too," I muttered as I watched him skidaddle as fast as his muscular legs would carry him.

It didn't matter, it wasn't as if I was even interested in men at the moment, but it was just typical of Clara. Well that had been my first test to see how guys reacted to the news of my separation, and it wasn't pretty. He didn't want to know, didn't want the baggage. How to lose a guy in ten seconds.

I left the bar without the drinks and walked back to the table with Clara.

"Why did you do that, Clara?" I asked.

"Do what, Lily? Are you embarrassed about your *divorce*?" she shouted the word again, and even Tom told her to stop making a scene.

"I'm not getting divorced," I said through gritted teeth.

"Lily – you're separated, next step is divorce. Once the obligatory four years is up, Marc will be express-mailing you those papers just you wait and see!"

She clicked her fingers in the air at a passing waiter and ordered a bottle of Tattinger.

"Don't you think maybe you've had enough to drink?" Tom said.

"Tom Kingston – if you think after five years straight of either being pregnant or breastfeeding that I am not entitled to a drink then you are sadly mistaken, my dear."

Tom put his head down into his hands. She was obstreperous now.

"Oh yeah, Tom you just bury your head in the sand like an ostrich! Am I not entitled to a break now and again?" she continued.

"Of course you are, Clara, but I think you might be taking it a bit too far tonight."

"Well you have some cheek! You don't know how hard I have it! Do you think it's easy for me going to the toilet with a toddler on my knee and another standing there watching me every time? And then they have to wave goodbye to Mr Pee Pee? Or don't you think I get sick of having to fake excitement every time I see a plane or a choo-choo train? Or listening to the bloody *Wheels on the Bus* or the *Happy Elf* on loop in the car? Or what's even worse is when I am alone in the car I still want to listen to the nursery rhymes because I don't know any of the songs on the radio anymore!" She was growing hysterical.

"Whoa, there, Clara – maybe Tom is right," I said softly. She was clearly plastered. She *never,* ever painted a bad picture of motherhood or showed us that she might find certain bits tedious or even hard.

"How dare you, Lily!" she turned on me then. "How dare *you* lecture me!"

"Look maybe you should go and sleep for a little while," Dad butted in.

"Sleep? *Sleeeep?* I haven't had a full night's sleep in over five years! *Five* years!" She was screeching now. "How would you feel if you hadn't slept in *five* years?" She was screaming hysterically now.

"But the boys have been sleeping through the night since they were six weeks old?" I said.

"Six weeks. Ha!" she spat. "Maybe by the time they're six

years I might get a night's sleep!"

Why would she not be honest over something like that? Why did she have to lie and say her boys were sleeping through the night when they weren't? It made no difference to me whether they slept or not but that was Clara all over though – her boys had to be the best at everything, even sleeping. She saw parenting as some sort of competition. She sulkily drank the remainder of the bottle of champagne to herself without offering the rest of us any.

We talked among ourselves and let her at it. A while later Tom said he was going to bed, and asked Clara if she was coming, but she refused saying the party was only getting started. Tom went off to bed on his own and Clara stumbled up from her chair. She shakily made her way to the bar, balancing precariously in her Prada heels.

When I saw her coming back with another bottle of champagne, I groaned. She was already in such a state – she would be paralytic after another bottle.

"Right – I think you've had enough now, dear," Dad said taking the bottle out of her hands before she had a chance to pour herself another glass. She was too drunk to argue with him. We watched her sway unsteadily in her seat until she suddenly jumped up, "I'm going to be sick." She started running towards the bathroom.

"You better go after her, Lily" Dad sighed wearily.

I got up and followed her into the bathroom. I found her in the cubicle down the end, the door still open with her head

211

hanging over the toilet bowl. The stench of vomit was unbearable. The other women using the bathroom were disgusted.

"Clara –"

I watched as she puked into the white ceramic bowl again. As you know from stain-gate, I am not good with sick at all. Clara's hair was hanging down in front of her face with clumps of vomit in it. I gathered it back as best I could and held it behind her head with one hand and pinched my nose with my other one, while she continued to spew into the bowl. When she was finished, she sat on the speckled grey floor tiles with her back resting against the toilet bowl. She must have been out of it because Clara wouldn't even use a public toilet, let alone sit on the floor of one.

"Thanks, s'Lily," she said before she fell asleep with her cheek resting against the toilet seat.

By the time I had finally managed to get her up the stairs and handed over to poor Tom to mind, I was exhausted. I fell into bed and was asleep before my head even touched the pillow.

***

The next morning Clara breezed into the breakfast buffet as though nothing had happened the night before. She seemed oblivious to it all. Either she didn't remember hanging her head over the bowl so that her tonsils were practically licking the toilet rim, or else she was just being pig-headed, and I knew which option I had my money on.

"How's the head?" I asked her eventually as I buttered a

slice of toast.

"Perfect," she replied. "Why wouldn't it be?"

I had to hand it to her. She looked remarkably fresh, dressed in an olive green silk wrap dress and heels, with perfect hair and make-up. If that were me, I would have been in a heap. The only giveaway that her head might be a little bit fragile was the huge pair of Tom Ford sunglasses that she was wearing indoors. Although with Clara you never really knew, she was the kind of person to wear them indoors just because she felt like it. We ate the rest of our breakfast in silence.

Chapter 22

The following week I was busy getting ready for the corporate gig. I had been up all the night before putting the finishing touches to cupcakes and had had no time to go to bed. Once the cupcakes were baked, I had to decorate them with cream frosting, and then I cut the company initials out of icing that I had dyed robin's egg in colour to match their logo. I had to drop everything off for eleven a.m. and set it up in time for the presentation, which was due to start at twelve. Frankie was picking me up and driving me to their offices. I knew I was going to have to learn to drive, and maybe get myself a van, but I couldn't afford it. The last mortgage payment had bounced, so of course the mortgage company had phoned me within days. I had to promise that it wouldn't happen again and I'd meet the repayment the next month. I just hoped I would be able to. Marc still hadn't put any money into our account and I was too angry to phone him and ask for it.

I was just starting to dress myself when my phone went. It was Clara in a complete panic. I balanced the phone between my ear and shoulder while I used my fingers to try and blend foundation into my face.

"It's Tatiana," she said breathlessly before I had time to

speak.

"What's wrong?"

"She's sick –"

"Oh, what's wrong with her?"

"It doesn't matter what's wrong, Lily!" she hissed. "What matters is that I am supposed to be hosting a charity luncheon in two hour's time and I have no one to mind the boys!" She was near hysterical at this stage.

"I'm sorry, Clara – I can't do it." I said quickly before she could even ask. "I have to deliver two hundred and fifty cupcakes into the offices of First Ireland Bank by eleven and set everything up. Sorry, if it was any other time of course I'd help you out."

"But you have to, Lily – this is so important. I'm being considered for the position of chairwoman of the committee – if I fail at this I can kiss goodbye to it!"

"I can't, Clara. I'm sorry. This is my first corporate gig and I have to get it right. Did you try Dad?"

"I couldn't get hold of him – he's probably off lolling around the golf-course!" she hissed.

"Well I'm sorry, Clara but I can't help you this time."

"But, Lily this is important to me."

"And so is this –"

"But you're only dropping off a few buns – the boys will be as good as gold I promise."

"It would look completely unprofessional if I brought them along with me."

There was silence on the other end.

"Clara are you still there? *Clara?*" I repeated but she had hung up.

I looked down at my phone waiting for her to call me back, but she didn't, so I dialled her number but she didn't pick up. I knew she was annoyed with me, but I had to stand my ground on this. How unprofessional would I look dragging two small boys with me?

I quickly finished off the rest of my make-up and spritzed myself with some of my Armani perfume. I headed back to the kitchen and spent the next hour putting the final touches to the cupcakes. I was just putting them into the boxes when the doorbell rang.

I assumed it was Frankie, but when I opened the door Clara was standing there with Jacob and Joshua on either side of her. There was a child's car seat and a booster seat on the ground beside her too. I almost closed the door in her face again.

"Please, Lily you have to –" she begged.

"Clara I can't believe you're doing this!"

"Pleeease, Lily," she pleaded.

Jacob looked up at me with a worried expression. His small face was wrinkled upwards as he looked from me to his mother in confusion, wondering what was going on. I couldn't bear to see him like that.

"Okay," I said purely for his sake.

"Oh thank you so much. Thank you, thank you, thank you,"

she gushed. Then she pushed the two boys in the door towards me and handed me a bag packed with their stuff, followed by the car seat for Joshua and the booster for Jacob.

I stood there holding the Cath Kidson hold all, stunned by what had just happened. We went back into the house and I switched on the TV to occupy the boys while I stacked up the boxes ready for Frankie's car. Then I realised that we wouldn't all fit in the car. Frankie drove a Mini Cooper and I had twenty-five boxes of cupcakes to fit in. God knew what state they'd be in by the time we got there.

When Frankie arrived, she was horrified when she saw Jacob and Joshua sitting in my living room, cross-legged in front of the TV drinking Coca-Cola and eating packets of crisps.

"What are they doing here?" she hissed pointing a finger in their direction.

"Shush!" I didn't want them to hear her. It wasn't their fault that their Mum was a self-centred witch. "Clara's *au pair* is sick."

"And what's that got to do with you?"

"Well Clara has some charity lunch on so I said I'd help her out."

"But, Lily in case you haven't realised, this is a huge opportunity for you. You can't bring them along with you!"

"I haven't any choice – she literally dumped the pair of them on my doorstep."

"When are you ever going to learn to stand up for yourself, Lily?" She shook her head in despair.

"I know, I know, Frankie. Look they'll be as good as gold. Won't you boys?"

They didn't divert their eyes away from the TV screen.

Frankie looked at me dubiously.

"C'mon," I said. "I don't want to be late."

She helped me to fit the boys' car seats, which took up the whole backseat of the Mini so I had to stack half the boxes up in the tiny boot and hold the other half on my knees. When we had the boys strapped in and the cakes loaded up, we set off. I held my breath as we drove over speed bumps and ramps, and that was only to get out of my estate. Then Joshua started singing *The wheels on the bus* and we all had to join in. On repeat. I could see Frankie tensing in the seat beside me as I did the actions once again for the "horn on the bus" with one hand while still keeping hold of the boxes, so I decided change tune to *Old McDonald* instead.

When we finally pulled up outside the offices of First Ireland Bank, Frankie's whole body was rigid. She let the boys out of their seats and helped me carry the boxes into the foyer. Their offices were on the fifth floor, so we had to bring the two boys and the boxes up and down until all twenty-five boxes were in the reception area. The receptionist phoned George's P.A., Sophie who came out to meet us. Frankie had to run back to the shoot she was working on. She was going to come back to pick me up in an hour's time.

"Childminder let you down?" Sophie asked me, nodding at

the boys.

"Something like that," I winced.

I followed Sophie as she led me into the empty meeting room, where in an hour's time, the presentation was going to be taking place. The two boys trailed behind us. There was a podium in front of a large screen, which was covered over with a red velvet curtain. The room was full with rows of chairs. The cupcake stand was located at the top of the room, over to the right hand side of the podium. It was really impressive. I had seen an image of it and Sophie had emailed me the dimensions but I had never seen anything quite like it before. There were three separate custom made stands in the shape of a 2, 5 and an 0. The whole thing was about a metre high off the ground and five metres long. It had been designed so that they would display exactly two hundred and fifty cupcakes. I bent down on my hunkers and got to work opening up the boxes and filling the stand with cupcakes. As I continued filling the 2, I could see Jacob and Joshua were getting bored – they had started play fighting with one another. Joshua kept elbowing his older brother, who would then retaliate with an elbow back. I bent down on my hunkers to work on the bottom of the stand, but when I got up again, the boys were nowhere to be seen. *Shit.* I stepped out of the door of the meeting room and saw them sprinting in laps of the open-plan office, Joshua in pursuit of Jacob. I nearly died. I hoped George didn't see or I could kiss goodbye to any repeat business. I mouthed sorry as I walked past all of First Ireland Bank's employees and hauled the boys back into the meeting room by the collars of their rugby shirts. I think it was because Clara normally had them so busy – she always had them doing some sort of activity, that whenever they were away from her, they tended to go berserk. Of course as soon as I would hand them back to her again, they acted like angels.

Once we were back inside the meeting room I sternly told them they'd have to sit down and stop messing. I managed to finish the 2 and the 5 and was just starting on the 0. It was starting to come together, and even I was impressed with how it had turned out. Thankfully the boys seemed to have calmed down. They were sitting quietly on two chairs in the front row.

"Nearly finished now, boys, just one more box to put up."

When the last cupcake went on the stand I stood back to admire the display. It looked amazing – it was completely unique owing to the stand; I was proud to put this on my portfolio. I took some photos to put on my website and then the boys helped me clean up the boxes. I was squashing them down inside a black sack, but when I turned around again I watched in horror as Jacob was trying to lift the 5 stand off the ground.

"Jacob – nooo!" I cried but it was too late. I watched in slow motion as he fell forward onto the stand, causing it to crash to the ground, sending the buns flying in every direction across the carpet.

Dear God, this cannot be happening. *This cannot be happening*, I thought to myself.

Jacob started to cry.

"I hurt my arm, Lily."

"Your arm? *Your arm*?" I was shrieking now. "Look what you've done to my cakes!" I pulled him up from where he had fallen on top of the stand. His clothes were covered in frosting. I stood there paralysed, just staring at the mess, not knowing what to do. The presentation was due to start in fifteen minutes. I was finished as soon as George and Sophie saw this. There was only one thing I could do to try and salvage the situation – I had to pick up the cakes that had fallen. I quickly started gathering them up off the floor, inspecting each one and picking off any bits of dirt or hairs that I could see as best I could before putting them back up on the stand again. I prayed nobody would eat those ones. I told the boys to help too.

We were all busy scrutinising the buns and putting them back onto the stand when a voice startled me from behind.

"Need a hand?"

"Jesus Christ!" I jumped up, nearly knocking the 2 myself.

It was an employee of the company – I remembered his face because he had been the only one to look vaguely amused when the boys were doing laps of the office.

"I was coming in to practice my speech, but I can see you've had a little accident there." He pointed at the buns, which still remained on the floor.

Sweet mother of Divinity, he had seen me picking them off the carpet. This was it now – I was a goner. I wanted to run out of the place and forget the whole thing. What did I, Lily McDermott, disaster central, think I was doing setting up a professional cake making business in the first place? Of course I would have to fail at it – I failed at everything else I had ever tried in life, why would this have been any different? I felt awful for Frankie because she had recommended me to the company. She would look bad now.

"Here let me help you," he said as he hitched up his slacks, bent down and started picking up the buns, inspecting them for dirt and hairs just like we had been doing, before putting them back on the stand.

I was too stunned to speak, and didn't know whether to laugh or to cry. I bent down and started doing the same as him.

"What happened?" he asked.

"The boys . . . fell . . . knocked it over." I was hyperventilating and could barely get the words out. My heart was thumping wildly.

"I see! That's a wild pair there you have," he said nodding at them. He had huge brown eyes, the kind that made him look like a nice person.

"Oh they're not mine. No way – they're my nephews." I had started to calm down. "My sister landed me with them at the last minute, they're lovely really, just a bit . . . hyper. This is Jacob and his little brother Joshua."

"Nice to meet you boys!" He put out his hand to shake theirs. "My name is Sam." I noticed his hands first. That's the first thing I always notice in a man – his hands. They were strong and muscular and dark hairs threaded his tanned skin. I would have to have a bath in Saint Tropez to ever go that dark.

"Hi, Sam," the boys chorused back.

"And you are?"

"Sorry – I'm Lily."

"I know you from somewhere –" Sam said as we picked up the last of the cupcakes.

"No, I don't think we've met before."

"No, we definitely have – I never forget a face," he said assuredly.

"Right, well . . . em maybe we met somewhere before." I really didn't want to get into an argument with the man – he was doing me a huge favour after all but I definitely had never met him before.

"The karaoke bar!"

"What?"

"The karaoke bar on South William Street – you know the one in the basement, with four tables and the glittery strips on the way to the toilet?"

"Erm, no," I tried to feign innocence.

"You fell off the stage beside me. I helped catch you before you hit the floor."

Dear God no, please don't do this to me. Could today get any worse? I wanted to crawl under the carpet tiles. No, no, no. Why do these things always come back to haunt me? This would never happen to Frankie. Not in a million, squillion years.

"Right . . . yeah – look I'm awfully sorry about that. I'm normally not so unprofessional," I said as I picked up the last cupcake, examined it and placed it back onto the 5.

"Don't worry – you and your friend – Frankie wasn't it? You were great fun."

Now that he said it, he did look vaguely familiar, but I had been so wasted that night that Kate Middleton herself could have offered me her entire collection of LK Bennett shoes and I still wouldn't remember.

"Hmm. There – all done now." I stood back to look at the stand again. You would never know the catastrophe that had just taken place. I had put all the wonky buns at the back and swapped them for better ones at the front.

"It looks great, Lily – well done!" Sam said.

"Right, look thanks again, we'd better go and let you get on with rehearsing your speech. C'mon boys. Say goodbye to Sam."

"Bye, bye, Sam."

"Bye, Jacob, bye, Joshua, bye, Lily," Sam said with a bemused look on his face.

Chapter 23

As Frankie drove us all home afterwards I filled her in on what had happened. She was horrified. She could remember Sam – at least one of us could. She kept on shaking her head saying, *"what are the chances"* over and over.

I was starving so we stopped off for some lunch and when we finally reached my estate, Clara's SUV was already there in the car park. She was sitting inside it waiting for us. I climbed out of the Mini and walked over to her.

"Where on earth were you, Lily?" she fired off.

"Just hang on a minute, Clara – I told you I had to deliver cupcakes into town."

"Well I've been waiting here for over half an hour – I tried phoning you!"

I remembered then I had turned my phone off so that it wouldn't go off in First Ireland Bank but I had forgotten to turn it back on.

"How did the lunch go?" I asked.

"Luncheon, Lily – it was a "luncheon"."

"*Luncheon* then – how did it go?"

"Yes, it was most enjoyable, we had a lovely afternoon."

She never even asked me how I got on, or how the boys

were for that matter. She climbed down from her Range Rover and came over to Frankie's car. She looked disapprovingly at the Mini before taking out the boy's car seats and putting them back into her SUV.

"Right, Lily I'd better go – the boys have swimming lessons at four."

She strapped them in before hopping into the driver's seat and heading off.

"I don't know how you don't throttle that woman, Lily!" Frankie said as she watched the SUV disappear out of sight. "She never even thanked you!"

"You know what she's like, Frankie – that's just Clara."

***

I decided to have a lie-in the next morning – after the stress of the previous day, I reckoned I deserved it but just after eight my phone rang. I didn't recognise the number.

"Hello, Lily?" It was a man's voice.

"Yes?"

"Lily – hi it's Sam – Sam from First Ireland Bank – we met yesterday?"

"Oh yeah – hi, Sam" I tried to make my voice sound like I hadn't just been asleep.

"Oh sorry, did I wake you?"

"No, no, I've been up for ages," I lied getting out of bed so I would sound more serious.

"I got your number from Sophie, George's P.A., and well I

just thought you might like to know that the cupcakes went down a treat."

"Well thank God for that, eh?"

"Yes, hairs and all."

I groaned.

"Don't worry no one went near the ones at the back of the stand, everyone was far too full by that stage."

"Phew! Look thanks again for helping me out like that. I really appreciate it."

"I hope you don't mind, but the reason that I'm ringing you is because I'm looking to have a birthday cake made – but not just any birthday cake, it has to be a dinosaur cake."

"Sure. When is the party?"

"This Saturday."

"This Saturday?"

"Right."

It was short notice but in fairness Sam got me out of a tricky spot the day before so I wanted to help him. "And what age is the child?"

"Cian is seven."

"And do you want any writing on it – 'Happy birthday Cian' or something?"

"Yeah, perfect."

"Great. Okay and where do you want me to drop it off?"

"The address is 99 Bull Island View, Clontarf."

I grabbed a pen and quickly scribbled it down. "Is one

o'clock okay?"

"Perfect, see you then."

There was no point going back to bed - I knew I wouldn't sleep. I put my dressing gown on and opened up my laptop to start researching ideas for dinosaur cakes. So much for having a lie-in.

***

The following Saturday, Dad picked up the dinosaur and me. I really needed to get some wheels – it was getting ridiculous having to get everybody else to transport me and my cakes everywhere. I knew Dad didn't mind, but what if he or Frankie weren't able to do it some day? Dad put the address into his sat-nav, and we headed for Clontarf.

I was delighted with the way the cake had turned out. I had moulded the chocolate biscuit cake vertically and covered it in icing to make a grey 3-D Tyrannosaurus Rex standing on its back legs, with its front legs raised and white teeth bared. He looked pretty fearsome – I just hoped Sam's son wouldn't be scared of it. I had shaped a 7 to look like it was carved out of rock, and stood it on the cake-board, which I had covered with red icing. Then I had written "Happy Birthday Cian" diagonally across the board in front of Rex. I was too afraid to put it in the boot or on the back seat of the car in case it would slide, so I put the board on my knee and had Rexy eyeballing me the whole way to Clontarf.

Eventually Dad pulled up on the kerb outside the house. 99 Bull Island View was a handsome red-brick two-storey house right on the seafront. He climbed out and went around to help Rexy and I out of the car. I walked up to the house and balanced the cake with one arm, while I rang the bell with the other. The door was pulled back by a woman dressed in a flowy white kaftan. She wore a pair of skinny denims cut off at the ankles on her endless legs and had a pair of flat Roman sandals. I noticed she had nice feet - her toes were all the right length, not like my deformed feet where my second toe was bigger than my big toe. She had her toenails painted with red nail varnish and not a chip in sight. Her blonde hair was tied up loosely on her head, and she had a pair of sunglasses perched on top. Even though she was casually dressed, she was still very glamorous. Her and Sam made a good looking couple.

"Hi – you must be Sam's wife? I'm Lily from *Baked with Love*. Here is the cake for your son."

The woman smiled kindly at me. "Wow, Lily it looks great – Cian will be thrilled – he is *obsessed* with dinosaurs. Do you want to come in? Sam is in the kitchen."

"Oh no it's fine, my Dad is waiting for me in the car." I felt like a teenager, I really was going to have to learn how to drive.

"Here put that down on the table. Your arms must be hanging off you!"

I placed Rexy onto the hall table, and just then Sam came into the hall with a child hanging over his back as he held him by the ankles.

"Lily, wow!" He stopped to look at the cake. "How long did

231

that take you? It looks amazing doesn't it, Cian?"

"Let me down, let me down. I can't see it," the boy cried. He couldn't see it from where he was hanging down Sam's back.

"No way – I told you if you scored that goal I would get you," Sam laughed.

"Put him down for God's-sake will you!" The woman said good-humouredly.

Sam put Cian down on the floor, and I saw he was a gorgeous boy with huge brown eyes like his Dad. "Wow the cake is so cool!" Cian said.

"Lily – this is, Marita, Marita – Lily"

"Nice to meet you, Lily," Marita held out a slender hand to shake mine.

"Will you stay for a while and try some of your creation?" Sam asked me.

"I'd better not – my Dad is waiting in the car for me." Sam looked over my shoulder towards Dad. Dad waved from the car, and Sam and Marita waved back at him. I cringed.

"Right so – look I'd better go. Enjoy the day. Oh and happy birthday, Cian."

"Well thanks, Lily, I really appreciate it."

We said goodbye and I walked back down the driveway and hopped back into the car, not missing Rexy's weight on my lap.

"Dad?" I asked as he pulled out into the traffic.

"Yes, Lily?"

"Will you teach me how to drive?"

Chapter 24

The next day my phone rang. I recognised it as Sam's number.

"Hi, Sam, how did the party go?"

"Lily, I'm so sorry! I completely forgot to pay you – I'm so embarrassed. You were gone off in the car when I thought of it."

"Don't be silly, I didn't want any money – after everything you helped me with that day, I'm just glad I could return the favour."

"No way – all I did was pick up a few buns from the floor. I insist – if you don't tell me where I can send it – I'll turn up at your bakery."

"I don't actually have a bakery," I mumbled. "I work from my own kitchen."

"Right then, I see . . . well, I'd better not turn up at your house. That might get awkward . . ." He started laughing. "How about you meet me for a drink instead?"

"Honestly, Sam - it's fine."

"Please, Lily?"

"I . . . ehm -"

"How about Young's? Would Friday at seven be okay with you?" He was insistent.

"Right, I'll see you then I guess."

I hung up the phone and felt strange. Maybe I was reading too much into it but it didn't really feel right – he was married with a child. I know I was technically just meeting him to get paid, but why did we need to go for a drink too? Marita had seemed like a nice woman, and after everything that happened with Marc, there was no way I would ever do that to another woman. No way.

***

With trepidation, on Friday evening, I got ready to meet Sam in Young's bar. I had decided that I would be polite and stay for one drink, but then I was going home. I made my way down the back of the darkened pub and I spotted him sitting alone at a table. He was dressed in a shirt and jeans, and his hair was styled up in an "I've-just-woken-up-but-really-it-took-me-an-hour-to-get-it-this-way" look. He stood up straight away when I reached the table, leaned over and gave me a kiss on the cheek like we were old friends. I could tell immediately from his body language that his intentions weren't innocent. This was all wrong and I felt really uncomfortable being there. I felt awful for Marita. We ordered a pint of Heineken for Sam and a white wine for me, which I intended to drink very fast.

"So how was the party?" I asked making polite conversation.

"Great – we had so much fun, but my God that cake was amazing. We had only got down as far as his teeth by the end of the party – we still have his whole body to go."

234

"Yeah – I probably got a bit carried away alright."

"Marita said we could freeze the rest of it and bring it out for all of Cian's birthdays until he's twenty-one and we still wouldn't get through it," he laughed.

"Did Cian like his presents?" I took another gulp of wine to drink it quickly.

"Well I got him a Lego Ninjago set – his Mam got him a bike so he did well."

"Lucky boy getting presents from both parents! Your wife seems lovely." I felt I ought to mention Marita – just so he knew the boundaries.

"My wife?" Sam looked at me quizzically.

"Yes – your wife, Marita?"

"She's not my wife."

"Sorry – I just presumed you were married. Partner is that the right word?"

"She's not my partner either," he laughed.

"Oh." I could feel myself going red. "Well if she's not your wife or partner what the hell is she?" I started to get flustered.

"My sister."

"Your sister?" I tried to piece it together. How on earth had I picked up that they were husband and wife?

"But Cian – he's your son, isn't he?"

"Wrong again, I'm afraid. He's my nephew."

"But he looks just like you!" I protested.

"Yeah – everyone always says that," Sam said shrugging his

shoulders.

It was slowly starting to click into place for me. "So Marita is Cian's Mum then?"

"Correct and right, Lily." He was laughing heartedly by this stage. "I can't believe you thought Marita was my wife – wait 'til I tell her!"

I started to laugh then too. I began to relax – he wasn't married, we weren't doing anything wrong by having a drink together. I sat back into the chair and took a slow sip of wine. When that glass was finished Sam signalled the barman to order another round.

We spent the rest of the evening chatting away. There were no awkward silences and we actually had a lot in common. Sam was very quick witted, and had me in stitches. By the end of the night my jaw was aching from laughter. The time went so fast, and I ended up staying longer than I had planned, so long that I ended up missing the last bus back to Ballyrobin. I rang Frankie and asked her to put me up again. Sam walked me to her apartment block, he actually only lived across the Liffey from her. We strolled along by the inky river, still talking away ninety to the dozen. When we arrived at Frankie's building, he waited until I was safely inside before heading on to his own place.

Frankie was still up when I went in. She made tea and toast and we sat facing each other cross-legged on the sofa. I told her the whole story about how I had met Sam for a drink and how I had thought he was married.

"Do you like him?" she asked.

"Not like that – no way, I'm not even looking at men at the moment. But it was a lovely evening and I really enjoyed myself. It's been aaaages since I laughed like that. It felt good."

"Well it's good to see you getting yourself out there again."

"No, Frankie I'm definitely not 'out there' again - maybe when I'm seventy I might consider it. What about you – when are we going to see some action from you? There's been no one since Anton."

"Lily, I like being on my own – you know that. I grew up in a house with six brothers and sisters, fighting over everything from food to toys and who got the first of the bathwater – if you were near the end, the water was all scummy and cold. This is the first time in my life that I have my own space – I spent nineteen years sharing a bedroom and I don't want to have to do it again anytime soon. Anyway I'm not sure if the whole getting married and having a baby thing is really my bag."

I knew she wasn't just saying that like some people do when really they're lonely and wish they weren't single – Frankie genuinely valued her independence and was quite happy on her own. Sometimes I wished I had her confidence – I was scared of being on my own. I had been going out with Marc since I was seventeen, and I didn't know anything else.

***

The next day when I was on the bus home my phone beeped. It was a message from Sam:

237

"Hope you got home okay? I really enjoyed last night, maybe we could do it again soon?"

I don't know why but as I read the message, my heart started to race and my head began to spin. I started to feel like there wasn't enough air on the bus for me. Although I had enjoyed his company immensely, it was too much. I wasn't ready for anything else. I pressed the delete button without replying and put my phone back in my bag.

Chapter 25

That same evening I had just arrived home when my phone rang.

"Lily, it's me –"

"What's wrong, Clara?" She sounded completely panicked. "What's happened?"

"It's Tom –"

"Is he okay?"

"No – he's not, Lily. He's not okay at all."

"Oh God what's happened?" A shiver ran down my spine.

"Please come over Lily, *please*," she sounded desperate.

"I'll be there as quick as I can, Clara."

I threw on my coat and ran to the bus stop. When I got there I tried looking at the timetable to see when the next bus was due, but some dickwad had scraped that piece off, so I had no idea how long I would be waiting. I decided to get a taxi, so I ran back down Ballyrobin Main Street to the dingy cab office.

"26 Shrewsbury Avenue," I panted as soon as I got in the door.

"Fifteen minutes, okay?"

"Have you anything sooner?"

"'Fraid not – all the drivers are out on calls at the moment, love."

"Okay." I took a seat on the wooden bench running around the wall. "How much will it be by the way?"

She looked up towards a piece of paper she had sellotaped to the wall beside her. Then she thought a bit, added a few more numbers to it, and because it was Ballsbridge multiplied it by seven and hey presto came up with the grand total of eighty-five euro. I nearly died – I didn't have that kind of money to be wasting on taxis.

"It is in *Dublin* love," she added. The way she said "Dublin" made it sound like I wanted to go to bloody Australia. I didn't have any choice this was an emergency, but because the stupid backwater town that I lived in still didn't have a proper public transport system, I had no choice but to swallow hard and pay it. I could be waiting for hours on a bus on a Saturday.

I sat down onto the hard bench listening to the radio bleeping over and back. Finally a driver came back to the base. When the controller gave him the address he looked me up and down and said, "Well *excuse* me, Miss Swanky Boots!"

I wanted to throttle him. As I got into his car my bare legs squeaked along the plastic covering on his seats.

"Pardon you!" he said and laughed hysterically at his own joke. "Paaaaarp!"

I glared at him. I had at least another hour left in the company of Mr Unfunny.

I rang Clara to tell her that I was on my way, that I was just getting into a taxi. "Thank God, Lily – just hurry," she had said, still in a terrible state.

When we finally reached Shrewsbury Avenue, I pointed out Clara's house to him. He pulled up in front of the electric gates. I hopped out to press the intercom and they immediately parted. I jumped back in and we continued up the driveway.

As we pulled up outside the house he let out a low whistle. "Nice gaff!"

"It's not mine – it's my sister's."

I paid him the eighty-five euro and he stared at me waiting for a tip.

"Here!" I said reluctantly pulling a tenner from my wallet.

"Ah thanks, love, sure that's small change to you!"

I shut the door before I said something I would regret and walked up towards the house.

Clara looked distraught when she answered the door. She was wearing a long dressing robe. Clara never lounged around in her dressing gown, *never*.

"What's happened?" I asked.

"Tom has left me."

"What?" I stuttered.

"He went to Gordon Jones' stag in Galway earlier and he won't come home."

"What do you mean, 'he won't come home'?"

"Well, he was meant to go for just a few hours – I never let him stay overnight at these things, they're far too raucous – but when five o'clock came and there was still no sign of him, I

241

phoned him to see if he was on his way and that's what he said. He said he wasn't coming home!"

"C'mon Clara – he's a grown man! He can't just not come home. I'm sure he'll be home in the morning."

"He was inebriated, Lily." She started to sob. "What kind of example is that for the boys? He has responsibilities! You have to go and get him, Lily," she pleaded.

"You want me to go all the way to Galway and drag your husband home?" I asked in disbelief. *Was she mental?*

"You have to, Lily – I can't go. I can't abandon the boys; it's bad enough that one of their parents has deserted them, without me leaving them as well. And Tatiana is off with Julio or whatever his name is!"

I put my head in my hands, why did she have to make everything so dramatic?

"Well I'm not going to Galway to drag your husband out of a pub in front of all his friends."

"But what if he meets some brazen hussy down there and never comes home? What then? The poor boys will come from a broken home that's what!"

"I'm not going, Clara. No way. Look he'll be home in a few hours' time – by the time I would get there, search him out in the pubs and then get him home, he'd already be back to you."

"You have to go, Lily."

"But how am I meant to get there?"

"On the bus of course."

"I'm am not getting on a bus to Galway to try and track down your husband, Clara, come on!"

"Please, Lily"

She looked up at me with tears in her eyes.

"Clara, it's ludicrous!"

"Maybe you're right," she sniffed as she dabbed at the corners of her eyes with a tissue. "It's just it is completely out of character - I'm worried about him."

I felt bad then, I had never seen her this upset in my whole entire life. She was normally so together, so composed. Her eyes were red from crying so much.

"Right, I'll go," I sighed.

"Oh thank you, Lily. Thank you!"

***

It was almost eight o'clock as I made my way down the aisle and sat into a seat. The bus was quiet. There were only a handful of people – a woman engrossed in a Maeve Binchy novel, a student with earphones in, and a man who was playing with his phone. I leaned my head against the window glass – I hadn't even thought to bring a book. The only plus about travelling at that time of night was that the roads were empty. I wasn't sure what I was going to do when I arrived in Galway or where I would even start looking for him. Clara had told me that they were staying in the G-Hotel but they wouldn't be there now – they would be out on the razz somewhere.

I had been to Galway once before – Marc had been working

on a film in Connemara and I had travelled down to the city at the weekend to meet him. The only places in Galway that I knew were Eyre Square and Shop Street, the pedestrianised street where all the restaurants and bars were – I supposed that was probably the best place of any to start my search.

The motorway lights lit the bus up in a soft orange glow as we drove along, and when I finally got off three hours later, I was tired. It was after eleven o'clock. I should have been going to bed, but instead I was only starting off on my mission of trudging through pubs and clubs trying to find my stray brother in law.

I searched pub after pub, but there was no sign of him. They were all wedged with people on a Saturday night. I squeezed past bodies as I searched out Tom's face in the dim lighting. I had rung Clara to tell her I had arrived, and she was ringing me every five minutes since to see if there was any sign of him. I could hear her pacing on her wooden floors every time. The longer time went on, the faster her paces became. Every pub seemed to be full of hen and stag parties, except for the one I was looking for. Everyone else was hammered, it felt odd being so sober in a pub that time on a Saturday night. And even if I got the pub right, how did I know Tom wasn't going to be gone to the toilet or something at the exact time I was searching for him? It was like looking for a needle in a haystack.

It was nearly two a.m. by the time I made up my mind to ring Clara and tell her it was useless, and that I was going to check into a hotel and would get a bus home again in the morning. I knew she would go ballistic, but what else could I do? I walked back up Shop Street heading towards Eyre Square, because I had seen a few hotels there when I had got off the bus.

I cut through Eyre Square, and just then I saw him. A lonely figure sitting on a bench eating chips from a Supermacs bag, smiling away to himself.

"Tom!" I said running over to him.

"Lily? What are you doing here?" There was a blob of mayonnaise at the side of his mouth and beer stains ran down the front of his white shirt. His tie hung loosely around his neck – he looked more like a bold schoolboy than one of Ireland's top barristers.

"Clara sent me down to find you – she's worried sick!"

He looked sheepish. "She's going to kill me, isn't she?"

"Uh-huh."

"I didn't mean to run off, I just wanted to cut-loose for a while. On the rare occasions where I do anything with the lads, I'm always the one having to leave early and go home to Clara – I get a lot of stick about it and well, this time I just wanted to have a bit of fun for once."

"Look I understand what you're saying but you know what Clara is like."

"I wasn't getting up to anything – we had a few pints and I'm on my way back to the hotel room, but I really enjoyed myself – all I want is to get away from things every once in a while. It doesn't mean I love Clara and the boys any less."

"I know."

"I can't believe she sent you all the way to Galway to find me!"

We both started laughing then.

"What the hell are we going to do now?" I asked.

"I think I'd better go home and face the music."

"How on earth will we get home at this time of night?"

"We'll get a taxi."

"But that will cost hundreds!"

"I know."

I should have known money would never be an obstacle – I don't know why I didn't make Clara pay for a taxi down for me, I had never even thought of it. Tom flagged a taxi for us and we climbed in, both glad to be able to sit down. Clara phoned me again but I didn't answer – I knew she would go off on one if she knew that Tom was beside me, and I figured it was best to let them sort it out face to face.

I woke up a few hours later with my head resting on Tom's shoulder. There was a damp patch where I had been drooling, and the side of my cheek was wet. I sat up, looked around and saw we were just pulling up outside their house. Tom paid the driver and we got out of the car. He let us in the front door and as soon as we stepped inside the entrance hall, Clara came out from the living room.

"Tom!" she cried.

"I'm sorry, Clara –"

246

"Where were you, Tom – I've been worried sick all evening." She started to cry then.

"Ah, Clara, don't cry, love." He walked over and put an arm around her shoulder.

I stood quietly in the corner.

"What were you thinking, Tom?"

"I just wanted a bit of freedom – I didn't mean to hurt you. I was there sober watching everyone else getting drunk and having fun, and for once I didn't want to leave early. I didn't want to have to go home – I wanted to join them so I did."

"But you hate those kinds of parties, Tom."

"Do I?"

"You do, Tom," she insisted.

"No *you* do, Clara – I really enjoyed myself actually."

"And look at the state you are in – look at your tie, and are those beer stains?" She admonished him like a bold schoolboy. I knew she disapproved of Tom drinking anything except wine.

"Look sorry to butt in," I said eventually. "But maybe you need to cut him loose a bit, Clara – he's a great husband and father and he's entitled to a bit of time-out with his friends." I was standing underneath the chandelier in the hall the whole time and every time Clara cried you could hear the crystal resonate.

"Oh and like you of all people, Lily should be offering me marriage advice!" she sneered.

I could feel the tension winding its way around my shoulder blades but I wasn't going to rise to it.

After Clara had finally managed to calm down and I was sure Tom wasn't going to be found buried alive in the orchard, I decided to go home to Ballyrobin. Besides my snooze in the taxi, I had been up all night and I was exhausted.

"Can you call me a cab please, Clara?"

"A taxi – at this time of night? But that will cost a fortune. No you can stay over here and I will drive you home myself after breakfast."

I groaned. All I wanted was to get away from Clara and Tom and to go home to my own bed. It amazed me how Clara could be so tight in some respects when she had money flowing out of her ears.

***

Any hopes of a lie-in the next morning were literally put to bed when Jacob and Joshua came in jumping on the bed at half six. I had only been in bed for an hour. I don't know how people who have children do those early starts. I decided to get up. I met Clara and Tom on the landing coming out of the bedroom together hand in hand.

"Morning," I grunted.

"Yes, good morning, Lily." She dropped Tom's hand instantly as if she had been caught in the midst of some lewd act.

I sat down at the breakfast table between Jacob and Joshua and ate the homemade sugar-free muesli that tasted like cardboard, sprinkled with Goji berries, which Clara insisted I eat. Clara asked the boys which placemat they wanted from their range of educational ones. Jacob chose one with musical notes on it - Joshua chose an alphabet one.

"Ni-ni have zoo one," Joshua said to Clara. She passed me a vinyl mat covered with zoo animals and their corresponding names. I felt like the third child.

Clara and Tom were like love's young dream, and I nearly vomited when I saw him playfully tip Clara on the bum while she juiced some oranges, when he thought I wasn't looking. They had obviously done a lot more than just kissing and making up last night.

Just then my phone rang and I saw it was Sam. My face went red as if Clara knew who it was. I didn't want to answer it.

"Auntie Ni-ni, your phone is ringing," the boys chorused.

I continued to let it ring, ignoring them.

"Well aren't you going to get that, Lily?" Clara said eventually.

I stepped out into Clara's hallway to take it so that she wouldn't be able to listen in on the conversation.

"Hi there, how are you?"

"I'm at a loose end later and I was just ringing to find out if you were doing any karaoke performances tonight?" Sam asked.

I found myself softening towards him. He was a nice guy, it's just the timing was all wrong, but that wasn't his fault.

"Nope," I laughed. "Right now I'm trying to emulate Harry Houdini and escape my demon sister."

"She can't be that bad?"

"Oh believe me she is."

"Do you want me to come and rescue you?"

"You're okay, don't worry. She'll drop me home soon. "

"I don't mind honestly."

"Are you sure?" I said hesitantly. After all who knew how long I'd have to wait for Clara to find the time in her busy day to drive me back to Ballyrobin.

"Where does she live?"

"Twenty-six Shrewsbury Avenue."

"I'll be there in twenty minutes." He had hung up before I had the chance to change my mind.

I went back into the kitchen and told Clara that there was a bus due soon. She seemed quite happy to let me make my own way home, and after I had said goodbye to her, Tom and the boys, I walked out into the cool morning air. I breathed in deeply as I walked down Clara's gravelled driveway towards the road. I wanted to meet Sam at the gate because I knew if Clara saw a member of the opposite sex picking me up, she'd have a field day.

Soon after a blue Audi sports car pulled up beside me.

"Get in, Rapunzel."

I sat on the soft leather seat, and this time there wasn't a squeak to be heard. I let out a long sigh as he drove me back to Ballyrobin.

"I can't believe you live all the way out here," he said as we passed field after field of countryside.

"Why does everyone always say that?"

"Maybe because it's miles away?"

When we reached my estate I invited him in. We went into the house, and I had a bit of panic when I realised that all the photos in my living room were of me with superimposed celebrities over Marc's face – he would think I was a complete loon if he saw them. I grabbed the one of Ryan Reynolds and I off the coffee table and moved it up to a high shelf. Thankfully he needed to use the bathroom, so I was able to whizz around the place hiding the rest of them.

When he came back out we sat on the kitchen chairs drinking the pot of tea that I made for us both. I had some of my orange cake in the fridge, and I cut us both a slice. As I spilled out what had happened with Clara earlier on, Sam listened in horrified amazement. "Poor Tom," he had said finally.

"I know – If I was him, I think I'd run away rather than face the wrath of Clara when she had been disobeyed."

"I just can't believe a person like that actually exists though."

"Ah I suppose she's not the worst."

He shot me a look. "Well you're not selling her to me anyway."

"This cake is divine, Lily - it's just perfect."

"I need a name for it actually."

"Well what about *Lily's Heavenly Orange Cake*?"

I smiled. "I like it."

We chatted loads more, just like we had the last time. We still hadn't run out of things to say to each other. He told me about his job in First Ireland Bank, I told him how I'd been fired from Rapid Response and then set up *Baked with Love*. He mentioned he had gone out with a girl for four years but they broke up six months ago because the spark was gone. It was all very amicable – they had turned into friends rather than lovers, and in the end they had both decided to call it a day. I still didn't mention Marc. We stayed there for two hours, talking about everything.

When it was time to go I walked out to the door with him.

"I really like you, Lily," he said suddenly and then leant over to kiss me. I felt the brush of his dark stubble against my cheek, and for a minute I seemed to forget where I was, who I was with. Then it hit me what I was doing. I pulled back straight away. "I'm sorry, Sam – I can't –" I whispered.

He looked stunned. "Right . . . look sorry, Lily . . . I obviously got it wrong, sorry. No hard feelings, yeah?" His large brown eyes were crestfallen and I knew he was wondering how he had misjudged it so badly. I felt terrible, absolutely awful. I didn't want to hurt him and I hoped he didn't think I had led him on. The thing was we got on so well – I really enjoyed his company and I loved being around him, but I just wasn't ready to move on again. It was too soon. I watched him take the steps down to the car park two at a time before going back inside and closing the door.

***

The next day the doorbell rang and when I opened it there was a delivery guy standing there with twenty-four long stemmed red roses. I assumed they were for my neighbours, and was about to point him in the right direction when he asked if I was Lily McDermott. They were for me.

I read the card, which simply said:

"I can wait . . . Sam xx"

Dumbfounded I took the flowers from him and went back inside. I felt awful. My heart somersaulted, and I felt sick with guilt every time I thought about it. You see the thing was I really liked him, I enjoyed his company, he was fun to be around and he made me feel good about myself. He laughed at my jokes and he was always paying me compliments, just little things like saying how my dress was lovely or my hairstyle suited me, but it had been so long since anyone had done that and I wasn't used to the attention. I couldn't let myself go back there again. I couldn't open myself up to anyone so soon after Marc. It had only been five months, for God's sake.

I was actually blown away as I read and re-read the card. It was one of the nicest things anyone had ever done for me – he clearly sensed that I had got cold feet, and to go out on a limb like that made me like him even more. However I didn't want to like him. The last thing I needed was to have my heart broken by two men in a row. Every time I thought about him I felt jittery inside. It was too soon though – Marc and I had only been separated for a few months. I didn't want to lead him on any more, but I had to acknowledge the flowers, so I dialled his number.

"Thank you for the flowers – you really shouldn't have," I said when he picked up.

"I hope everything is okay?" he asked nervously.

I smiled. "I don't deserve them."

"Well, to me, you do. How are you feeling?"

"Like shit."

"Do you want me to come over – I can bring a DVD? We can just chill - no pressure –" he added quickly.

"I'm sorry, Sam but I don't think that's a good idea." Even though I would have loved nothing more than to see him, I needed to nip things in the bud right then, because I knew what would happen if I let it grow into something more. It would just be another disaster in a long line of Lily McDermott type disasters. Sam was a nice guy, he was one of the good ones, but I didn't need anymore stress in my life.

"Okay no worries, Lily."

The disappointment in his voice was unmistakable. I longed to be able to tell him that I was sorry, and to come over and we could spend the whole night laughing and talking, but instead I found myself saying goodbye and hanging up the phone. I was doing the right thing I told myself - it was going to be head over heart for once in my life.

Chapter 26

In the days that followed, I felt miserable. For every cake I made, I ate one. I didn't know why I was feeling so glum, but it wasn't a nice feeling. I went out for cocktails with Frankie, because cocktails always made me feel better, but even they didn't work. I couldn't sleep at night; I spent all night lying awake and thinking of Sam's bright smile. I was afraid to let myself like him, because I knew as soon as I did, then it would all go wrong. The funny thing was that I seldom thought much of Marc anymore except when it came to our mortgage, and the fact that soon I was going to have to face up to my problems.

Mrs G had rung me a couple of times. She was dumbfounded by the behaviour of her own son. She had learnt of Nadia's pregnancy from another magazine, and she was devastated. It broke my heart seeing him mistreating the woman who had brought him into the world so badly. She had been almost like a mother to me at times. I felt awful for her because I knew she had given Marc everything a mother possibly could, but he still didn't care about her feelings. If I ever had a son, I would hope that he'd treat me with a bit more respect than the way Marc treated his Mum at times.

Dad, although unaware of Sam, knew I was going through a

low patch, and he brought me out for lunch to cheer me up. We went to my favourite restaurant from when I was a little girl, Carlito's. I ordered their Hawaiian pizza and the chef, Carlito, put the pineapple into a smiley face for me like he had been doing since I was a toddler. I forced a smile for his sake. I took a bite of pizza, but I wasn't in form for it and I pushed the plate away. I stirred the ice in my coke with my straw.

"What's wrong with you, Lily?" Dad asked. "I'm worried about you."

"I think I like someone else," I blurted.

"I see," Dad said taken aback. "Who is he?"

"Do you remember Sam, the guy in Clontarf where we dropped off the dinosaur cake?"

"But he's married, Lily!" Dad was horrified.

"No – that's what I thought too, but that woman is actually his sister."

"Oh I see. Well that's alright then."

"He's wonderful, Dad. He makes me feel so good about myself. But it's too soon!"

He shrugged his shoulders.

"Do you think people are like Tupperware Dad?"

"How do you mean?"

"Well there is a lid for everyone –"

"A lid for everyone?" He looked bewildered.

"Like everyone has a perfect fit out there? I've always thought there is one person out there for everyone, but maybe

256

not?"

"Oh I see what you mean – well yeah, I like to think so but sure I'm an 'oul romantic. You know your mother was the only woman I ever loved and I haven't even so much as looked at another one since."

"I know, Dad."

"We were so good together your mother and I. She was my best friend too." He had a sadness in his eyes. "She was a real lady, it took me months to work up the courage just to ask her out, y'know."

"I miss her too. Every day. Especially at times like this - I'd love to be able to ask her what I should do."

"And she'd say just the right thing too – far better than me."

I smiled at him.

"You're more and more like her every day. I bet she's smiling down on you right now."

"I hope so, Dad."

"Oh she is – I'm sure of it."

I took a sip of my drink and put it down again. "I'm so scared to let myself like anyone else again."

"Look, Lily – you have to take a risk with love. You have to open your heart to let someone in, or else how will they get in?"

"But what if I get hurt again?"

"Look why don't you give him a chance – take it slow."

"But what will people say – I'm not even six months separated!"

"Who gives a toss what they say – let them talk, what does it matter? I think it's about time you gave yourself permission to be happy again, Lily."

Chapter 27

When I went home that evening I flopped down on the sofa and exhaled heavily. I thought about what Dad had said to me about giving myself permission to be happy. I was scared about moving on and exposing my whole self to somebody new. But was Dad right? Was it time to take a chance and open my heart to Sam? I had been hurt so badly before, and the worst part of it all was the devastating shock – the blow that I had not seen coming, the trust that Marc had stolen from me. I didn't think I could ever feel secure in another relationship – Marc had robbed that from me. I looked up at the photo of Mam smiling down at me from the bookshelves. I wondered what she would say to me if she were here today. That's one of the things I missed about not having a mother to talk to. Dad was great but I envied people who could go to their mothers for advice, or just to have them lend a listening ear.

Then I thought of Sam with his honest and open face where I couldn't imagine any secrets or lies hiding, but I had been fooled before and as the saying goes "once bitten, twice shy." The sensible part of me said that, in the interests of self-preservation, I should never let another man into my heart, but God I longed to just do it, jump right in and have Sam take me in his strong arms.

I wanted to feel the firmness of his lips against mine, the brush of his stubble against my cheek.

I knew I was completely crazy rushing into a new relationship so soon after my marriage ended, but I couldn't stop myself, and with shaking hands I picked up the phone and dialled Sam's number. My heart was racing and I thought about hanging up again.

"Lily?" He sounded surprised to hear from me. "How are you?"

Just hearing his voice made me feel calmer. There was something about Sam that told me, it would be okay – he wasn't like Marc.

I took a deep breath. "You know when you said you'd wait for me?"

"Yeah?"

"Well I think I'm ready now," I practically whispered.

"Really?" I could almost hear the smile in his voice. I imagined the broad grin that was spreading across his face.

"Uh-huh," I said laughing.

"You won't regret this I promise!" he said excitedly. I was so glad to hear that after my rejection of him, he still hadn't given up on me.

***

The following morning my doorbell rang and when I answered it, Sam was standing there.

"I thought you might like this," he said smiling at me as he handed me a chocolate cake in the shape of a heart. The top of it was covered with halved strawberries held in place with a thick chocolate ganache.

"You're always baking for everyone else so I thought it might be nice for someone to bake for you for a change." He handed the cake to me and I was lost for words.

"Thank you," I said, genuinely touched. "Come in."

He followed me inside and we sat down on the sofa.

"Did you make it yourself?" I asked amazed.

"I sure did – I don't know how you do it, Lily. It took me ages to get it right."

"Well it looks great, hang on until I grab a knife and we can try some."

I went into the kitchen, grabbing the photo of Bressie and me off the hall console table and stuffing it into the drawer underneath as I passed.

I brought back two plates, forks and a knife and cut us both a slice.

"Well – be honest," he said as I chewed a forkful.

"It tastes good."

"Really?" He looked chuffed with himself.

"Uh-huh," I nodded. "Things always taste better when someone makes them for you."

He grinned. "Now when you're finished that I'm bringing you to the beach."

"The beach?"

"Yep – Lily, it's a beautiful day out there and I'm not taking no for an answer."

I started to laugh. "I haven't been to the beach in years!"

"I don't believe it!" He was horrified. "Well then we're definitely going, no ifs, ands or buts."

I quickly put on my converse trainers and threw a cardigan into my bag in case it got cold later. I didn't have time to bother with my hair or make-up.

Even though it was late September, it was a bright, sunny day and I had to put on my sunglasses to avoid the glare through the car windscreen as Sam drove us towards the coast. When we finally pulled up on the strand road, it was hard to get a parking spot. The road was busy with families unloading their cars, keen to enjoy one of the last warm days of the year before winter came around the corner.

"You've thought of everything," I said as I watched him take out a picnic basket and a rug from the boot of his car.

As we strolled along the wooden boardwalk leading down to the strand, I wasn't sure where we slotted in among all the families and couples. We weren't exactly together; we hadn't even kissed yet but you couldn't really say we were just friends either.

We found an empty patch on the honeycomb coloured sand, Sam spread out the blanket and we sat down onto it. He handed me a roll with ham and cheese and it tasted great in the fresh sea air.

We sat there enjoying the sound of waves crashing and breaking on the shore in front of us, while children ran across the beach, zigzagging around people. After a while Sam suggested we go for a walk. I followed him as we climbed up through a path in the dunes. We climbed higher still until Sam came to a stop at the top, he reached down for my hand and pulled me up to stand beside him. I looked down at the beach that was now far below us.

The view was magnificent. The land dipped and peaked for miles around covered with a hair of grassy reeds. Wispy white clouds were pulled delicately across the peacock-blue sky. A passenger ferry cut a silvery wave through the water below us looking like a toy boat from up there.

"It's amazing up here," I said eventually.

"On a clear day you can see all the way to Wales," Sam said proudly.

"Do you come here often?" Then I realised it sounded like a cheesy pick up line, and we both started to laugh.

"Well this was the beach that Marita and myself always came to as children. I have great memories from this place, if I ever need to get away from it all, I find a walk here usually sorts me out."

I couldn't imagine the usually so cheery Sam ever having a bad day, he seemed to be permanently in a good mood.

After the beach, we had worked up an appetite. We managed to find a cosy pub in the harbour and we slotted into a little snug down the back. We ordered a feast of Dublin bay prawns, which the waitress told us were landed only yards away. Sam's arm was draped around my shoulder and it felt good. Beyond the window, dusk was starting to fall over the pretty white fishing boats and yachts that were docked in the harbour. A tea-light flickered on the table in front of us casting a warm glow around the panelled walls.

"So is this our first date?" I asked taking a sip from my wine.

"I suppose it is."

Sam dropped me home when we were finished, and as we sat in the car talking at the end of the night, I didn't want the day to end. I had had the most amazing time – it had been so long since I had had that much fun.

"I really, really enjoyed today," I said. "Thank you."

"You don't need to thank me, I'm glad you had fun."

"Sam?"

"Yeah?"

"Why are you so nice to me?"

"Because I like you, Lily. Isn't it obvious?"

"I wanted to say sorry."

"For what?"

"Well when you went to kiss me that time . . ."

He raised his hand to stop me. "You don't need to apologise."

"I want to explain, Sam. I love being with you, I have so

much fun in your company . . ."

"I sense a but coming –"

"But, I've been badly hurt before . . ."

He reached across the gearstick and placed his hand over mine giving it a squeeze.

"You know we can take it as slowly as you need – I'm not going anywhere and I'm not going to break your heart." Sam gave my hand a reassuring squeeze.

"How do you know you won't?" I asked.

"Because I'm a man of my word – look I don't know what happened before, and maybe someday you'll feel ready to tell me, but I promise you, Lily I won't do anything to hurt you. Just give us a chance, please. You won't regret it."

I knew this was the right time to be open and honest with Sam about Marc but it was like a stubborn tie had come over my tongue, I just couldn't bring myself to do it.

Whether it was his kind words or because I was caught up in the wonderful day we had just had, suddenly I didn't care about Marc, I didn't care that my head told me that it was too soon. The moment felt right. I felt myself drawn to him like some magnetic force that was pointless trying to resist. Before I knew what I was doing, I had leant forward across the gearstick and our lips met. They were soft and full and felt gentle against mine. He kissed me back with a longing and intensity that I couldn't remember ever having felt before. It felt good. Really good. I was expecting it to be weird but it wasn't at all, in fact it felt completely right.

My heart was racing; it had been years since I kissed anyone but Marc. And although the way Marc had behaved told me never to trust another man again, something told me that Sam was different.

"Goodnight, Sam," I whispered as I got out of the car.

"Goodnight, Lily," he said with a wide grin spreading across his face.

I walked across the car park and climbed the steps to my duplex. I put my key in the lock and let myself in, and as I shut the door behind me I jumped up and down and squealed.

Chapter 28

I was careful not to rush things with Sam – I was enjoying being with him so much that I didn't want to ruin what we had. At the weekends we would go for a walk along the beach and browse the farmers' market. He would always drop me home afterwards, but I would never invite him in. I was not ready to take the next step yet. I knew he was probably wondering when I would stay over in his or invite him to stay in mine, but if he was, he never let on. I still hadn't plucked up the courage to tell him about Marc. I had hidden all the photos of us that were in my home, and there was none of his stuff left after I got rid of it all. Sam had asked me casually about my exes, but I just blew him off. I didn't want to scare him away by offloading all my baggage onto him. I knew I would have to say something soon but how? I didn't want there to be any secrets between us – secrets brought trouble with them. I of all people knew that. I had met all of his friends, but he had only met Frankie – I wasn't ready yet to introduce him to other people, plus I was worried they would let it slip about Marc and I, and I wanted him to hear it from me first.

I could tell Frankie was impressed by Sam – not only was he a hottie, but he was a gentleman too, which made him even sexier. He was old fashioned in a black and white movie kind of way; he held open doors, and if we were out to dinner and I got up from the table, he stood up too. He always let me choose the movie when we went to the cinema. He was really close to his family, which I always think is a good sign. He was the polar opposite to Marc in lots of ways, which could only be a good thing. I was worried that people would think that I was moving on too quickly. I told Dad about him, and he was delighted for me and told me not to give a fiddler's what people thought once I was happy myself.

One day a few weeks later, we brought his nephew Cian and his younger sister Ava to Playfactory, a children's entertainment centre. With only a few days left before Christmas, Marita wanted to get some last minute shopping done so Sam had offered to mind the kids for a few hours and she had gladly accepted. He had suggested that I bring Jacob and Joshua too, but I told him there was no way I would be able to control them in a place like that, and he hadn't disagreed.

Sam was a natural with his nephew and niece, he had dived into the ball-pool with them, and when little Ava had been too scared to come down the slide, he had squeezed through pipes and climbed up the padded steps before bringing her down on his knee. I could never in a million years imagine Marc playing with children like that – in fact he had always seemed quite scared of them, like he was just waiting for them to be sick on his suede shoes.

Just as we were coming out of Playfactory, we were holding

Cian and Ava's hands between us when I spotted Clara, Tom and the boys coming along the path towards us. I tried turning to the right so she wouldn't see me, but my human chain was too long and Cian started asking where I going. It was too late, Clara had spotted me. Oh God, how was I going to explain this, I thought? I purposely hadn't told her about Sam because I was afraid of how she would react.

"Lily!" she exclaimed. "What on earth are you doing here and who owns those children." She pointed at Cian and Ava. Even though she had children herself, she looked upon other people's kids with disdain.

I took a deep breath and prayed that Clara wasn't going to make things difficult for me. "Clara – this is Sam, his nephew Cian and his niece Ava."

"Sam – this is my sister Clara, her husband Tom and you know the boys."

Tom looked quite sheepish; he was still mortified over his antics in Galway.

I didn't offer any explanation of who Sam was and I could see Clara getting irritated.

"Nice to meet you." Sam held out his hand to shake Clara's but she looked at him like he was diseased. Tom shook it then.

"How do you know, Sam?" she turned and asked the boys hoping they might provide a clue as to what was going on, but my little soldiers remained tight-lipped. I flashed them a smile.

"Look, we'd better go, Clara – Ava is exhausted," I said.

"But – but, Lily?"

"Yes?"

"Erm – I was just . . ." She paused, "look I'll give you a ring tonight."

I groaned.

"Right I'll talk to you later on."

"Well that was awkward," Sam said as soon as they had gone inside the door.

"It's just typical of Clara – she will ring me this evening and interrogate me, just you wait and see!"

"And that's the husband that didn't come home from the stag party?" Sam asked laughing. "She must have taken off his shackles for the day."

We dropped the kids home before heading back to Sam's apartment in Spencer Dock. He had a beautiful home; it was all high-end furnishings and minimalist sleek lines. All of the walls were painted white, which contrasted with the warmth of the polished oak floorboards. The living room had a red, L-shaped sofa scattered with huge multi-coloured cushions to brighten up the otherwise muted decor. There was a 40-inch flat-screen TV hanging from the wall, and colourful canvases hung randomly. His kitchen had white high gloss cupboards with soft close drawers beneath. I noticed that the worktops were empty, not littered with things like in my kitchen. The appliances were all Miele and finished in stainless steel. His bathroom had dimmed spa lighting and a standalone basin with a central tap and mocha coloured tiles. The bathtub stood in the centre of the floor and it looked like a heavenly place to unwind after a long day.

When you stepped outside through the floor to ceiling glass doors, he had a roof garden with views over three sides of the city. The views across the rooftops were amazing – you could see the Ringsend chimneystacks on one side and the Spire when you went around the other side. He had lots of large plant containers with tropical plants and bamboo along the other side to give some privacy.

The first time I had seen the place, I had been in complete awe. My mouth had hung open, but Sam modestly had said that he couldn't take any of the credit - his sister Marita had done it all for him. She was an interior designer. I decided that if I ever won the lotto, I would be hiring her.

We sat down onto the swinging chair on the balcony and I rested my head against his chest as we sipped our wine. Even though it was December, it was quite a mild evening, and we were able to sit out there with our coats on.

After eight my phone rang as expected. It was Clara. She was so predictable, I knew she would just have put the boys to bed and now was ringing me to find out what was going on. It had probably wrecked her head so much that it had ruined her day. I knew what the conversation was going to go like, plus I was comfy lying back in Sam's strong arms, so I didn't answer it.

"Aren't you going to answer that?" he asked.

"Nope – I couldn't face Clara now."

271

"But what's wrong with you having a boyfriend – you're thirty-two years of age for God's sake!"

I felt guilty again for not being completely honest with him, but the more we got to know one another, the harder it had become to tell him. I really liked him and now the longer my secret about Marc remained hidden, the more I was afraid that the truth would jeopardise everything.

Earlier that day I had decided that that was the night I would finally stay over in Sam's. I had thought it over a lot, and I couldn't hold out any longer – I wanted him. I was bloody nervous though – Marc was the only person I had ever slept with, and he was the only one that had seen my wobbly bits in all their glory. I was afraid that once Sam saw me naked, he would make an excuse not to see me again. I supposed I looked alright with my clothes on, but taking them off was a whole different kettle of fish. And where was I meant to get changed? Would he expect me to do some half-fangled striptease dance? I used to get changed in the bathroom when Marc was there, and then I would get into bed in my pyjamas and he would undress me under the covers so no one saw anything, but I didn't know what everyone else did in the bedroom nowadays? I felt so inexperienced. Luckily I had put on nice underwear that morning – well what I hoped Sam thought was nice – I didn't know what single girls were wearing these days – crotchless knickers might be the norm for all I knew! I had chosen a simple set in Marks and Spencer's the day before. I had gone for a navy plunge bra with a cerise pink trim and matching French knickers. I had spent so long agonising over what colour to buy that the security guard began to hover around me, but it was a hard decision to make. The colour was important - white was too boring, black too obvious and red was too raunchy. Then there was the worry of what to do with my lady garden. I knew Brazilians and even Vajazzles were all the rage these days or even completely shaven, but I had only got my regular bikini wax. I really wished I had asked Frankie – she would have told me what to do.

I was so nervous as Sam kissed me and we made our way to the bedroom because we both knew what was coming next. I tried to just relax and enjoy it, but my mind wouldn't switch off. I was going to have sex with another person that wasn't Marc. Then Sam began to undress me, and I was relieved that there were no striptease performances expected as we found our way down onto the bed. We had slow, tender sex and it felt bloody amazing. As he moved inside me, it felt right and I didn't feel nervous anymore. We both climaxed in a shuddering heap and as I lay there in the crook of his arm afterwards, I felt on top of the world. And the best bit was that Sam didn't tell me I was doing it wrong, or ask what in the name of God was that? He didn't jiggle my wobbly bits or grab the higher roll of flab on my tummy and pretend that it was talking to the bottom one like Marc used to do after we had sex, instead we lay there and he stroked my shoulder and told me how happy I made him.

Chapter 29

Sam dropped me home the next morning and we kissed passionately in the car park, neither of us wanting to say goodbye. It was amazing how close we had become in the space of a few months. Reluctantly I climbed out of his car and headed for my duplex. I was only in the door five minutes when my bell rang, and suddenly Clara was on my doorstep.

"Clara," I exclaimed. "What are you doing here?" I had managed to put Clara out of my head after her phone call the night before.

"We need to talk, Lily," she said walking past me and straight into the living room. "God I'd forgotten how small this apartment is."

"It's a duplex," I said through gritted teeth. "It has a doorbell."

"What's that got to do with anything?"

"Apartments have buzzers, I have a doorbell."

"Right, Lily – let's not be pedantic. If you want to call it a *'duplex'*, we'll call it a *'duplex'*." She was being patronising, and it sounded like she was talking to one of her children. "Why didn't you call me back last night?" she demanded.

"Sorry I forgot," I lied.

"Hmm. I was talking to Dad," she continued.

This sounded ominous. "And?"

"Well, he tells me that you've met someone else?"

I knew Dad wouldn't have said it unless Clara probed him for information, which I'm sure she did straight after she bumped into us yesterday.

"Yes, I have actually."

"Well don't you think it's a bit soon?" Her eyes flashed at me.

"I'll tell you what I think, Clara – I think it's none of your business. That is what I think!" I couldn't believe I had spoken to her like that – never, ever before had I done that. All the years of biting my tongue and internalising my rage, had in that instant come to a head and I just snapped.

"But you've only been separated for a few months!"

"It wasn't like I went out looking to meet someone new – in fact that was the last thing I wanted, but sometimes these things just find us."

"There you go again spouting your romantic 'fate and destiny, loves finds us' nonsense. When are you ever going to grow up and join the rest of us in the real world? When are you going to become a responsible adult?"

"I like to think I already am one actually."

"Lily, you're thirty-two years old, you're separated after a mere three months of marriage, you got fired from what has to be the world's easiest job, and then you decide to set up a bakery even though you have no formal qualifications. You can't drive, yet you live in an apartment in the middle of bally-go-backwards and expect everyone else to ferry you around the place. Well Mam would be very proud of you!" Her eyes flashed with anger.

"How dare you, Clara. How dare you say that about Mam." It felt like she had punched me. Her words stung me like they were physically piercing my skin. She had gone a step too far, even for me.

"You think you can just sail through life *sans* responsibilities. Well I think we're all growing a bit tired of the Daddy's little girl act at this stage, Lily."

"Clara, what are you talking about?"

"I know what you and Dad are like – the pair of you together whispering 'oh there goes Clara again' and laughing at me behind my back, do you think I can't see you?"

"But what has that got to do with me and Sam?"

"Because, Lily what I'm trying to say is that I'm sick of always looking out for you and trying to help you, steering you in the right direction and then you go off and do stupid things anyway."

"You don't look after me!"

"Lily, I have been looking after you since you were two years old."

"I think you'll find it was Dad who brought me up thanks."

"No he didn't," she sneered. "He was grieving. He was a mess, I was the one who held it all together." Her face had gone red and her nostrils flared slightly.

277

"But you were only five!"

"Exactly, Lily!" She lowered her voice and I could see tears in her eyes. "I was only five years old." And with that she walked back out the door, leaving me stunned and wondering what had just happened in my own home.

Clara and I had always had a tumultuous relationship, but we had never had a fight like that. I had never seen Clara in tears before. I just couldn't understand her problem – okay so I knew she was fed up of me not getting my life together, hell *I* was even fed up of me not getting myself together too, but it was my life and it was none of her business. I thought about ringing Dad, but I knew he would get upset if he thought his two daughters were fighting, plus he'd feel awful for letting the cat out of the bag about Sam. I wondered if what she said about Mam were true – would she be disappointed in me? Would she be disappointed with how I had turned out? That upset me more than anything, the thoughts of Mam looking down on me in despair from wherever she was. I went over and picked up the photograph from the bookshelves and traced my finger along the outline of her face. What would she have thought of all of this – Marc and I breaking up, then meeting Sam so soon afterwards?

"I'm sorry if I've disappointed you, Mam," I whispered. "I don't mean to make such a mess of everything – it's like I can't help myself."

I placed the picture down again and sat on the sofa and flicked through the channels. A really old episode of Home &

Away was on, it had Pippa and Tom, and Bobby and even Donald's evil sister Morag was in it, it was that old. When I was a child I always wanted to go to Australia and live with Pippa and Tom, and be one of their foster kids. I thought all my problems would fade away living in that wooden clapboard house. I sat watching the TV absently, thinking over all Clara had said. My phone rang then and I saw it was Sam, but I didn't answer it. Maybe Clara was right. Maybe it was time I grew up.

Chapter 30

Sam rang me several times that evening. He eventually left a message saying that he hoped everything was okay between us. I felt terrible not answering him, but it was for the best. Clara's words had hurt me and even rung true. What *had* I been thinking, moving on so soon?

I didn't sleep a wink that night as the argument with Clara replayed in my head. I saw every hour on the clock. I didn't like fighting with people, it unsettled me. I wasn't tough like Clara, who was probably fast asleep now, not giving it a second thought. An argument would play on my mind, and anxiety would curl around my gut until it was all sorted out again. Although the next day was Christmas Eve, I certainly wasn't feeling the Christmas spirit.

I was exhausted when I got up the next morning. Sam phoned me again, and I wasn't going to answer it but then I decided I owed it to him to be upfront.

"Lily," he said. I could hear in his voice. "Are you alright? I was getting worried about you, I rang you last night?"

"I know – sorry."

"Look did I do something wrong?" Sam asked.

"No, of course not – I just think that maybe we're better off leaving things as they are. Before we get in any deeper," I sighed.

"Oh –" he said clearly taken aback, "I see."

"I'm so sorry, Sam."

"Can I ask why?"

"Look, it's just for the best."

"I just don't understand? Was it the other night, if it was too soon for you then I'm sorry –"

"It wasn't that – the other night was perfect, but I'm sorry Sam, I can't be with you any more."

"I don't get you at all," he said in obvious frustration. "But, well if that's what you want . . . then take care of yourself, Lily."

I hung up the phone and bawled. Big full on fat tears with snot and everything ran down my face and wet the front of my t-shirt. My life was a complete mess. But the thing was I liked Sam, I really, *really* liked him. That was why I had to do it. I hadn't been honest with him about Marc, and I was pretty sure he wouldn't want to get involved in all that hassle and drama that was inevitably going to come down the line. I was doing him a favour in the long run – I had to keep on telling myself that.

My phone rang later that day from a number I didn't recognise.

"Hello?"

"Lily, hi, it's Marita here – Sam's sister."

"Oh hi, Marita." What was she ringing me for?

"Well firstly I just want to say thanks for bringing the kids to Playfactory at the weekend – they had a ball, and went straight to bed after you dropped them home – they were that tired!

"No worries – we had a great day. They're lovely children."

"Well the real reason I was ringing was to ask you over for Christmas drinks tonight? It's a family tradition – everyone comes to my house for mulled wine and mince pies on Christmas Eve. Now the kids will be up to ninety waiting for Santa but it's normally a bit of fun. Will you come along with Sam? I'd love to get to know you better."

"You obviously haven't been talking to Sam then?"

"No, why?" she asked.

"Well Sam and I have decided to go our separate ways I'm afraid."

"Oh really? God I'm so sorry. I should have talked to Sam first before I rang you . . . Sorry, Lily. God I'm so embarrassed now."

"Don't be. You weren't to know."

"Me and my big mouth – pass me a shovel so I can dig myself out of this one," she laughed nervously.

"It's okay, really, Marita."

After we hung up I felt really bad. His family, well the ones I had met anyway, were so lovely and welcoming – it was like breaking up with them too.

I held my head in my hands and sighed. Why could life never be straightforward?

I had to do a wedding cake that was being collected on St Stephen's day, and I didn't want to spend all of Christmas Day sweating over it in my kitchen so I knew I should make a start on it. I smashed bags of digestive biscuits that I was using to make a chocolate biscuit cake on the worktop with unnecessary force. I rattled cake tins and pounded out icing with the rolling pin – this cake was definitely not *Baked with Love*.

A while later there was a knock at the door. My heart leaped a little, hoping that it might be Sam. I opened the door, but it was Dad.

"Hi there," I said trying to mask my disappointment.

"Well hello to you too." He sat down on the sofa. "There's a lovely smell in the place."

"Chocolate biscuit cake. I'm making it for a wedding," I said grumpily.

"Are you all set for tomorrow?" He was referring to Christmas dinner in Clara's.

"I'm not going."

"What do you mean?"

"I'm not going."

"Did you and Clara have a falling out or something?"

I said nothing.

"Well there is something wrong or my name isn't Hugh McDermott – you've a face on you that would turn milk sour!"

"Look Clara and I had a fight yesterday – she called over here and said some pretty nasty stuff."

"Ah," he said. I knew by his tone, he knew more about this than he was telling me.

"Come on spit it out?"

"Well it's probably my fault so –" He stopped. "Look, Clara rang me telling me that she'd met you with some fella outside Playfactory, and I said well actually he's not just some fella, his name is Sam and that you seemed to be very happy with him but that was it, she just went off on one. I'm sorry, Lily I should have pretended that I knew nothing about him."

"Look it's not your fault – she said lots of hurtful things, Dad and I'm not going to stand for it anymore. I've been listening to her for years bossing me around – well not anymore!"

"But it's Christmas – we always go to Clara's for Christmas dinner?"

"Well I'm not going. I'll get a frozen turkey in Tesco or something."

"Aaaah, Lily."

"You should have heard what she said, Dad!"

"Go on what did she say?" he groaned.

"Well, where will I start – first of all she started by ranting at me for moving on so quickly after Marc. Then it just snowballed." I didn't want to tell him what she had said about Mam because I knew it would upset him too. "Anyway she'll be happy now because I've finished with Sam."

"Why?" He was shocked.

"I don't often say this, Dad but Clara is right. It's far too soon for me to be rushing into another relationship. It isn't fair to Sam to get me on the rebound – he's a lovely guy and deserves

285

someone with no baggage."

"But you liked him, Lily!"

"I know, Dad. I know," I sighed.

"Look Clara will come around – don't be worrying about what she thinks. She just feels she has to look out for everyone."

"That's exactly what she said to me the other night – that's why she is so angry with me because she said she's been spending her whole life minding me."

"There's probably a bit of truth in that," he said quietly.

"What do you mean?"

"Well for a while after your mother died – I wasn't there for her, for both of you as much as I should have been. I know that now. But at the time . . . well grief does funny things to you. You were okay – you were too young to understand really and Clara took on the role of mothering you. But Clara . . . well . . . Clara had no one to do that for her I suppose." He paused. "I regret that every day. Look, I know she goes on a bit, Lily and I know she gives you a terrible time of it sometimes but she means well, and she was so good to you when you were small. If you saw the way she used to mind you, Lily - and she only a small thing herself!" His voice broke and his eyes filled with tears. "I'm sorry, Lily –"

I was shocked by what he had said. Dad had never spoken about this before. I was too young to remember the immediate aftermath of Mam's death, so this was new to me. I could only ever remember Dad being a good father to us. I was lost for words.

I could feel myself starting to cry as well. I always did that as a child if I saw a grown-up crying, it frightened me so I ended up crying with them. "Go on, Dad. It's okay," I said softly.

"She's not as bad as you think, Lily – she has a hard front but she's a big softie underneath it all."

I had never thought of things from this perspective before. I had just seen Clara as a bossy, interfering older sister, but maybe this was the reason why she was like that.

"Nobody ever spoke about it, you know?"

"Well that was probably my fault, people didn't want to upset me, you see? I'm sorry, Lily, I'm sorry that you never felt able to talk about your mother or to ask questions about her. I suppose I never thought of it from your point of view – you probably don't even really remember her, you're bound to be curious."

I nodded gently. "It's okay, Dad, honestly. I know it wasn't easy on you or Clara either. She was a few years older, maybe I was lucky to be so young."

"Who knows, Lily," he sighed, "who knows. I'd bet my life that Clara is just as upset as you are right now."

"Do you think?"

"I'd bet money on it, Lily. Why don't I drive you over there now and you two can make it up. Huh?"

I looked back at him sulkily.

"Come on, it's Christmas, " he cajoled.

"Alright," I mumbled.

Chapter 31

Dad pulled up the handbrake and silenced the engine. We were outside Clara's house. Through the bars of her formidable electric gates, I could see that the house was decorated like a house from an American Christmas movie. The whole façade was illuminated with strip lighting like it was a giant Christmas present waiting to be opened. Garlands tied with huge red bows hung in every window and a bushy wreath arched over the front door. Fairy lights were strewn gracefully across the branches of the trees in the driveway. It must have cost tens of thousands to light up the house and grounds like that, I thought.

"Clara's been busy," I said nodding to the lights that were twinkling magically in the evening twilight.

"She hired professionals," Dad said.

"I see . . ." I paused for a moment. "So are you going to come in?" I asked nervously.

"I think you two need to sort this out by yourselves without me being there." He put his hand over mine and gave it a squeeze. "It's for the best, Lily."

"Yeah, you're probably right," I sighed. I was usually able to let Dad do the talking for me but it was probably time I did it myself now.

"Ring me afterwards, won't you and let me know how you get on?"

"Of course, Dad." I gave him a kiss on the cheek and got out of the Nissan Micra.

The gravel crunched under my feet as I let myself in through the pedestrian side gate and trudged towards her front door. The sky was heavy, with grey woolly-looking clouds. I took a deep breath and pressed the doorbell.

"What are *you* doing here?" Clara said icily as she opened the door to me.

"I wanted to talk to you," I said.

She held back the door and directed me into the living room.

"Where are the boys?"

"Tatiana has brought them swimming to try and burn off some excess energy – they're exuberant about Father Christmas."

Father Christmas? Since when did she call him that? It was always Santa when we were growing up.

"The house looks great," I said by way of conversation.

She merely nodded at me.

I sat down onto the formal Chesterfield sofa, which was quite hard and always made me sit up straight. Clara took one of the armchairs.

I decided to come straight out with it.

"Look, Clara – you said some hurtful things last night, but I've been talking with Dad, and well I realise that maybe you didn't have things as easy as I thought growing up . . ."

"How do you mean?"

"Dad said you used to look after me – after Mam died."

"He did?" She looked shocked.

I nodded.

"Well I had no choice, Lily – you were only two. Dad went to pieces, so someone had to step in."

"I never knew that before," I said quietly. "Nobody ever talks about her."

"It's not a big deal. Someone had to hold it all together and that person was me."

"Well thank you – for doing that for me, even though I don't really remember it – thank you."

She looked up at me and there were tears glistening in her eyes.

"I'm sorry for everything I said yesterday, Lily. I didn't mean it – really I didn't and I know some of what I said was truly awful. Of course Mam would be so proud at the way you turned out."

This was enough to set me off too, and soon the two of us were a sobbing mess.

"You were too young to remember, Lily, but I was five and I understood everything. She dropped me off to school one morning and then didn't come back to pick me up. The thing was that Mam always picked me up on time – she was always the first mother there. I stood waiting and waiting with my teacher Mrs Byrne in the schoolyard as one by one every child went home with its parents, until suddenly I was the last child left. Even then I felt very anxious, it wasn't like Mam to be late. Mrs Byrne said it might be better to wait inside, and she brought me up to the principal's office and gave me a Rich Tea biscuit. I'll never forget it – I had never been inside it before. She kept trying to ring Mam from the school phone, but there was no answer." Her voice was now a whisper. I knew there was something wrong because I could see it on Mrs Byrne's face. Then the school rang Dad at work, because it was almost an hour later and still no one had come to collect me. So Dad tried ringing her and she still didn't answer the phone, so he knew something was up. Dad came then and picked me up and when we went home, we found Mam lying on the kitchen tiles. That was it – a brain haemorrhage had taken her instantly. I'll never, ever forget seeing her lying there on the floor. I was only five, but I knew something was very, very wrong and then Dad started shouting – I can still hear it now. I don't really remember what happened after that but I remember wondering why Mam would want to sleep on the kitchen floor. When Dad went to check where you were, you were sleeping soundly in your cot – you had slept through it all."

"I never knew that," I whispered. I had known that a brain haemorrhage was what had killed Mam, but no one had ever told me the full details of what happened that morning, and I had always been too afraid of upsetting people to ask.

"We were robbed of so much, Lily. So much." Her voice broke and she started to sob. "We didn't even get to say goodbye."

"I know," I whispered. I had never really thought about it from Clara's perspective before, what must it have been like for a five-year old girl to see her mother dead on the floor?

"Auntie Flor came and helped out for a bit and Granny too, but with families of their own they couldn't stay forever, so soon it was just the three of us left on our own to get on with things, and Dad went to pieces. He loved her so much, Lily – he took it very badly. He was caught up in his own world of grief so we stuck together you and I."

I smiled at her.

"Sometimes I was jealous of the girls in my class in school – they still had mothers to mind them – for silly reasons like to plait their hair or iron their uniforms. Mrs Byrne was very good to me, she took me under her wing, but I still missed my own mother. So I had no choice really – I had to grow up fast. You were my little sister, and I loved minding you. And all the things Mam used to do for me, I tried to do for you so that you wouldn't miss out on anything. When you started school, I did your hair as best I could in the mornings and I packed your lunches every day and made sure you always had your homework done. I even made your costumes for the school concert."

"Thanks, Clara," I mumbled. This all had come as such a shock to me. Everything I thought I knew about my childhood had been turned upside down.

"She was so beautiful, Lily. Really classically beautiful. She had such delicate features, pale flawless skin and dark shiny hair. I used to think she was the most beautiful woman in the world. She'd always put on her make-up every morning – even if we weren't going anywhere and I would stand beside her at the mirror, and she would hand me her red lipstick or her mascara and I would put them on too. I'm sure I made a mess, but she never said – she just said how I looked so pretty."

"You're lucky to have memories of her. I would give anything to remember her. I only have the photos Dad gave me."

She smiled wistfully at me.

"It's not fair – life isn't fair. I spent so many years being angry as a teenager about it all, but I was only wasting my energy – it wouldn't bring her back. She was only twenty-seven, too young to be taken away and to leave two young girls without their mother. That's why I'm so full on with the boys – I just want to give them everything that I didn't have as a child. I'm so scared that something might happen to me and I won't be around to see them grow up. I know I probably go overboard, but no matter what happens at least they'll grow up knowing that they're loved. I feel that I have to hold it all together, because if I don't, we all go to pieces and I don't want to lose any more of my family."

It felt as though everything in my life now made sense. I finally understood Clara and why she was like she was. She had been through so much, and I had never appreciated that before. I always just saw her as my bossy older sister, but there was a reason she was like that.

"I'm sorry, Clara."

"What are you sorry for?"

"For everything – for all you went through after Mam died, for caring about me still even though God knows I manage to royally fuck things up at times!"

"Lily, I'm sorry too – I know I can say hurtful things to you sometimes but if I'm completely honest I'm probably a little bit jealous . . ."

"You? Jealous of me?" I asked in disbelief.

"Uh-huh." She nodded. "Sometimes you seem so carefree and you're so easy-going about life, well sometimes I wish I could be more like you actually –"

"I don't think you would like to be like me, Clara," I laughed.

She laughed too. "How are you and – Sam, isn't it – how are you getting along?"

"We broke up actually."

"You did?" Her face dropped. "But why?"

"Well I was thinking of everything you said, and you were right. It was too soon after Marc. I mean what was I thinking launching straight back into another relationship after only a few months?"

"But I didn't mean what I said – I was just angry, I didn't mean for you to break up with him!"

"You didn't?"

"Of course not, when I saw you walking out of Playfactory

that day I couldn't help noticing how for the first time in so long you looked genuinely happy."

This just made me feel worse. *What had I done?*

"I was happy. I really like him. I've been miserable ever since."

"Well go after him then."

"What?"

"Tell him that, tell him that you're miserable without him, and hopefully he'll be willing to try again."

"Do you really think so?"

"Well I could tell by the way he looked at you that he felt every bit as strongly as you felt about him."

"I hope you're right."

We stayed chatting easily to each other. For the first time in our lives we were talking properly like sisters rather than the mother/daughter type relationship we normally had. She asked me with enthusiasm how *Baked with Love* was going, and when I told her how I was limited by the size of my oven she suggested she would talk to Tom that night to see if he might have something suitable for me to set up a proper bakery. Unbeknownst to me, he had a huge property portfolio, and Clara reckoned he would be willing to give me a good deal on a small unit to help me get off the ground.

Tatiana came back with the boys soon after.

"Auntie, Lily," Jacob cried when he saw me.

"Auntie, Ni-ni," Joshua said following his older brother

over.

"Jacob, Joshua! Come over here and give me a hug!"

They ran over and I wrapped them into my arms. Suddenly I understood Clara. I knew why she was like she was, and why she was a contender for extreme parenting. Most of all though, I knew she was only looking out for me. I was lucky she was my sister.

Chapter 32

After my heart to heart with Clara, there was still one more thing to be resolved. I hopped into Clara's SUV and we headed for the city centre. What should only have been a ten-minute journey took over half an hour with all the last minute Christmas Eve traffic. The roads were bumper-to-bumper with people heading home to start on their festive preparations. As we sat through another change of red lights, I felt myself grow ever tenser and I found myself getting more impatient. I knew it was only because I was nervous. Finally we turned onto the quays and soon we reached Sam's apartment block. Clara pulled up outside and before I jumped down from the dizzying heights of her Range Rover, I leaned across to the driver's seat, to give her a hug. She wished me luck, and made me promise to ring her to let her know how I got on. I got out and headed over to the door. I waved goodbye to Clara, and then pressed the buzzer to Sam's apartment. My heart was almost rattling against my ribcage.

"Hello?" he answered huskily. God it was so good to hear his voice again.

"Sam – it's me, Lily."

"Lily – I -" he sounded distracted. It hadn't been the reaction I had been hoping for.

"I'm sorry, Sam," I continued.

"Who's that, Sam?" I heard a woman's voice ask in the background.

I froze on the spot. Who was she?

"Is that Marita?" I asked hopefully.

"Em sorry, Lily – I . . . er . . . can I call you later? This isn't a good time for me."

"Right, yeah . . . of course," I said trying my best not to sound completely devastated.

Tears sprung into my eyes, and my heart felt as though it had thudded to the floor. Once again, I had been a fool. This was the price you paid for opening your heart to someone. All I knew was that I needed to get away from there quickly. Thankfully Frankie's apartment was so close. As I hurried along, I had to wrap my scarf double around my neck and bend my head from the piercing wind being channelled up the river as I walked over the graceful arc of the Samuel Beckett Bridge. I steered left and right to avoid the crowds of last minute Christmas shoppers laden with bags. The Christmas lights from the surrounding office blocks twinkled off the surface of the water. I couldn't believe he had moved on so soon – I thought we had had something special, but maybe I was just one woman in a long line of conquests for him. Bloody men, they were all the same. Why on earth had I thought that Sam would be any different? Well I wasn't going to waste anymore tears on him – I remembered what Dad had said, no man is worth your tears. Soon I was outside Frankie's block. I wiped my eyes with the back of my hand and pressed the buzzer.

I waited a minute but there was no answer. I tried it again but she wasn't home. I took out my phone and dialled her number. It rang for ages before she eventually answered. It was hard to hear her over the noisy din in the background and I could just about make out that she was in a pub. She sounded well on. She told me to come and join them, but there was no way I could face that so I said goodbye and hung up the phone. I had been doing pretty well at holding back the tears up to that point, but then they just came and I stood there sobbing on the street. I decided to walk back down the quays and get the bus home to Ballyrobin.

I was lucky to get on the last bus back to the sticks; they were all finishing earlier, because it was Christmas Eve. As I made my way down the back of the bus, I saw that all the seats already had one person in them, so I sat in beside a girl the same age as myself but if I thought there'd be some Christmassy goodwill in everyone's hearts I was wrong. She threw me a filthy look for choosing the seat beside her because it meant she had to put her handbag on the floor. This was the trigger that made me cry even more. What was it about me crying on buses? I supposed it had been an emotional day.

When the bus finally pulled into Ballyrobin, I walked home in the biting cold. It felt strange being out at that time on Christmas Eve, usually I would be tucked up warmly at home, watching a movie and finishing the last of my wrapping.

My phone rang just as I was putting my key in the door – it was Sam. I knew I shouldn't answer it – he didn't deserve another minute of my time, but of course being the sucker that I am, I answered it.

"Hi there. Look sorry about earlier –" he said quickly.

"No worries," I said coolly. I didn't want him to know how upset I was.

"How've you been doing?" he asked.

"Grand."

"I've missed you."

I couldn't hold back any longer. "Well it didn't take you long to move on!"

"What do you mean?"

"The woman in your apartment earlier?"

"Oh you mean Gina?"

"Yes *Gina*!" I said as if I had known her all my life.

"Gina is my friend Derek's wife."

"Oh my God how could you!" I was horrified.

"Eh . . . I'm going to be the best man at their wedding in a few days time, and she just wanted to run through some stuff with me for the day."

Foooooooook. Fuckedy, fuck and double fuck. Why did I always have to make a complete and utter holy show of myself?

"Oh – I see, right well em' I'll go now then . . ."

"Lily?" He was laughing. "Why do you always put two and two together and come up with two hundred and twenty-two?"

"Sorry, Sam." I was happy, so, so happy. He wasn't a complete dickhead after all.

"Don't mention it."

"So how come you were in my neck of the woods earlier then?"

"I wanted to talk to you."

"Oh, what about?"

"Well I've been doing some thinking – can I meet you?"

"I'm sorry, Lily – I'm just on my way to Marita's – it's a family tradition, there's no way I can skip it."

"I know."

"You do?"

"Well she rang me earlier and invited me over – it was a bit awkward actually."

"Look why don't I call over tomorrow morning – I have something for you anyway. I picked it up before –" he broke off.

"Thank you, I'd like that."

***

Later that night I managed to finish up my cakes and wrapping my gifts and had just climbed into bed when my bell went. My heart started racing as it always did whenever anyone called so late at night. I wrapped my dressing gown around me and made my way to the door. I looked through the spyhole to see a distorted Sam standing there. I pulled back the door.

"Sam?"

"Sorry, Lily – sorry it's so late. I know it's only me and

Santa up at this hour but I couldn't wait until tomorrow to see you."

He was barely in the door when I threw myself on him and started kissing him deeply.

"I'm sorry for everything – I've been miserable without you," I said as breathed his scent in.

Soon we were grabbing each other, stripping one another naked and making the most passionate love I have ever made in my life.

We lay there breathless and panting afterwards.

"That was amazing," I said.

"I need to ask you, Lily, why did you get cold feet? I thought it was all going so well, and then the next thing I knew you were telling me it was all over!" Sam asked, as we lay there naked together afterwards.

"I'm sorry – I'm all over the place at the moment. But I'd a lot of things to sort out in my head and well . . . there is something that I need to tell you before we go any further . . ." I took a deep breath.

Then as if on cue there was a loud bang against the wall.

"What was that?" Sam nearly jumped off the bed.

"Here we go again," I groaned.

"What is it?"

"It's next door having sex." It wasn't just any old sex; no it was full on, bed banging sex.

"Jesus do they do that often?"

I was slightly embarrassed.

"Mmmh, a few times a week," I lied. It was more like a few times a night. It had been the same when Marc had lived there, except I think he used to get off on it.

I knew we had just done the same, but there was no way we were that loud.

"Have you ever tried talking to them about it, y'know asking them to keep it down?"

"No way."

"Well they should invest in a solid headboard – it's the least they could do."

We sat there waiting for them to finish for an age until finally they both gave it a rest.

"I feel slightly inadequate after that," Sam said and we both laughed.

"So what was it that you wanted to tell me?" he asked seriously.

But the moment was gone then and I couldn't say it. "Just that I'm so happy that you didn't give up on me," I said instead.

He hugged me tight in his arms and we spooned each other. I lay awake as he snored softly behind me. I felt awful – I had wanted to start afresh with no secrets, but now I had wasted another opportunity. The longer this went on the worse it was going to be. And I was so afraid that when I finally did tell him that I was going to lose him.

Chapter 33

Sam dropped me off at Clara's house on Christmas morning. I had tried to tell him about Marc as we drove along through the countryside, but he was chatting away excitedly about his friend's wedding, and then when he asked me to go with him as his plus one, I didn't have the heart to do it. I didn't want to spoil the moment, especially on Christmas Day, but I knew that I needed to do it soon. Time wasn't on my side, I wanted to be able to introduce him to my family but to do that; I knew I needed to tell him about Marc first.

We pulled up outside Clara's house.

"The place looks like bloody Narnia!" he said open-mouthed.

"That's Clara for you!" I said laughing.

We kissed deeply in the car neither one of us wanting to be apart from each other. I would see him that evening anyway, he had invited me over to his parents' house, but the thoughts of spending a whole day apart from him seemed like an eternity.

I opened the door and went to climb out of the car, but Sam pulled me back and planted a kiss firmly on my lips before letting me go.

I took my presents out of Sam's boot before making my way

towards Clara's front door.

"Lily!" Clara greeted me warmly.

The boys ran up and hugged my legs, their eyes fixed firmly on the presents in my arms.

"Happy Christmas, my darling," Dad said giving me a kiss on the cheek. "You look radiant this morning."

"Do I?" I asked surprised.

"You do, you're glowing," Clara chimed.

I blushed thinking back to the night before with Sam.

We followed Clara into the kitchen where Tom had just popped the cork on a bottle of champagne and was busy handing out glasses. Clara was like another woman. Normally she would be stressing about the turkey timings or barking orders at Dad and myself to chop vegetables, but today she was completely chilled. Even Tatiana had gone all festive on us – she came down for dinner wearing a red and green striped bandage dress, if she wasn't such a ball of sexiness, she would have looked like a Christmas tree decoration. The dinner was a relaxed affair, and Dad and I were relieved to see that Clara seemed to have taken a departure from her usual formalities. Normally she was uptight about every little thing from using the right knife, to the boys' table manners, but when Joshua picked up his turkey and ate it using his fingers, she didn't seem to care. She even let Dad drink Heineken – he wasn't a big wine drinker and normally Clara wouldn't buy beer, but she had bought him a few bottles especially for the occasion. Even Tom joined in and used the bottle opener to pop the lid back on one.

After dinner was finished, we all sat around wearing our party hats, and Clara didn't complain when Tom opened the top button on his trousers, or when the streamers from the party poppers were left trailed around the floor. It was the best Christmas Day I'd ever had and we were all well on when Sam came back later on to pick me up.

"What are you doing for New Year's?" Sam asked as we drove across the deserted city streets to his parents' house.

"I haven't really thought about it to be honest." This wasn't true at all. The truth was I had thought of nothing else for the last few weeks. "I hate New Year's anyway," I lied.

Unlike most people, I used to love New Year's Eve, that's why Marc and I had chosen it as our date to get married, but as this New Years' Eve was to have been my first wedding anniversary, I had a huge sense of dread. It wasn't because I was still sad about Marc, but I was sad that our marriage was over. All the hopes and dreams and excitement that I had had this time last year were gone, and it was scary to think how radically your life could change in the space of a year. Plus I had been doing so well over the last few months since Sam had come into my life, and I was worried that the looming date would set me back again.

"Well I was wondering if you want to come down to Marita's cottage with me, in County Clare?" Sam was chatting away. "She said it's free and we're welcome to have it for a few nights - if you'll come?"

"What a great idea. I'd love to, Sam."

I knew that a change of scenery would do me the world of good. I didn't want to spend it moping around my duplex on my own. I could think of nothing nicer than ringing in the year in Sam's arms, just the two of us on our own.

Soon Sam was pulling up outside a small three-bedroomed semi-detached house in a quiet estate.

"Are you ready?" he turned to me with a grin.

"You make it sound like I'm going into a den of lions."

"Nah, not lions . . . more like wolves."

I slapped his arm playfully, and we got out of the car.

I followed Sam around to the back of the house, because nobody used the front door, he told me. We came in through the kitchen, and as soon as I had taken a few steps across the tiles, it was like stepping into a circus - the house was teaming with people. I had brought a box of cake-pops I had fashioned into the shape of reindeers.

"Who are all of these people?" I whispered to Sam.

"These are all the relies."

"You said it was just your family?" I said panicked.

"This is my family, Lily – here, meet Uncle Charlie."

He thrust me in front of a rosy cheeked man who was obviously well on, because he gave me a big bear hug and told me, how happy, how really happy he was to finally meet me.

"This is my Mam," Sam said, introducing me to a rotund lady in her sixties. She looked quite like him – they both had the same dark, kindly eyes.

"It's so nice to meet you," I said shaking her hand. I handed her the box of cake-pops, and felt like I was giving her a peace offering.

Before I knew what was happening she had thrown both arms around me and was wrapping me into a bear of a hug, "It's so nice to finally meet you, Lily."

She let me go and linked my arm, "Come in and meet everyone else, they're all dying to meet you."

Marita came over then and squeezed my hand. "I'm so glad you and Sam sorted things out," she whispered kindly in my ear before linking my arm and introducing me to relative after relative, until my head was a jumble of names and faces. Everyone was warm and welcoming, and it made me think about Marc's parents. His family had been the same – it was just a pity he wasn't like them. I still missed his mother. She rang me the odd time, but it was strained now. There was an unmistakable awkwardness because neither of us wanted to speak about the elephant in the room. I knew she would never forgive Marc for what he had done.

We had a great evening, and when it was time to go home Sam drove back to the city centre.

I woke the next morning wrapped in Sam's arms with my head resting against the firmness of his broad chest.

"Good morning, beautiful," he whispered softly as I opened my eyes.

"Well I survived!"

"Were you that nervous?"

"Uh-huh."

"Well you shouldn't have been."

"Do you think I passed the test?"

"They all loved you. The cake-pops helped."

I laughed. "Bribery always works."

We lay there cuddling in the morning light, laughing and chatting and so at ease. I remembered on this very day the year before I had collected my wedding dress from the bridal shop, and now here I was in the arms of another man. I knew now would be a good time to tell Sam about Marc.

"Sam, there is something that I need to tell you –"

"Sounds ominous."

"Well there is something about me that you need to know."

"What? That you're gorgeous, talented not to mention a supremely talented baker – I know all that already."

"There's something else –" My heart was racing and I thought I might get sick with the nerves.

"What is it?" His face grew concerned. Frown lines converged in the centre of his forehead.

The doorbell rang then. "Back in a sec, Lily," Sam said hopping out of bed.

Sam came back a moment later with an apologetic smile on his face. "It's Derek, he wants to practice his speech for the wedding tomorrow - I'm sorry, Lily."

"Don't worry about it," I said climbing out of bed. "I probably should head on anyway, I've a couple coming to collect a cake later on."

"Take your time in the shower, and I'll have a nice breakfast waiting for you, okay?"

"Sure," I said. I felt deflated. It seemed that every time I plucked up the courage to tell him about Marc, we would get interrupted. The timing just never seemed to be right.

Chapter 34

Slowly the world began adjusting back to normal after another Christmas. The days seemed to be sneaking past me, and I still hadn't worked up the courage to tell Sam. We had a great day at the wedding. Although Sam was a groomsman, he was attentive to me throughout the day, and made sure that the wives of his friends looked after me. I will admit to feeling emotional as the church organ played. It was so close to my own anniversary and it brought all the memories back to the surface.

Sam and I were both so hungover the morning after the wedding that I just couldn't face telling him. I knew I needed to be in the right frame of mind before embarking on something like that.

I was really looking forward to escaping with him on our mini-break in County Clare. On the day before New Year's Eve, I decided to run into Brown Thomas to get some nice new underwear. I wanted everything about this weekend to be just perfect. There would be none of my M&S sets this time.

As I stepped outside, I discovered it was bitterly cold out. I had put on my red woollen coat as well as my hat, scarf and gloves, but the icy wind still cut through me. I caught the bus into town and as I strolled down Grafton Street I couldn't resist stopping to look at the beautiful displays in the shop windows. There were winter scenes of Victorian families ice-skating together; another window had carol singers gathered in a snowy churchyard and in another, children tossed snowballs at each other. They were all beautiful.

When I reached Brown Thomas the doorman held the door open and the warm air welcomed me inside. I took off my hat and gloves and breathed in the heady scent of the perfume hall. The shop was still extravagantly decorated with lots of fir garlands tied with elegant gold and silver bows. As I coasted up the escalator, I could hear the orchestral version of *Oh Come All Ye Faithful* playing in the background. Even though I loved Christmas music, there was something about it being played in the days just after Christmas that made me feel a teensy bit icky.

I could never come into Brown Thomas without paying the shoe department a little visit, so that was my first port of call and even though I couldn't actually afford to buy shoes there, I still could admire those little beauties. As I walked around the displays I picked up a few, but the price made me put them down just as quickly again – to think that Rosie and Clara wore shoes like that on a daily basis! Even if I did own a pair I would be too afraid to wear them.

I took the escalator up to the second floor, and walked through the archway leading to the lingerie section. Pretty bras hung along the walls and the matching knickers were displayed in open drawers underneath. There were basques with ribbons tying up the back and matching suspenders and stockings. There were satin baby dolls and little balconette bras that would look ridiculous on my large bust, but always looked so pretty on models. Even the racy thongs and lacy French knickers were all made with beautiful silks and delicate laces, with not a hint of polyester to be seen.

"Can I help you there?" The sales assistant came up beside me. Her dark hair was severely pulled up into a high ponytail on the crown of her head.

"Yes, I'm looking for some underwear."

"Yes, that tends to be why people come in here," she said. "What type are you looking for? Is it for a special occasion?"

"Well, I'm going on a mini-break with my new boyfriend, so I wanted something special, you know?" I could feel myself reddening. I was in my thirties for God's sake. Why did I feel embarrassed admitting I was going to be having sex with my boyfriend?

As I followed her over to a display, her ponytail swung behind her head steadily like a metronome.

"How about a 'demi bra'?" she said taking one down from the rail and handing it to me.

"But where is the rest of it?" I asked bewildered. It looked like the machinist had forgotten to finish off the cups properly.

"That's the point of them – hence the name, *demi* meaning half."

"Yeah I know what demi means – I know Italian."

"It's French actually. Now these are really popular for people looking to move away from traditional lingerie sets without going down the whole kinky route."

"But where do your . . . *y'know* go?"

"Excuse me?"

"Y'now – *nipples*," I whispered. I could feel myself blushing. God I hated saying that word out loud.

"Your breast is meant to sit over the top of the trimming here so your *nipple* - she practically shouted the word - is partly on display."

"I see. Well are they half the price?" I laughed nervously.

She shot me a look to say she didn't appreciate my joke.

I walked over to the flesh coloured sucky in knickers – now I was more at home.

"Are you trying to impress this new man or not?" she said dragging me away from them.

Okay, relax there, Gok Wan, I thought to myself.

"Over this way please," she said as she led me over to the "real" bras. I picked out a few that I liked. Then she showed me into a fitting room, and after she had measured me she brought in armfuls of them for me to try on. I winced when I looked at the price tags – the bras were over a hundred euro each and the knickers were half that again, but as soon as I tried them on, I knew why. They did amazing things for me. My breasts were held firm where they belonged, and the knickers were so flattering on my curves. In this underwear I felt confident about my shape. I decided to go with a midnight blue, satin plunge bra and matching knickers. It had a delicate black lace trim and I thought it looked sexy without being overtly so. I also picked a nude-coloured sheer mesh bra, which seemed a bit racy to me but the assistant told me to trust her and that I was being a prude. She tried to convince me to take a see-through baby doll too, but at €250 it would be staying where it was. She spent ages wrapping up my purchases in layers of tissue paper, fitting the packages neatly into a box and then tying it with ribbons before handing it over to me. I wanted to squeal with excitement. I had never spent so much on underwear in my life, and I knew I would have to bake a lot of cakes to pay for it, but I felt very proud of my purchases. I couldn't wait to show Sam. To celebrate, I decided to treat myself to a hot chocolate. As I made my way to the café I passed by rails of gorgeous clothing. I saw the kids' designer clothes and I couldn't resist having a look – even though I obviously didn't have children, I loved the cuteness of all the little miniature outfits.

I was just picking up a white, broderie anglaise Chloe baby girl dress when another girl snatched it straight out of my hands. I turned around and saw she was pregnant so I let her have it. I supposed she had more of a right to admire it than I did.

"Lily? Is that you?"

My eyes moved from her bump up towards her face and I saw that it was Nadia.

"How are you, Lily?" She held out her hand to shake mine

but I left it hanging there in the space between us. I was frozen to the spot, I knew my mouth was hanging open, but I couldn't close it. Her bump was so neat on her tall, slender figure. It just looked like she had eaten a big dinner. I did a mental calculation and she must have been seven months pregnant at that stage. She hadn't a pick of weight on her anywhere else. She was wearing a casual jersey dress layered with leggings and a jersey cardigan. Her dark hair was styled in waves around her face. Her skin was glowing. I hated to admit it but pregnancy suited the bitch.

"It's a lovely dress isn't it?" She admired the white dress in her hand. Suddenly the white dress signified everything – she had taken away my husband and now she had grabbed the white dress from under my eyes too. I reached across and tugged it back out of her hands.

"Oh here, sorry did you want it?" She released the dress and then I was left holding it, feeling silly because I didn't really want it at all.

"Lily, look I'm so, so, sorry about everything. I know I'm probably the last person you want to see right now but if you have a few minutes, I would really appreciate it if you could grab a coffee with me?"

I looked at her like she was daft.

She reached across and put her hand over mine. "Please, Lily, I'd really like to talk to you." Her almond shaped brown eyes were begging me.

Reluctantly I agreed.

Wordlessly we took the escalator to the third floor café together. We were just walking over when an older lady stopped us.

"Nadia – Nadia Williams? Is that you? I absolutely loved you in *Our Endless Days*, I can't believe it's you – I know you're out and about and I hate to ask you but can I have your autograph please?"

"Sure!" Nadia smiled easily at the lady. Her teeth were perfectly even and white.

"There you go -" she said breezily as she handed back the notebook where she had scrawled her signature across the page that the woman had folded back.

"Thanks, Nadia!" she beamed. "And can I just say you look fantastic!" She pointed to Nadia's bump. "It suits you – I saw you and your partner in *Social Importance* magazine, you're a very glamorous couple."

"Oh you're very kind." I watched as Nadia smiled good-naturedly at the woman and flicked her hair with her slender wrist. I wondered would the woman still think that the sun shone out of her arse if she knew what a home wrecker Nadia really was?

There was queue outside the café but when the hostess recognised Nadia, she quickly made space for us and showed us over to a table in the corner. Nadia immediately took the bench seat running along the wall, so she had a view of the restaurant, and I took the seat opposite her. Marc used to do this too – he

321

would always grab the inside seat first so he would have the view, it didn't really bother me but it was a big deal for him and he would sprint across the restaurant floor just so he would get to it first. The waiter handed us both menus and told us what the specials were.

We both read our menus silently - I still couldn't speak. My heart was thumping wildly. Why did she want to talk to me? She had practically begged me to go for a coffee with her.

"Ladies, what can I get you?"

Nadia pointed to me, "You go first, Lily."

"Okay, well I'll have a cappuccino and a slice of the lemon meringue pie."

"And I'll have the fruit cup and a bottle of San Pellegrino please," she said before closing the menu and handing it back to the waiter, giving him a wide smile.

The fruit cup and fizzy water? What the fuck? She was pregnant – she was supposed to be eating for two! I knew if I were pregnant it would be a calorie-free-for-all. No wonder she looked so great. I instantly regretted ordering something so piggish – now I would be totally self-conscious eating it in front of her.

We sat in awkward silence for a few minutes while we waited for the waiter to bring our food. I kept thinking about her inverted nipple.

"So when are you due?" I finally said after I couldn't take any more awkwardness.

"February."

"Wow, you've only a few weeks to go so."

"I know." She rubbed her bump absently.

I couldn't believe that that was Marc's baby in there. My Marc's baby.

"Look the reason that I wanted to talk to you, Lily –" She leaned across the table to me but we were interrupted by the waiter bringing our food.

"The pie?"

"Me thanks," I mumbled. I was sure that he thought I was a pig as well.

"And the fruit cup for you, madam." He placed the silver dish on the table in front of Nadia. He was just walking away when he stopped and turned back around.

"Sorry, it is you, isn't it? You're Nadia Williams?" he reddened.

"Yes it's me."

"I loved *Our Endless Days*!"

"Why thank you." She smiled that same smile again. It was obviously her "I'm all sweetness and light" smile reserved for annoying autograph hunters.

"Well, I don't want to interrupt you so I'll let you and your friend get back to your food – it was great to meet you, Nadia." He walked backwards still smiling away at her until he bumped into the table behind him. Even pregnant, Nadia had an amazing effect on men.

"Sorry, Lily – where were we? Oh yes, sorry, baby brain! It's Marc, I'm worried sick. Ever since he found out that I was pregnant, he's been . . . well, really distant. We've been arguing a lot, and then a couple of weeks ago he said we needed time apart, so he stayed with his parents for Christmas. I just don't know what to do any more . . . I'm at my wits' end. It was all going great – we were having so much fun. Marc loved the invitations to launches and premieres every night of the week. He loved being invited to the best restaurants in town or getting into the VIP area in nightclubs. Then, when I found out that I was pregnant, he went ballistic. Honestly, Lily, I was devastated by the way he reacted. Although we didn't plan to have a baby, I was secretly thrilled when the test was positive and because things were going so well between us, I had thought he would have felt the same. But instead he started roaring and shouting at me and asking how I could have let it happen – like I did it all by myself!" She stopped to take a mouthful of her water before continuing. "He wanted me to have an abortion y'know – he kept on telling me that my career would be over as soon as the production companies knew I was pregnant. He said that no one would cast me, but I still couldn't do it, Lily, I couldn't go through with it and do that to our baby."

I was stunned. She kept tossing chunks of pineapple and strawberries around with her fork. I didn't know what to say to her. I knew that I was probably doing a good impression of a goldfish right then, but I was just so shocked by how open she was being.

"Eventually he came round, but things were still strained between us. For the sake of our relationship, I tried to be 'fun' Nadia again – we kept on going to parties, but I was so exhausted after a full day of filming and then being the only sober person in the nightclub while everyone else around me was getting pissed. So eventually I stopped going out, which made Marc really angry again. He kept on calling me boring and telling me that I had changed. He said that I was letting the baby take over my life!"

She speared a chunk of melon with her fork and brought it towards her mouth, but she didn't eat it. My pie was calling me, but she still hadn't eaten any of her fruit and I didn't want to look like a complete pig by diving in first.

"After the first trimester passed I couldn't hide my bump any longer, so I had to tell the director of the film I was working on, but he wasn't prepared to shoot the rest of my scenes with props covering my bump or editing it out so he fired me! In fairness it was written into my contract that I wasn't allowed to get pregnant, but I thought he would have at least tried to accommodate me. And to make matters worse a contact I had, had promised Marc a big role on an upcoming feature being shot, but he just dropped him when I was no use to him anymore – so Marc went ballistic. Of course I asked a few other contacts that I had – people I had worked with previously – if they knew of anything available but the work just dried up. Marc was right – nobody wanted to know me when they heard I was pregnant. And that was the straw that broke the camel's back – Marc started going out with all of *my* friends without me, and some nights he didn't come home at all. I spent so many nights at home alone crying myself to sleep. Deep down I think Marc loved the perks of being with me more than actually being with me if you know what I mean?" And just like that tears started to run down her face.

"God, Nadia – don't cry." I reached out across the table to rub her arm.

"I just don't want to lose him, Lily," she said in a whisper. The tears started to flow faster. I couldn't believe it – the glamorous composed woman who had been sitting across from me just minutes ago was now a sobbing mess.

"You must really hate me after everything I have done to you." She dabbed at her eyes with the linen napkin. Amazingly her eye make-up didn't budge through it all.

"Of course I don't hate you," I lied. She didn't need to know that I regularly fantasised about sticking steel pins in her mouth to make her fillings tingle. "The last few months have been some of the worst of my life but I'm doing okay now. . ."

"Well I'm sorry, Lily – genuinely. I know nothing I can say can excuse my behaviour or what I've done to you. I'm not proud of myself – not one bit. I guess what goes around comes around, huh?"

I felt really uncomfortable. "Nadia, I . . . Marc and I, we've a lot of history, we were *married* but I really believe that everything happens for a reason. Look I don't know what is going on with you and Marc right now, but even if you have to do it on your own, you're obviously a strong woman – you'll get through it. It'll be okay," I said softly. I couldn't believe I was sitting here counselling the woman who I had found in bed with my husband. Only me. Anyone else would have told her to fuck right off, but of course I was a walkover as usual. I felt sorry for her though, because no matter what Marc had put me through, I wasn't left bringing up a baby on my own.

She took out her Chanel powder compact from her Mulberry handbag, opened it up and checked her appearance in the mirror. She proceeded to pat it across her cheeks. When she was finally satisfied she snapped it closed and put it back into her bag.

"I'm sorry, I have no right to off-load onto you after everything I have put you through – blame the pregnancy hormones," she sighed heavily. "But when I saw you, I just had to talk to you – you of all people know Marc better than anyone else. I don't know what I'm looking for – maybe some insight into what is going on inside his head?"

"I can't help you there I'm afraid, Nadia – I spent a long time trying to figure that out myself."

"But has he been back in touch with you, Lily – please be honest with me, I don't think I could take any more lies," she sniffed.

"Well, no not for a while now."

"Phew." She let out a long sigh of relief. "I was so afraid

327

you were getting back together again. Lately every time he goes out the door I imagine he is going to see you. He wants you back y'know, Lily? He talks about you all the time – I know he misses you and regrets ever meeting me, I'm sure. He told me before he left that it was the biggest mistake he ever made – leaving you. Can you imagine how that made me feel – I'm carrying his baby! If it was anyone else I'd tell him to get lost instead of desperately clinging on to him but . . . it's not just me I thinking about – we're having a baby together whether he likes it or not."

Was what she was saying true? Did he really say that to her? I had enough of staring at the pie, I couldn't resist it anymore so dug into it with the fork and took a bite. The tartness of the lemon perfectly contrasted the sweetness of the sticky meringues it was divine. I needed to add this onto my list for *Baked with Love*.

"I don't want to do this on my own," she said suddenly. Her eyes were wide with fear. "Please don't take him away from me, Lily. Please."

"Look, Nadia – what do you want me to say? Marc chose to be with you. He left me to be with you!"

"I know, you're right, Lily," she sighed heavily. "It's just that I wanted so much more for our baby, y'know?" She continued, "I grew up in a broken home, my Dad walked out on my Mum when I was only three months old, so I never really knew him – I have vague memories of him taking me off on a Saturday afternoon, but I just remember screaming every time he came to pick me up. Basically he was a stranger to me and I was expected to go off and have fun with him! So eventually I'm sure he had enough of listening to me bawling and crying, and his Saturday visits petered out altogether, until it was just a token visit for an hour on Christmas morning. I always swore when I had my own children that I wouldn't let that happen and that's what upsets me the most, because now here I am about to let history repeat itself all over again."

"You don't know that, Nadia – it just takes men longer to get their head around these things. Once he sees his little baby he'll fall in love with it, he won't be able to resist his little son or daughter."

"It's a boy you know."

"You're having a boy?"

"Yep – that's why I need Marc on board – I don't know the first thing about little boys! Imagine me trying to play diggers and dumpers or whatever it is little boys play these days?" She started to laugh.

"Well Marc always wanted a son, so I'm sure once your little boy arrives, he'll be a changed man."

"I hope you're right – I really do. I envy you, Lily y'know?"

"You? Envy me?"

"No really, Lily I do – I know everyone thinks I'm confident and in control of everything and in some ways I am but I don't have freedom like you do. Look at you there eating that cake –"

I self-consciously swallowed down the bite I had been chewing.

"I can't remember the last time I had the guts to order cake – I mean I'd love to eat cake, but the little voice in the back of my head says 'remember the camera adds ten pounds and no director wants to cast a fatty'. Even now I'm pregnant, I thought this would finally be a great excuse to relax on my diet, but I can't do it. Now I feel under pressure to be the skinny pregnant woman – I know it's wrong, but I take it as a compliment when people tell me that my bump is tiny. So that's why I'm sitting here with a fruit cup watching you relishing that pie."

"Do you want some?" I said through a mouthful.

"No, you're okay thanks, you look like you're enjoying it. Sorry it's just this pregnancy has made me reassess everything in my whole life," she said as she massaged her temples. "I've been acting since I was seven years old – my Mum pushed me into it and I always thought it was what I wanted to do but now I'm not so sure – yes there are many benefits to it but there's an awful lot to be said for a simpler life like you lead."

"Well, thank you very much!"

"Sorry, I didn't mean it like that – fame is great and everything, but there are a lot of negatives as well. The constant scrutiny and the pressure of being in the public eye – it makes you so self-conscious. It's like every day I get up and I put on a mask – I have this public persona that I constantly have to live up to even though half the time I'd love to just tell everyone to fuck off. You saw it there, in the twenty minutes we've been here and I've been approached twice, imagine that all day, every day?

330

People saying the same thing all the time *'We loved you in Our Endless Days, Nadia'*, " she mimicked. "God listen to me you must think I'm such an ungrateful bitch."

"Well . . . look, Nadia just give him time."

"I'm afraid it might be too late . . ."

We chatted some more and when we asked for the bill the manager came over and shook Nadia's hand and told us our food was on the house. Nadia feigned surprise, and kissed the waiter on both cheeks before telling him she would be back again soon. I could tell she was used to this kind of treatment. We parted company, and as I strolled back down Grafton Street, I thought over everything she had said. I couldn't understand it but I felt strangely deflated, compared to how I felt on my way into town that morning when I hadn't had a care in the world. A few months ago I would have given my right arm for this day, but now it had tossed everything up in the air again just as I was starting to move on with my life. Meeting Nadia had stirred up all that emotion and hurt once more.

I was supposed to call into Sam when I was finished shopping, but the conversation with Nadia had unsettled me and I just wanted to be on my own. I texted him to say I wasn't feeling well, so that he wouldn't worry and then I headed for the bus stop to take me back to Ballyrobin. There I was with my fancy schmancy underwear, and all the excitement of the previous few hours had disappeared. There was only one thing for it - I *needed* to see him.

Chapter 35

I quickly rang Marc's number hardly daring to breathe. I felt bad doing this to Nadia after everything she had confided in me earlier on but he was still my husband and we still had a lot of unresolved business.

He answered after the second ring.

"Lily – great to hear from you!"

"Marc, we need to talk . . ."

"Is everything okay? I tried calling you a few times but you never answered so I presumed you wanted me to leave you alone . . ."

"Don't worry everything is fine – there are just a few things I think we should discuss."

"Yeah of course – do you want to meet somewhere or will I come over?"

"Can you come over here to my - I mean - *our* place?"

"Sure."

I went into the bathroom and touched up my make-up. Then I tried to puff up the roots of my hair using hairspray to give it a bit of volume. I stood back and looked at myself in the mirror, I was wearing my mustard coloured dress with a swallow print. I turned to the side and looked at my tummy. Even when I sucked it in, it was still bigger than Nadia's, and I wasn't seven months pregnant.

Just over an hour later the bell went. My stomach somersaulted. I knew how important this was. It was one of those defining moments where the whole pathway that my life was going down would be decided over the next few hours. Fifteen years together was a long time. I didn't enter into our marriage lightly, and I certainly couldn't walk away from it easily if I thought there was a chance, even just a small chance that we could work it out. I didn't want to spend the rest of my life wondering what would have happened if we had tried again. I needed to be sure. Obviously it was made complicated by Marc and Nadia having a baby together, but if we were to make a fresh start then I would support his involvement in the baby's life.

I took a deep breath and opened the door. Marc was standing there with a huge bouquet of long stemmed red roses. I was taken aback. In the fifteen years that I had been with Marc, he had only ever given me carnations bought hurriedly from the petrol station down the road from the house, usually because he was trying to get back into my good books. He was wearing a black V-neck jumper with a grey polo shirt underneath, jeans and trainers – the type of clothes that I was more used to seeing him in before he met Nadia.

"You look great, Lily," he said as soon as he came through the door. He handed me the flowers.

"They're lovely, Marc – thank you."

"No worries." I could tell he was nervous. "Sit down."

He made his way over to the sofa. I put the flowers in a vase and then sat down on the armchair beside him.

"So how've you been? Did you have a nice Christmas?" He leant forward towards me.

"I did actually." An image of Sam flashed into my head and I felt a huge pang of guilt. I pushed his face out of my head again.

"How about you?"

"It was okay."

"Only okay?"

"Well – Nadia and I – well things aren't going so great between us actually so I spent Christmas Day at home with Mum and Dad."

"I know."

"You do?"

"Yeah just one of those bizarre coincidences – I was in Brown Thomas and we were both eyeing up the same dress." I didn't tell him it was a baby's dress.

"You women – you're all the same - a shop full of dresses and you both go for the same one!"

"We went for a coffee actually."

"Oh yeah?" I could see he looked worried. "You know about the baby then?"

"Well considering it was front page news on *Social Importance* magazine, I could hardly miss it."

"Look, Lily I don't know what she said but the truth is I

335

don't want to be with her anymore," he blurted.

"I know she told me that too. She's very upset about it."

"It's all such a mess," he groaned. "But the spark is gone – it was so intense you know at the start, but it burned out so quickly. We're different people. And we were always fighting – we're just not suited at all. I don't think it would be fair to bring up a baby in that environment, having its two parents shouting and screaming at each other, but I'm going to do my best to be there for them both. I'm actually going over there this evening to tell her it's over."

"She's not going to take it well."

"I know," he lowered his head. "Look, Lily I've been a complete fool – I've given up what we had, which was wonderful and perfect – for a fling with Nadia. I was such a weak person – my head was turned so easily because she was this famous actress I looked up to – I overlooked you, my own wife. I'd do anything to win you back. I think because we were together from such a young age I always felt that I never had a chance to sow my wild oats – the lads always used to give me such a ribbing about it, and then when Nadia came along and paid *me*, Marc Glover attention - well I was flattered. You know what they say 'the grass is always greener on the other side'. But I'm sorry, Lily, it's no excuse for what I put you through. I will spend every day for the rest of my life trying to make it up to you if you'd only let me prove it to you."

I had to give it to him – he was saying all the right things.

For the first time in his life, he wasn't just thinking about himself. He had certainly grown up a lot in the space of time in which we had been apart.

"I'm sorry, Lily – for everything that I've put you through. I've made a huge mistake – the biggest mistake of my life. Nadia is nothing like you – I don't know why I didn't see that!"

"How could you leave me for someone else – we were only married a wet week?" I had waited so long to get an answer to this question.

"You know what I'm like – God you of all people know me better than anyone. I'll admit it, I'm always looking for something bigger – something more exciting and then Nadia came along and I could tell that she liked me. She is so successful – I mean she has an Oscar nomination for God's sake! People in the acting world respected her, not like me – I'm the lowest of the low. She had the lead role – she was everything I aspired to, and then when she showed an interest in *me* and well, em, I'm not proud of it but . . . well I suppose I let my big fat ego get in the way." He lowered his head.

"How long had it being going on?" I wasn't sure I wanted to hear the answer but I knew I had to. If we were to have any hope of moving on then we needed honesty. We had to have everything out in the open.

He hung his head.

"Look, Lily that's not important."

"How long?"

"A few weeks."

"And you were prepared to give up everything we had for someone you had only known for a few weeks? You hurt me so badly, Marc! How can I even begin to trust you again?" My voice was shaky and I knew I was close to tears.

"I know, Lily – God I am so, so sorry. I've been a complete dick. I'm willing to do whatever it takes or wait however long you need to have you back again. I've changed. I know I have responsibilities to Nadia and the baby, but the time I spent apart from her over Christmas has given me lot of time to think. I miss you, Lily – Nadia is nothing like you."

Oh my God, he had finally said the words I had wanted to hear for so long. Ever since the day he left me, my confidence had been shattered. Hearing those words was like a balm for my soul.

"I've made a lot of mistakes over the last year, but I know what my priorities are now. Even if Nadia and I are no longer together - I'm still going to be a part of my child's life. I've started putting money aside to give to Nadia when he's born – even though she earns far more than me, I still want to be able to pay my share and help her out."

"I'm glad to hear it. She doesn't want to do it on her own, you know."

"I know – I feel terrible about it all –"

Silence fell between us and his crystal clear blue eyes met mine. He got up and walked over to the armchair where I was sitting and sat down beside me. His fingers stroked the skin on my face and we sat there staring into each other's eyes. It felt familiar and good – like putting on a comfy old tracksuit after a hard day. His other hand moved up and brushed the hair off my face.

"I meant every word that I said, Lily," he whispered.

I moved my head in towards his and our lips touched. Warm and firm, exactly how I remembered them to be. His hand moved down to my shoulder and soon he was pulling me up and we were moving down onto the sofa. My head was spinning and suddenly I felt as though I couldn't breathe.

"I can't do it," I pulled back instantly. "I'm sorry, Marc – I can't do it." I thought of Sam and his smiling eyes that I loved so much. The way *his* lips felt against mine. That was what I wanted. I wanted Sam. I belonged with Sam.

"What?"

"Sorry, Marc – everything has finally just clicked into place for me," I moved out from underneath him and sat up feeling ecstatic.

"But, Lily, you were giving me signs there, I wasn't imagining it!"

"Sorry, Marc I'm not trying to mess you around honestly. It's over now . . . for good. I'm sorry."

"But, Lily – you're my wife. Come on – we're Marc and Lily, *Lily and Marc*. We'll be just how we used to be!"

"Exactly – that is exactly it! I can't go back there. Look,

Marc the last few months have been so hard for me but I've come out the other side of it and I'm a stronger person for it. I wish you all the best – I really do and you'll always have a special place in my heart you know that – we can't just erase fifteen years."

"I just can't believe it. Are you serious, Lily? If this is some kind of ploy to make me beg you back then it's not funny."

"I'm sorry, Marc – we're done. Go back to, Nadia – try and make a go of it for the sake of the baby. Please, Marc – you have a chance to do the right thing here." I squeezed his hand in mine.

He looked stunned as he got up off the sofa and walked back out the door and left our apartment.

After Marc had gone, instead of feeling sad I just felt relieved. It was like a huge weight had been lifted off my shoulders. For the first time the decision hadn't been made for me – I had made it myself. Everything was finally clear. I knew now what I wanted.

There was one person I needed to talk to. I picked up the phone and dialled Sam's number straight away.

"Lily! How are you feeling?" Just hearing his voice on the other end of the phone made me smile.

"Much better thanks – everything is much better now," I practically sang down the phone to him. I felt bad lying to him like that, but it had taken seeing Marc earlier to realise that it was finally finished between us.

"Glad you're feeling better. I was worried you wouldn't be well enough for our trip tomorrow."

"I wouldn't miss it for the world."

"I'm looking forward to it myself – just me and you together with no distractions."

"Sounds like heaven."

"Make sure you wrap up warmly – the forecast says it's going to snow."

"Really? Ooh I love snow!"

"Me too. Well get a good night's sleep, and I'll pick you up at nine, if that's okay – I want to get down there before the weather gets bad, and at least we'll have the rest of the day ahead of us."

"I can't wait."

"Okay, well sleep tight, my dear."

"You too, see you in the morning."

I had decided to tell Sam about my marriage as soon as I saw him in the morning before we set off for Clare. I needed to get this secret out in the open, I was sick of carrying the weight of it with me. It was nearly the start of a new year and I wanted a fresh start with Sam. I just hoped he felt strongly enough about me not to run a mile.

Chapter 36

I hopped out of bed the next morning and pulled up the blind letting the string ping as it wound itself up. The ground as far as the eye could see was covered in soft white snow. It made my cardboard box housing estate look pretty, and that was saying something. Everything was remarkably still and quiet outside. I stared at the falling flakes, enthralled. I felt like a giddy child with excitement. I couldn't wait to get away with Sam.

The cottage had sounded blissful when he had described it to me; set up on the cliff top all on its own; open fires with the crashing waves of the Atlantic down below. Mobile phones didn't work there so we could really switch off. There was no TV either, so Sam was bringing books and board games. I was looking forward to ringing in the New Year, just Sam and I together with no interruptions. I imagined cosy nights by the open fire, mugs of steaming hot chocolate – it reminded me to grab marshmallows from the press so we could toast them on the fire. The snow made everything much more romantic.

It was so strange to think that this time last year I had been getting ready to marry Marc. If you had told me that my marriage would be over but that I'd already be happy with someone new, I would have had you committed. However I didn't feel sad about it – of course I was sad that my marriage had failed after such a short time, but I had accepted it and was ready to move on now. Sam had made me happier than I ever could have imagined. I loved being around him. He made me feel good about myself. I had never felt more comfortable with a man, and that included Marc. I didn't feel self-conscious when I was naked in front of him or that I wasn't cool enough for his friends whenever we went out with them. This day marked the end of an awful year and good riddance to it. I couldn't wait to see the arse of it. With the start of a new year, I could start afresh, wipe the slate clean.

I spent ages getting ready that morning. I wanted everything to be just right for our trip together. I had packed my Hunter Wellies because Sam had warned me that the weather would be worse the further west we went. As the forecast was for snow, lots of it, I had my thick wool coats, scarves and hats, jeans and woolly jumpers. And my new fancy-dan underwear too - this weather was not going to get the better of me. I looked at the mountain of stuff I was packing for a three-night break, and knew it wouldn't fit into my holdall. Why did winter stuff have to be so bulky? I was going to have to go for a full on suitcase, but I didn't want Sam to think I was insane. I heard the bell ring, and knew it was him so I went out to let him in.

"Hello there," he said, coming in and taking me in his arms and kissing me deeply.

"I'm nearly ready – well I'm all packed. I just want to jump into the shower."

"Take your time, but we wouldn't want to leave it too late to set off – it's really coming down out there. I hope you've packed warm clothes? It's going to be a cold one. I borrowed Marita's jeep in case the roads are bad."

I left Sam with a mug of coffee and a plateful of scones while I went back into the bathroom and jumped into the shower. I did my usual multi-tasking ritual - putting conditioner in my hair for the recommended five minutes while I exfoliated and shaved my legs. Then when I had dried myself off, I put on my lovely posh Jo Malone moisturiser all over. I spritzed some perfume into the air and walked into the mist as the droplets fell down around me. Then I put on my jeans, Ugg boots, a pink and beige fair-isle jumper. I dried my hair with the hairdryer, and tied it up loosely into a ponytail. I put on my make-up, keeping it natural, with a bit of blush to have that winter, red-cheeked glow.

"Do I need to bring towels?" I shouted out to Sam. I really hoped I wouldn't – I'd never fit them in too. He didn't answer so I went out to the living room. "Sam, do I . . ."

"Hello, Lily," he said turning towards me. "Happy anniversary."

He was plonked in the exact same place on the sofa where I had left Sam just half an hour ago, remote in hand.

"What are you doing here, Marc? Where's Sam?" I said panicked.

"That's no way to greet your husband on the morning of your first wedding anniversary!" he slurred.

"Are you drunk? How the hell did you get in here?"

"I have a key. Remember? This time last year, Lily, I was standing in the church waiting for you to make me the happiest man alive."

"Oh leave it out, Marc, spare me the crap – we all know how happy I made you. It only took you a matter of weeks to leave me for someone else."

"Well, look who's the kettle calling the pot black. I met Sam. He seems like a nice enough fella – harmless really."

My blood was boiling.

"Where is he gone, Marc?" I was starting to panic.

"It didn't take you long to move on! Well it seems that you weren't entirely honest with your new flame, Lily. I can't believe you didn't tell him you were married. I'm quite hurt actually." He let out a heavy sigh.

"Look here, Marc – I didn't do this. This was your choice. I did enough waiting around for you to come home and I'm finally moving on again. I won't let you ruin it for me. No way."

"We had something special, Lily."

"No we didn't, Marc – I thought we did. I thought we were soul-mates but in the short time since I've been with Sam it has made me see that what we had wasn't very special at all."

"How can you say that, Lily – we were good together? Can we not try again?"

"We weren't, Marc – being away from you for the last few months has opened my eyes. I'm not the girl I was before. And in

346

case you've forgotten Nadia is pregnant with *your* baby."

"She kicked me out. I've nowhere to go, Lily."

"Well you're not coming back here, get that idea out of your head. You haven't paid a penny to the mortgage or bills. Since you've gone, I've struggled on my own."

"Yeah sorry about that – Nadia has every penny I earned gone on buggies and baby-grows."

"Look I don't care about that now – tell me what you said to Sam?" I said impatiently.

"I didn't say anything!"

"Marc, what did you say?"

He knew by my tone not to mess around anymore. "I just said it how it is – that you're my wife."

"You bastard," I roared. "How dare you!"

"Well legally you are," he said smugly.

"Yes, legally on paper we are husband and wife but that's all it is – just a bit of paper. There is nothing more to it than that. Nothing!" I was shouting now. "Where did he go?"

He shrugged his shoulders "How the hell am I supposed to know?"

I snatched his key back from his hands and then I told him to get out. I grabbed my phone and dialled Sam's number, but there was no answer. I hurried down the steps of the duplex past Marc and ran across the car park to see if there was any sign of Marita's jeep. Usually coming outside to freshly fallen snow would have made me ridiculously excited but now it was just a hindrance. I saw Marc's car, which just made me madder because he was drink driving. As I tried to scan the car park for Sam, all I could see was grey.

I glanced behind me, and saw Marc was still staggering down the steps, which were treacherous with snow.

I could only imagine what was going through Sam's head. What must he have thought about another man just letting himself into my house like that? Whatever Marc had said to him had shocked him enough to make him leave. I knew I should have told him from the start. Now my worst fears had been realised, he had heard it from someone else first. And what was worse was that he had heard it from Marc himself. How awful must he have felt when Marc had told him?

I tried ringing his phone again but it just rang out. God only knew what Marc had said. I cursed myself again for my lack of driving skills. I watched Marc clinging desperately to the side railing as he was still trying to make his way down the icy steps without falling. He finally made it to the bottom and stumbled across the car park towards me. I needed to get to Sam but I couldn't even ask him for a lift. My phone rang and it was Frankie wishing me a happy New Year before we headed west, as she knew the signal wouldn't be great.

"What's wrong, Lily you sound distracted?" she asked.

"It's Sam – he came over earlier to pick me up, but while I was in the shower Marc called in drunk. By the time I came out he had gone so God only knows what Marc has said to him. I've tried phoning him but he's not answering."

"Oh God, Lily - you really should have told him before now."

"I know, Frankie, I know."

"Well why don't I come pick you up and bring you to his apartment – I'm sure he's probably just gone home."

"Would you? Oh thank you so much, Frankie – you're a star. I owe you one big time."

"I'll leave straight away, try not to worry!"

"Thanks, Frankie."

***

An hour later I sat anxiously in Frankie's Mini and flicked on the radio. It was one of those seventies hours. I turned it off again as it was getting on my nerves.

"Stop biting your nails," she scolded.

"Sorry," I said removing the offending hand from my mouth and sitting on it. I didn't even realise I was doing it. When we reached Sam's apartment block she parked up on the kerb and I went inside to the foyer and pressed the buzzer but there was no answer. I pressed it another three times but there was nothing. I wasn't sure if he just wasn't there or if maybe he was ignoring me. I went back outside and walked down the ramp into the underground car park to check if his car or Marita's jeep were there but his space was empty. I went back to Frankie's Mini.

"He's not there," I sighed.

"Well what about his sister – the one you made the cake

for?"

"Marita – yeah, it's worth a try I suppose." I didn't want to tell Marita what had happened. She would think I was the worst girlfriend possible for her brother after breaking up with him out of the blue and now this. I would hate me, if Sam were my brother.

When we reached Bull Island Road, we slowed down as I scanned the house numbers. When we finally came to 99, Frankie pulled into the driveway. I hopped out and pressed Marita's doorbell.

"Lily, this is a nice surprise but what are you doing here? I thought you and Sam were supposed to be on your way down to the cottage?" She was wearing jersey layers in neutral tones that complemented her peachy toned skin.

"We are – were, but something has happened. I guess he's not here then?"

"No, he's not. Don't you know where he is?" she said worriedly.

"Look, Marita I need to get hold of him urgently if you see him will you tell him to call me?"

"Of course, Lily." I could tell she was curious as to what was going on. "Look I don't want to pry, but is everything okay?"

"I hope so, Marita." And before she could say anymore I ran and climbed back into Frankie's car.

As we pulled out onto the road again, the snow was falling heavier now and I knew it wouldn't be long before the traffic came to a standstill as cars began to find it difficult to get around in the weather. I couldn't ask Frankie to stay out driving me around for much longer. I needed to find him soon.

"No luck then?"

"Nope. I wish he'd just answer his phone!"

"Think, Lily - where would he have gone?"

"That's what I'm trying to do!"

"Well how about the cottage – would he have gone down there without you?"

"I don't think he would drive all the way down there on his own."

"Well what about his friends, do you have any of their numbers?"

"No," I wailed. "God this is hopeless."

"Well this snow is getting worse, Lily, I think we'd better head home and maybe he'll get in touch when he calms down?"

Suddenly I had an idea. "Wait! I just want to try one more place and if he's not there then we'll go."

"Okay, Lily" she sighed. "Where are we going?"

"The beach."

"The beach? But why on earth would he be there?"

"It's just a hunch. Please, Frankie."

She shook her head at me but turned the car around so we were heading towards the strand where Sam had brought me on that sunny September day a few months back.

Visibility was poor as thick flakes rushed up against the

screen. Frankie leaned forward to try and see better, but the harder she stared, the more it blinded her, so she gave up and sat back again. We drove dead slow, the roads were slushy and non 4-wheel drive cars were having difficulty getting up even gentle slopes.

"C'mon," I shouted at a BMW driver whose rear-wheel drive car was fishtailing across the road in front of us. Finally we reached the deserted car park. There was one other car there, which was covered in a thick blanket of snow but I didn't know if it was Marita's jeep or not. Frankie parked the car, and we picked our steps on the slippery boardwalk leading to the dunes.

"I'm not really dressed for this," Frankie said. She only had on a light polo neck with a furry gilet over it.

"I won't be long, I promise."

"But where are we going, Lily?"

"This way," I panted.

We bowed our heads and ran on.

"This is madness!" Frankie said. She was trying to keep up with me in her high-heeled boots. I still had my Uggs on so I was okay.

And then I saw his outline. That stature that I loved. He was standing with his back to me just staring into the water.

"Is that him?" Frankie asked completely shocked that I wasn't losing the plot after all.

"Yes."

"Well go on – go and talk to him. I'll wait in the car." She crossed her arms across her body.

I was nervous as hell as I walked up behind him. I tipped his shoulder and he swung around instantly. The hurt in his eyes was unmistakable.

"I'm sorry," I said. "I should have told you."

"So it's true then? Were you ever going to tell me? I feel like such a fool."

"No, Sam please don't say that."

"Well how am I supposed to feel?" he asked bitterly. He swung around to face me head on.

"It isn't like that. We're separated, we have been for a few months now."

"But why didn't you tell me? That's what hurts the most – some poncy looking arsehole calling himself your *husband* had to tell me!"

He had only met Marc for five minutes but already had figured out what it took me fifteen years to learn.

"I wanted to tell you – I was going to – on Christmas Eve I was all set to tell you then - but then next door kicked off, and then there were other times too, but we always seemed to be interrupted and I don't know . . . the moment was gone."

"But there were so many other times you could have told me."

"I was so afraid I'd lose you. That was the reason I broke up with you because I didn't want to bring you into this mess, but I missed you too much."

"But how do you think I felt hearing that the woman I love has a husband who she never told me about?"

He had said the love word. He hadn't said that before.

"I was just there in your home, Lily and in he strolls! So obviously I asked him who he was and what he was doing in your house, but then he tells me he's your husband and he asked me who *I* was!" he continued.

"I'm sorry – I didn't want you to find out like that. You didn't deserve that. He's a prat. He had no right turning up like that."

"So how long were you married for?" he said as he turned back to face the grey-green water.

"Three months."

"Three months?"

"I know it's pathetic. I came home from work early on the evening of our three-month wedding anniversary, and there he was in bed with somebody else! Today should have been our first wedding anniversary."

His face softened. "God, Lily, I'm sorry."

"Yeah it was pretty awful at the time, but you know I'm doing really well since. It's funny how things change though, because I can honestly say it was the best thing to ever happen to me."

"Why?"

"Because I wouldn't have met you, Sam."

He stayed silent.

"Do you really love me, Sam?"

"I do – I did. I mean I'm just so messed up right now. You hurt me badly, Lily – I thought what we had was special. I thought we were good together and then I find out you had this whole other part of your life which I knew nothing about, so now I'm wondering if I ever really knew you at all?"

"You did know me – you *do* know me. What you know is the real me, that's it. I have no other secrets or skeletons in the closet. It's actually a relief to have it out in the open now. It was such a weight carrying it around wondering how I was going to tell you and what way you were going to react."

"But how am I meant to trust you again, Lily?"

"Please, Sam, if you can just give me one more chance, I will make it up to you. I promise I have no more secrets. That's it – this is me. Please, Sam – can we start again?"

"I don't know, Lily, you really hurt me." His eyes were wounded.

"Sam, please if you love me, please I'm begging you. Give us another chance."

He lowered his head and was silent for an eternity. "I'm sorry, Lily – I can't –"

I was devastated; my heart felt like it had sunk down into my boots. "Oh . . . right well, again I'm sorry, Sam – I really am. You deserved more than how I've treated you." I started to walk away. My boots compacted the snow into a crunch as I walked. That was it, just when I had found happiness; I had ruined it once again. Why hadn't I been honest with him from the start? If I just had told him the truth from day one, I wouldn't be in this mess.

"– I can't imagine my life without you in it." I heard his voice from behind me. I swung around to look at him. "I've waited my whole life to have a relationship with someone that came close to the relationship that my parents have with each other. And then I met you – I've never met anyone like you before, Lily and I'm not sure if that's a good thing or a bad thing, but now that I've met you – I don't want to ever let you go."

"What? Did I hear you right?"

"Come here, Lily."

Snowflakes rushed against my face as I ran back towards him and flung my arms around his neck.

"I love you," I said as the snow fell magically around us.

"I love you too, Lily McDermott,"

This was it, this was so right. Wrapped up in Sam's arms was where I belonged and where I wanted to stay for the rest of my life.

As we stood kissing in the snow a huge snowflake landed on my nose and Sam brushed it off. Then I remembered Frankie.

"We'd better go, Frankie is waiting for me."

As we walked back, hand in hand towards the car park, I saw that the snow had settled thickly covering my footprints already. I couldn't help but think back over the last year and how my "mishap" as Clara had termed it, instead of being the worst moment of my life, had actually turned out to be the very best thing that had ever happened to me.

THE END

Recipe for Lily's Heavenly Orange Cake

Ingredients

225g butter, plus some for greasing

225g caster sugar

225g plain flour

3 eggs

Finely grated zest and juice of 1 orange

1 teaspoon baking powder

Pinch of salt

Cream Cheese Icing

60g butter

180g soft cheese

100g icing sugar, sieved

1 teaspoon orange juice

Grease a 23cm diameter tin with some butter. Preheat the oven to 180°C, 350°F, Gas 4. Put the butter and the caster sugar in a bowl, then cream them together. Beat in the eggs, the orange zest and the juice (make sure to keep a few drops to flavour the icing). Sift in the flour, the baking powder and the salt, and mix gently.

Tip the mixture into the greased tin, then *Bake with Love* in the oven for 20-25 minutes; insert a skewer into the middle to check if it is ready – the skewer should come out clean. While the cake is cooling, you can start making the cream cheese frosting.

Combine the butter and cheese in a bowl. Sift in the icing sugar and the orange juice and mix until smooth. Then spread over the top of the cooled cake.

Enjoy xx

Want to know what happens next for Lily and Sam?

Turn over to read Chapter 1 of **Baked with Love**, the second book in the Lily McDermott series . . .

* * *

I'm always telling people that cake has magical powers.
Everyone knows that feeling when a buttery sponge melts on your
tongue and suddenly a bad day is set to right. Or the moment you
bite into a lighter than air pastry, flakes falling down around you,
and the problems in your life are temporarily suspended. A slice
of cake can be five minutes of magic in the middle of a chaotic
day. A thick chocolate ganache is a heavenly balm for a crisis of
the heart, while the crunch of a meringue on a fine summer's day
can make us feel warm inside. Cake is food for the soul and each
little bite you take is a little piece of enchantment. And if you
don't believe me, then let me show you . . .

* * *

CHAPTER 1

Can't breathe . . . can't breathe . . . can't breeeeathe . . .

"Ehm, Lily, why is your face turning purple?" Sam asked, his face a mixture of concern and amusement.

I was looking at my reflection in the glass and sucking my stomach in so much that I thought I was going to starve my brain of oxygen. I exhaled and let everything hang out again. It was useless; I'd never be able to keep that up all night.

I was standing in my newly appointed *Baked with Love* and it was a few minutes before the first guests were due to arrive for the launch party. I couldn't believe that I was about to open my very own bakery – me, Lily McDermott, a bakery owner? It sounded ridiculous even to me.

"Are you sure I look okay?" I said, turning around to him.

"You look great, Lily – I've told you a million times already!"

"I don't look like a person who should have their own bakery though, do I?" Although I had had my hair blow-dried and I had bought a gorgeous new tea dress, the nerves were starting to get the better of me. Whenever I looked at my reflection in the mirror, I didn't look mature enough to own my own business. I felt like an imposter.

"What are you talking about?" Sam asked with a laugh.

"Me . . . this –" I said, gesturing around the café with a sigh. "Oh God, I think I'm in over my head . . ." You know when for once everything in your life is going right and you finally think you have your act together? Nope, me neither because here I was yet again in a situation where I felt totally out of my depth.

My best friend, Frankie, had invited lots of journalists and PR people and I knew they would be expecting somebody confident, somebody assured, somebody who knew what they were doing, not someone who was completely winging it. I felt like this was all a big charade. I was waiting for somebody to jump out and say, "Haha, Lily, you didn't really think we were going to let you open your own bakery, did you?"

"Relax, Lily, it'll be great!" Sam reassured me, taking me into his arms.

"But what if nobody turns up?" I said for possibly the hundred and seventh time that day.

"Well, then me and you will have a lot of cake to get through –"

I glared at him. "That's not even funny!"

He grinned back at me. "Lily, stop fretting, of course they will. You've had loads of RSVPs. You've worked hard for this, try to relax and enjoy your special moment."

"You're right." I sighed, wondering once again why I had decided to do this. Was I completely mad?

As I looked around the room, I couldn't believe that this place was mine. A wooden sign with *Baked with Love* now hung proudly over the door and the fringe of a huge red and white candy-striped awning billowed gently underneath. In good weather, I would be able to put a few tables under it. The original oak floorboards were still intact, and two old bottle glass windows looked out onto Bluebell Lane where inside I had created a tower of macarons to entice people through the door. A traditional style glass counter ran along one wall, which was now full with cakes and treats. I had an old-fashioned, push-button till at the end of the counter. A comfy sofa ran along the back wall beside the gas stove which I hoped would give the place a warm, cosy feel during the long winter months. The room at the back was fitted out as my kitchen, and I was so excited to have proper catering ovens, an industrial-size fridge, and tonnes of space to work. I felt like a child at Christmas over the last few days as I tested out the new equipment. I would be able to double, if not treble, my output every day. I had bought some mismatched tables and chairs which, as well as being cheaply purchased in the charity shop, gave the place a relaxed and welcoming feel. I had also picked up vintage-patterned plates and teacups, saucers and bowls; none were from the same set but somehow, collectively, they all worked together. The end result was that *Baked with Love* was cute and homely and exactly what I had imagined my dream bakery might look like way back when I had been working out of my kitchen in Ballyrobin.

I had viewed unit after unit over the past few months, but inevitably they were too small, or too big, or didn't have space for a kitchen, or were on the quiet end of the street. Every place I had looked at hadn't been right, but this little shop was just perfect. I could feel it in my bones.

I would be eternally grateful to my brother-in-law, Tom, who had a large property portfolio around Dublin and was cutting me a deal on the unit. The previous tenants had only vacated the building recently, and Tom had said it was mine if I wanted it. There wasn't a chance I could ever hope to afford the rent on a prime location like Bluebell Lane without his help. I turned back around and looked around the room and once more a nervous feeling began bubbling its way up inside me.

It wasn't long before my Dad and Frankie came through the door, followed shortly by my sister, Clara, and her husband, Tom. I was relieved to see Clara hadn't brought her boys, Jacob and Joshua, with her. I had visions of my brand-new bakery being destroyed by her "energetic" sons. Frankie arrived next wearing an electric blue coat over a cerise pink dress. Most people with Frankie's pale colouring and wiry auburn hair would shy away from wearing bright colours but not her. Her job as a freelance fashion stylist meant she wasn't afraid to experiment with clothes.

"Are you ready?" she asked, kissing me on both cheeks.

"Do you think anyone would notice if I ran away right now?"

"Don't worry, you'll be great," she said, giving me a squeeze.

Soon the rest of the guests began to arrive, and I watched in amazement as Frankie turned into my PR woman. She had invited Ireland's top journalists and food bloggers and other people who she said were social media "influencers" – whatever they were. She confidently greeted people and introduced them to me until my head was spinning trying to keep up with who was who.

370

Frankie had insisted that we needed a theme, so we were simply going with "Cake and Cocktails." We had designed strawberry mojitos to complement the Eton-mess, which were served in a shot glass alongside the cocktail. There were sticky toffee apple martinis to match my bite-sized sticky toffee puddings, and Frankie had suggested gin-gin mules to pair with the key lime cupcakes. Dad and Sam had been given the job of serving the guests, and Frankie directed them through the crowd with their trays so that everyone had a drink and matching cake in their hands.

I was so busy running around meeting and greeting the journalists and PR people that Frankie was introducing me to and trying to make a good impression that before I knew it she was tipping a spoon against the side of a wine glass calling on me to make a speech. My stomach flipped over; I had been dreading this bit. I managed to catch Sam's eye across the room, and he gave me a reassuring wink.

I swallowed back a lump in my throat and began. My voice trembled with emotion when I gave a special mention to Frankie for encouraging me to set up my own cake-making business in the first place. It was hard to believe that an idea that was conceived over a bottle of wine one night was now almost a fully fledged bakery. I could never have imagined when I first took those tentative steps into business that I would one day have a café with my name over the door. To see *Baked with Love*, my own bakery, alive with people eating and chatting and laughing was everything I had ever dreamed of. I finished by saying: "Thank you, everyone, for coming, I think we have the recipe for a perfect night: a great crowd, some lovely cocktails, and hopefully some tasty treats."

The rest of the night went past in a blur, and before I knew it I was saying goodbye to everyone as they assured me that they would be giving *Baked with Love* a big thumbs up.

As soon as we had closed the door on the last guest, I let out a huge sigh of relief and collapsed onto a chair.

"I think it was a success!" Sam said, coming over and wrapping me into a hug.

"I don't think I said anything too stupid . . ."

"You need to work on your public speaking, but otherwise I think people actually enjoyed it," Clara said.

"Of course they did!" Frankie said, cutting across her. She had no patience for Clara's antics.

"I'm proud of you, Lily," Dad said.

After we were finished cleaning up, Frankie, Dad, Clara, and Tom headed on leaving just Sam and me alone together.

"You were amazing tonight," he said, taking me into his arms. "Come on, this calls for some bubbles!" He took me by the hand. We locked up and stepped out onto the pedestrianised street where the aprons of cafés and bars fronted. Office workers walked past us, blazers draped over their shoulders and ties loosened on the warm evening.

We walked over to a nearby bar and took a seat outside under the canopy. Sam disappeared inside and returned a few moments later with a bottle of champagne. He uncorked it and the froth rushed over the neck and down onto the table. He poured us both a glass.

"To *Baked with Love*," he toasted.

"To *Baked with Love*," I echoed.

He put his arm around my shoulder, and we sat back and watched the busy street life unfold before us.

"I never thought I'd say it but my life it pretty perfect right now, Sam Waters." I reached for his hand and gave it a squeeze. When I thought back over how things had gone for the last two years, a whirlwind didn't even begin to describe it. In that period, I had married Marc and separated. I had been fired from my job in Rapid Response pregnancy tests and had set up *Baked with Love* from my own kitchen. I had met Sam when he had come to my rescue after a disaster involving a stand of fallen cupcakes and my nephews, Jacob and Joshua. After a few false starts, we had finally got it together and now here I was, relaxing in his strong arms, looking across the street at my new bakery. I almost had to pinch myself to believe it was true. From one of the lowest points of my life, all these good things had happened to me and it was all because of the magic of cake.

It was then that I noticed Sam lowering his gaze towards the cobblestones on the ground.

"What is it?" I asked.

"It's nothing – sorry . . ." He smiled at me and squeezed my hand.

We sat chatting and people watching and staring across at *Baked with Love* with a mixture of pride and amazement until the cool evening air began to make its presence felt. I began to shiver, and Sam took his jacket off the back of the chair and draped it over my shoulders.

After we had finished the bottle we strolled home hand in hand along the Grand Canal towards Sam's apartment. It had become my apartment too over the last year. He had let me take over his kitchen with my baking on the condition that I saved him some of whatever I had made that day. I figured it was a win-win for both of us, so I had put my house in Ballyrobin up for rent and moved in with Sam the very next day.

I felt as though I was dancing on air the whole way home. The sun began to set in shades of pink and orange over the Grand Canal basin, glinting off the water below and bedding down somewhere over Boland's Mill. Dublin really could be the best city in the world on a sunny evening like this, I thought.

When we reached the apartment, I walked over to the floor-to-ceiling length windows. Dusk had started to fall, and a field of city lights lay twinkling beyond the pane. I drew the curtains across and flopped down onto the red L-shaped sofa that ran the length of the wall.

Sam sat down beside me and took me into his arms.

"I'm proud of you. I know you'll make it a success."

"I hope so," I said, nervously biting down on my bottom lip.

"You make me so happy, you know that don't you, Lily?" he said suddenly.

I smiled and looked up at Sam's handsome face, the cutting cheekbones dotted with dark stubble. But he wasn't smiling; instead, his face had clouded over. His brow was furrowed downwards emphasising the crease above the bridge of his nose.

I was taken aback by his serious expression. "I know that, Sam, I love you too." I laughed to try and lighten the situation, but I noticed that he wasn't meeting my eyes. A cold feeling washed over me and I didn't like it one bit. It was unsettling. I had been here before.

Suddenly, his face relaxed and his mouth broke into a grin and I relaxed then too. There was something about his smile that always seemed to calm even the worst of my neuroses. I was just imagining it; everything was fine.

Izzy Bayliss

Acknowledgements

This book has been a while in the making and as is the case in life, lots of things have happened in the meantime. In that time I got married and had children but throughout all this, the character of Lily remained firmly in my head so I feel as though she has been a part of my life for a long time now and I'm so glad she finally gets to tell her story. I hope you will like her just as much as I do.

I wish to thank my ever-present family who put up with my constant daydreaming and reluctance sometimes to come back from my fictional worlds and join them in reality (pah!).

I must also thank fellow author Janelle Brooke Harris who has been an invaluable help to me in writing this book and is also a great coffee & cocktail date. My fellow Scribblers and Paupers, for their encouragement and advice. Najla Qamber (http://www.najlaqamberdesigns.com) for her brilliant cover, you have been a pleasure to work with and excuse the pun but it's great to be on the same page.

Sarah Perkins for her editing eye (http://www.the-proof-angel.co.uk)

Lastly, thank you for reading this book, it never ceases to amaze me that people take the time to read something I created in my head - I have to pinch myself that I get to do this for a living and I'm very lucky. So, as we say in Ireland, míle buíochas! I hope you will love Lily McDermott just as much as me,

Izzy xx

Made in the USA
Monee, IL
04 December 2020